MURDER AT THE ALTAR

Murder at the Altar

The Ellie Quicke Mysteries

VERONICA HELEY

HarperCollins*Publishers*

HarperCollins*Publishers*
77-85 Fulham Palace Road, London W6 8JB
www.**fire**and**water**.com

First published in Great Britain in 2000 by HarperCollins*Publishers*

1 3 5 7 9 10 8 6 4 2

Veronica Heley asserts the moral right to be
identified as the author of this work.

A catalogue record for this book is
available from the British Library.

ISBN 0 00 274073 7

Printed and bound in Great Britain by
Creative Print and Design [Wales], Ebbw Vale

Murder at the Altar

Too late, she understood.

She understood why Ferdy had been killed in that place, and at that time of day.

The police had been wrong. She had got it wrong herself.

But she had been right in thinking her every move had been watched. She had been afraid, and she had been right to be afraid.

She wanted to scream! She was only just coming to terms with Frank's death. Now she, too, had run out of time.

She backed up against the door of the church. It did not yield and let her in as it had yielded for Ferdy.

The murderer took a step forward …

It was two days since the funeral.

Ellie had told everyone she would be perfectly all right on her own, but of course she wasn't. The pills the doctor had given her weren't helping, either. She couldn't sleep at night, and felt half asleep all day. She knew she would feel more alive if she stopped taking the pills, but she wasn't sure she could cope if she did.

She stood at the French windows and stared down the slope of her back garden, across the alley and up to the church. The trees around the church had just started to turn yellow when Frank had been taken to hospital. There had been a sharp frost the night he died and now there were more leaves on the lawn than on the trees.

They ought to be cleared up, or the grass would suffer.

Frank had never been interested in growing things, but it had been the joy of Ellie's life to transform a privet-bound patch of straggly grass into a pretty garden, massed with flowering shrubs and herbaceous plants. A sundial sat in the middle of a circle of lawn, reminding passers-by that 'Time Passes, and Man is Left to Account for it'.

Frank had passed on with Time. Ellie was still trying to account for it.

The soft green walls and comfortable furniture of the living-room behind her had once seemed a serene refuge from the world outside. Now there was dust on the scattered mounds of sympathy cards lying on the table in the bay window overlooking the road. A couple of half-empty coffee mugs sat abandoned on the sideboard, flowers drooped and died in their vases, and there was a litter of newspapers on the cream-coloured carpet by the settee. You must get moving, Ellie told herself. Start clearing out Frank's clothes, get out of the house to buy some food, return the overdue library books.

She tried to think positively. There was still plenty of colour in the garden even in November. The door of the garden shed had drifted ajar. She must go and secure it. Her shed was haunted by stray cats and a neighbour's small boy … which reminded her that she hadn't seen the boy since Frank died.

The sun was trying to come out, turning the stone of the garden seat and urns on the patio to a golden glow. Just before Frank had been taken ill, she had filled the urns with winter-flowering pansies and variegated ivies. They were doing well.

The sun was getting brighter, making the church spire stand out black against the sky. It didn't often stand out as clearly as that. It meant it was going to rain.

The grandmother clock in the magnolia-painted hall behind her chimed sweet and low. Time to get Frank his mid-morning cuppa. She started. No more mid-morning cuppa for Frank. Why couldn't she remember that?

A heavy-set woman burst out of the side door of the church, arms flailing. Ellie registered that this was unusual, but did not move.

Mrs Dawes ran down the path from the church. Ellie felt a faint stir of interest. She'd never seen the stately Mrs Dawes run before.

Mrs Dawes fought her way through the gate which led from the church grounds into the alley. Crossing the alley she wrenched open the gate into Ellie's garden. Mrs Dawes' face was red and her padded olive-green coat flapped around her as she pounded her way up the garden and banged on Ellie's kitchen door.

Ellie went to let her in, moving like a sleepwalker.

At first Mrs Dawes couldn't speak properly. She tore the flowered scarf from her throat and gesticulated.

She needs help, thought Ellie. She felt something stir inside herself in response to Mrs Dawes' need. She said, 'Sit down,' and ran some water into a glass. 'Drink this. Don't try to talk for a minute ...'

'Phone!' Mrs Dawes knocked the glass away, spraying water around. 'Police! Dead man in church!'

Ellie blinked.

'Stupid girl! Do it!'

Ellie blinked again. At the age of fifty, she no longer considered herself a girl.

'Ring the police! You're the nearest. I think it's one of the workmen, the heating engineers, you know? They've been in and out all week. Thought he was drunk! Tried to pull him up ...!'

She rocked, podgy fingers over her face.

Mrs Dawes, respectable widow and head of the church flower-arranging team, was not a woman to fall apart unless she had seen something particularly nasty.

Grief and shock over Frank's death tried to keep their hold on Ellie, but she forced herself to be practical. Mrs Dawes had come to her for help, and help she must have.

Ellie rang the police and administered tea and sympathy to Mrs Dawes. Wait till Frank gets home and I tell him, she thought.

Oh. Why do I still keep thinking of things to tell him?

She persuaded Mrs Dawes into the sitting-room. Mrs Dawes took Frank's chair, the best chair. Of course. She was a woman of ample proportions. Even so, Ellie winced at seeing someone else in Frank's big armchair.

'I've put two sugars in. Have a biscuit. Good for shock.'

Mrs Dawes' colour was a little better but her breathing was still uneven and her dark-dyed hair was coming down. She put up shaking hands to deal with it.

'I didn't notice him at first. I'd just finished the flower-arranging class in the church hall, so I thought I'd pop into the church to see what needed doing to the flowers since the funeral ...'

Frank's funeral.

'Yes,' said Ellie in a steady voice. 'You do the flowers at

4

the church so beautifully. Everyone remarked on it the other day.'

Mrs Dawes found the compliment soothing. She inclined her head and finished her tea. Her hands still shook but she held out her cup for a refill.

'I took in some chrysanths to replace any which might have gone over. As I went up to the altar I nearly fell over him. You don't expect to see anyone lying on the floor in front of the altar, do you? Touching it. With both hands. Lying on his face.'

'Who ...?'

'I didn't see his face. I thought he was drunk.' She began to cry.

Ellie fetched some of Frank's beautiful linen hankies. Frank wouldn't need the hankies so they might as well be used. Ellie still had to tackle the disposal of his clothes, his shoes, his books, his papers. She wouldn't think about that for the moment.

Mrs Dawes blew her nose and mopped up as the police rang Ellie's doorbell.

Mrs Dawes repeated her story to the police, finding it not unpleasant to be the focus of attention for two nice-looking young policemen. She refused to accompany them back to the church. The side door to the church was open, she said. They could go in and see for themselves. She herself was not going back till the body had been removed. Ellie could show them the way, couldn't you, dear?

Ellie showed the policemen the way down through her garden, across the alley and up to the church. A stir of curiosity surprised her. She had to acknowledge that it would have been interesting to have gone into the church with the police, just to see if what Mrs Dawes had said was true.

The police said she should return to sit with Mrs Dawes. They also refused to admit the central heating engineers who arrived at that moment.

Ellie checked them off: the foreman and both of his helpers. So it wasn't one of them who lay dead in front of the altar.

She got back to find Mrs Dawes combing her hair in front of the mirror.

'More tea?'

'No, but I'll use your loo, if I may.' Mrs Dawes' fingers twitched at the bunch of lilies which Ellie had shoved all anyhow into a vase. It had been kind of people to give her flowers at the funeral, but she'd been too distracted to arrange them properly.

'You shouldn't cram lilies into a small vase like this,' said Mrs Dawes, once more on familiar ground. 'You should have cut an inch and a half off the stems and—'

'I know, but …'

'Come to my flower-arranging classes,' said Mrs Dawes. 'Thursday mornings, 10.30 prompt in the church hall. Those nice young policemen want me to make a statement. Not that I can tell them much. I pulled on his arm, you know, to try to make him get up.' She shuddered.

Ellie listened and nodded and made more tea for Mrs Dawes and for the policemen when they eventually returned. A different lot of policemen this time, but still requiring tea and biscuits. Familiar actions, listening, nodding agreement, providing food.

She still felt only half awake, but they didn't seem to notice.

The large house opposite the church had been empty for months. The fat man had parked his dark-green Saab under the For Sale notice in the drive. Perhaps someone was interested in the house at last, even though gossip said the owner was asking too much. Perhaps one of the playgroup helpers from the church hall had parked the car there, out of the way.

The Saab had been parked in that particular place so that the driver had a good view of the comings and goings at the church.

Mrs Dawes' arrival ... the watcher wound down the window, heard her scream. So the body had been discovered. Good.

The fat man noted which house she went to for help. Ah, now wasn't that the house where the woman was supposed to have been standing, watching everything that had happened the other night?

The fat man pinched in his lips. In his opinion, the killer ought to have dealt with the witness then and there, instead of losing his head and rushing away from the scene of the crime. If the old biddy told what she'd seen, the killer would have to be sacrificed, even if he were the boss's right hand man.

And if he went ... the fat man smiled ... someone else could step in, couldn't they?

The police car arrived. The fat man watched as the woman showed the police the way up to the church. She didn't go in with them, but returned to her own house. The driver counted the backs of houses. Hers was the fourth out of eight semi-detached houses, all backing on to the alley and looking out over the church. Passers-by began to collect.

He waited while senior officers arrived, then forensics. The fat man cowered in his seat until he remembered that his windows were tinted. He could see everyone, but they couldn't see him.

He waited till the senior policeman and sidekick came out of the church and went down the path to take statements from the witnesses. The boss would soon find out whether the woman had seen enough to identify the killer or not.

The fat man started the engine and after carefully looking both ways, slid out into the traffic on the main road.

Ellie walked Mrs Dawes back to her own house two streets away. Mrs Dawes needed someone to lean on and Ellie was selected. A familiar role.

Mrs Dawes said she couldn't wait to ring her daughter to tell her what she'd seen.

Ellie decided not to ring her own daughter Diana till after six o'clock. Diana wouldn't be back from her part-time job yet, anyway. There was a sore place inside Ellie when she thought of Diana. Diana sometimes made it difficult to give her unqualified love. For instance, after the funeral Ellie had been reminiscing with a distant cousin about Frank's earlier days, when Diana had interrupted saying, 'I do wish you wouldn't go on about Father. You know how much it upsets me!'

This was the first time Ellie had left the house since the funeral. Now she was out in the fresh air she decided to make the most of the day's thin sunshine and walk right round the local park. Returning by way of the alley she paused to see if there were any sign of the policemen. What a shocking thing to have happened! She could hardly take it in. Poor Mrs Dawes, stumbling on a body …

It was a pretty, Victorian Gothic church, much favoured by brides who liked traditional wedding photographs. There was no churchyard as such, but the building was surrounded by a grassy area planted with mature trees. The Green, as it was called, was criss-crossed by tarmac paths in every direction.

Ellie knew how much it cost to keep the church going, since Frank had been on the parish council. His chief concern had been the thirties-built church hall next door to the church, well past its sell-by date and in urgent need of replacement. Well, Ellie thought, at least Frank doesn't have to worry about that any more ...

Frank had always said how fortunate they were to have a likeable middle-of-the-road vicar who attracted a reasonable congregation. Ellie wondered how the vicar had received the news of a death in his church.

She wondered when the man had been killed, poor thing. Last night some time? He couldn't have been there for long, or someone would have found him.

Having been quiet for so long indoors, Ellie felt oppressed by the noise of the traffic on the main road beyond the church.

A bus screamed to a halt outside the church hall. A car tooted at an elderly man using the pedestrian crossing. Soon the children would be trooping out of the primary school opposite.

It wouldn't take me long to pop along to the shops in the Avenue to get some food, thought Ellie.

Until Frank went into hospital, Ellie had worked part-time in the charity shop in the Avenue. She hadn't been back since. Did she feel up to answering kind enquiries from her co-workers? No, not yet.

She turned her back on the main road, grateful for the seclusion of their own house. Frank had been born and brought up in one of the grand houses at the other end of the parish, but they had enjoyed living in this unpretentious area beside the church. Ellie had been concerned that he would find a small house claustrophobic but for some years they couldn't have afforded anything larger, and later on Frank had found other uses for his money.

Ellie had no idea whether she could afford to continue to live there. She wasn't sure she cared.

The side door into the church was closed and cordoned off with tape. A policeman stood on guard, fending off the excited enquiries of some passers-by. Seeing Ellie, they called out to know if she'd seen anything. Ellie made herself smile and shake her head.

One of them persisted, running over to speak to her. 'They've set up an incident room in the church hall! I don't know what the playgroup is going to do! They're asking everyone if they'd seen anything suspicious!'

Ellie found it difficult to be sociable, but did her best. She said, 'Yes, they asked me if I'd seen anything, but I'm afraid I haven't been noticing anything much.'

'Ah yes, of course. After Frank ... so sorry to hear ...' An understanding nod.

Ellie nodded back. She went through her gate, climbed the slope up her garden and let herself into the kitchen.

She made a sandwich but the bread was stale and she only ate half of it.

She found herself weeping. It was all right to give way, now and again ... widows were permitted ... though she knew she mustn't do it in public, because it made other people uncomfortable.

Diana, for instance. If she'd been there, she would have said, 'Pull yourself together, mother!'

Ellie still had to tackle the leaves on the lawn, the clothes in the cupboard, the library books which must be returned, the paperwork, the toiletries in the bathroom. The stack of letters of sympathy, the cards. The lack of fresh bread or indeed any other fresh food in the fridge.

She went to stand in her favourite place by the French windows, looking out over the garden and up to the church beyond.

'Diana, it's mother. How are you?'

Normally when Ellie rang, she had to listen to Diana complaining about her boss, the woman who ran the nursery where her toddler went, the damage done to a new blouse by the dry cleaner ...

Ellie didn't like to think badly of anybody, but it had occasionally crossed her mind that Diana enjoyed finding fault with other people. Like ... Ellie stopped that thought before it could get any further. And then substituted a more acceptable one. Like Frank's Aunt Drusilla.

But after that cutting remark of hers at the funeral, Diana had changed and been very loving to her mother. She worried whether Ellie was eating properly, and urged her to pay them a long visit up north. Today Diana wanted to know whether Ellie was still taking her pills ...

'Diana dear, sorry to interrupt, but a most exciting thing happened here today ...'

Diana was shocked. She wanted her mother to pack a bag and go up north at once, that very day. 'You mustn't stay there any longer, and that's flat!'

'No, no, dear. It's quite all right ...'

When Ellie had lifted the phone to call Diana, she'd been half hoping that her daughter would renew her invitation to go up north to stay with them. But once the offer had been made, Ellie discovered she did not want to go. Anyway, it had been more of a command than an offer, and Ellie really did not like being bossed around by her daughter, however well-meaning.

Today I am going to be very positive, Ellie told herself. I am not going to take any more pills. I am going to set myself a job to do and I am going to do it. I will not get distracted. I will return our library books. I will be good and phone Aunt Drusilla to see how she's getting on. I will buy and cook a proper meal and eat it.

But first she must throw out the half-dead flowers; and in particular the lilies which were fading to brown in their unsuitably small vase. As she picked them up Ellie glanced at herself in the mirror to see that she was neat and tidy.

Frank hadn't liked her to flaunt herself in bright colours or wear makeup other than a little pink lipstick. Her short curly hair had turned silver early. Ellie thought this made her look dowdy and had been surprised to overhear a neighbour refer to her as 'an attractive little thing!'

That had been a boost to her morale.

She never wore black, as Frank had believed it was too harsh for her fair skin. Today she wore a cream and blue wool top and a blue skirt, which had pockets in it and was full enough to be comfortable.

Her mother – long dead – had always said, 'Cover your knees, dear, and always keep them together in company.'

Aunt Drusilla had said, 'Why don't you go on a diet?

Men can't be expected to be faithful to women who let themselves go.'

Ellie shook her head. Frank had been faithful to her, she thought. And if he hadn't been, she did not wish to know about it.

Ellie saw that Mrs Dawes had left her comb behind on the table under the mirror. Another job for her to do ...

Mrs Dawes ushered Ellie into her tiny terraced house.

'Come in, dear. I'm glad to see someone. Could you get me one or two things from the shops? I'm all of a twitch, daren't go out. The doctor said I should keep warm and try not to think about it. So did the vicar. Did you know he was talking to the lad just before he died?'

Ellie was pushed down into a chair. The room was small, overcrowded with brown furniture and too warm for comfort. Resignedly, Ellie set herself to be the listener Mrs Dawes needed.

'It wasn't one of the central heating men, dear. Chloe came in to see me after she finished work last night ...'

Ellie thought she ought to know who Chloe was, but for the life of her she couldn't remember.

Mrs Dawes tutted with impatience. 'Chloe, my grand-daughter? Taking a year off before going to university? She's saving up to travel round the world, wants to go back-packing in Australia – sounds dreadful to me, but that's what all these young people want to do. Anyway, she needs money so she's working part time at Sunflowers, the new café in the Avenue where they have all those good pastries. Well, Chloe says the central heating men went in the café after the police had finished with them. So it wasn't one of them. Which is a blessing in disguise really because if it had been one of them, the heating would never have been back on again for Sunday, would it? And there's nothing worse than a cold church, I always say.'

'So do they know who ...?'

'Mmhm. The vicar told me when he called to see if I was all right. He'd gone into the church yesterday lunchtime. He used the main door, of course, because that's the one nearest the vicarage. Anyway, he found the police there, photographing and all that. They asked him to take a look just in case he knew the man and of course he did, so that made things easier.'

'And who ...?'

Mrs Dawes sniffed. 'That no good son of Mrs Hanna's, all mouth and trousers and both of them needing a good wash out with soap, if you want my not-so-humble opinion. He'll not be missed.'

Again Ellie found she couldn't put a face to a name.

'Had a big stereo in his van, you could hear him coming a mile off. Flashy. Earrings and nose stud. No job, of course.'

Ellie nodded. She knew who it was now. Mrs Hanna worked in the bakery in the Avenue. A nice woman, her speech still heavily accented after all these years in Britain. Young Ferdy had been both the pride and despair of her life.

'How do they think ...?'

'Hit and run, the vicar thought; though the police wouldn't say, of course.'

Ellie's imagination produced a vision of young Ferdy being run down inside the church by a giant tank. She suppressed a smile. Mrs Dawes would not appreciate such levity ... any more than Frank would have done, come to think of it.

Mrs Dawes continued, 'It must have happened outside the church on the main road. That corner's ever so dangerous. I've always said they'd have a fatal accident there one day, and now it's happened. Then the driver panicked. He wouldn't want to leave the body in plain sight, would he? He must have spotted that the church was open because of the central heating men ... they're always in and out, leaving the door open and never mind the draughts and security ... well, the driver must have dragged Ferdy into the church and left him there, so as to give himself time to get away. I don't suppose they'll ever find him; the driver, I mean.'

What you really mean, thought Ellie, is that Ferdy's death is good riddance to bad rubbish.

Ellie didn't think Mrs Hanna would agree. She wanted to say, 'Let's hope the sinner found peace by ending up in the church,' but she felt that would be considered frivolous. Certainly Frank would have said it was in bad taste, and perhaps it was.

'I must go,' she said, getting to her feet. 'If you'll let me know what you need at the shops ...? And take it easy, won't you?'

'Oh, I just can't face going out. My legs start to shake as I get to the front door. Tell me if you hear anything else at the shops, won't you?'

Ellie thought that with any encouragement, Mrs Dawes would lapse into a victim frame of mind and stay there. Ellie herself knew just how easy it was to fall into that trap. She had only just escaped from it herself ... and could easily slip back into it again. Perhaps somebody tactful might be able to help Mrs Dawes, and prevent her sinking into premature old age?

She opened her mouth, hesitated, closed it. It surely wasn't up to her to say anything. On the other hand, if she didn't say anything, who would?

Ellie said, 'Now don't you worry about the flowers for this Sunday. I'm sure one of your team will be only too happy to take over. If they can't do it at such short notice, perhaps our organist can bodge something together ...'

Mrs Dawes' impressive bosom inflated. 'Nora? She's about as much good at it as you are! Nora touches my flower arrangements over my dead body!'

'I'm sure she will do her best,' said Ellie, craftily. 'Though of course ...'

'Her best is not good enough!' said Mrs Dawes. She thought for a moment and then reached for her coat. 'I'll just pop around to the church now and see what's happening. If the main altar is roped off, perhaps we can hold the services in the Lady Chapel. I'd better see the vicar about it. I left an armful of chrysanths in a bucket at the back of the church ... I wouldn't put it past those policemen to knock them over and then where will we be?'

Ellie did her shopping in the Avenue, which was buzzing with the news of the body found in the church. Did Ellie know anything about it? No? She hadn't seen anything? Well, not surprising, really. She'd probably have had the curtains drawn, that time of day. Would it make the national newspapers, did she think? She'd expected to be asked how she was feeling after the funeral, but only a couple of people remembered to do that.

Ellie told her fellow workers in the charity shop that she hoped to be back with them the following week. She could see that they were ready to shove all their problems back on to her again. So and so had said this, to which She had taken exception, et cetera. Ellie told them she was sure they were managing beautifully. They agreed, looking doubtful. She hoped they would refrain from quarrelling outright till she got back.

Ellie had held down a good secretarial post until she was married and had Diana. After that she had worked as much as she could while suffering a shattering series of miscarriages. By the time they had given up any hope of another child, Frank had been doing so well that there had been no need for her second salary. Frank had urged her to take up charity work instead. Ellie hadn't minded the loss of independence because she'd enjoyed being a home-maker. Only now there was no one at home to look after.

There was no reply when she returned to Mrs Dawes', so Ellie assumed the dear lady had overcome her trembling legs enough to return to her usual routine.

Ellie put in an unpleasant afternoon's work sorting out Frank's clothing and ate an early supper in front of the television. Frank would never eat on a tray in front of the television. She felt guilty about letting her standards slip, but was too tired to care. She ducked ringing Aunt Drusilla. She would do that tomorrow.

She drew the long green and cream patterned curtains in the big room and then went into the kitchen to draw down the blinds there. With her hand on the blind over the back door, she stared out over the dark shadows in the garden and up to the church.

She hadn't bothered to put on the kitchen light, but she could see well enough as there was a street light in the alley, used as a short cut night and day. And the church and grounds were lit by the lights of the main road beyond. Some people thought the church grounds looked creepy at night, but Ellie had always loved the view. Until now. Now it did look a little sinister.

What nonsense! That was all in her mind, remembering Ferdy's death.

Only ... a woman was sitting on the bench by the side door to the church.

Ellie got her coat and went to join her. Mrs Hanna, the dead boy's mother, was sitting as near as she could to the place in which her son had been found.

Ellie sat beside her, unable to find the right words. She found herself stumbling into silent prayer. Please, help her, help me ... I don't know what to say ...

After a while she felt better. Quieter in her mind.

It began to rain. Not much. A drizzle.

From across the road, the fat man in the Saab watched the two women.

2

Mrs Hanna sighed and got to her feet. 'Have to be up early.'

Ellie nodded. Of course, Mrs Hanna worked at the bakery.

Mrs Hanna said, 'Show you something.' She opened a large leatherette bag and took out a wallet. Inside the wallet was a photo of a beautiful dark-haired young boy. Ferdy, aged five or six. Mrs Hanna showed it to Ellie, without letting go of it.

Ellie said, 'It's so sad.'

The drizzle misted everything, their coats, their faces.

Mrs Hanna asked, 'Why? That's what I want to know.'

Ellie lifted her hands, helplessly. She didn't know why.

'You live in that house? I see you draw the curtains. You must of seen something. You saw who killed my boy, no?'

'No, I'm sorry. I didn't see anything.' Between her grief and the pills she'd been taking, she wouldn't have noticed if a flying saucer had landed in the church grounds two nights ago.

Of course, Mrs Hanna didn't know about Frank's death, the funeral, Ellie's shock and grief. How should she? It was only natural she should think Ellie had seen something.

Mrs Hanna pushed her face close to Ellie. 'You did, didn't you?'

Ellie shook her head. 'No, I didn't see anything.'

Yet something lurked at the back of her mind. A voice crying out, footsteps, someone rushing along the alley ...?

No, that had been one of her nightmares, she was sure of it. Anyway, the memory – if it was that – had gone now.

She said, 'If I could help, I would.'

'You think. Then you tell me, right?'

'Right,' said Ellie, not knowing what else to say.

Mrs Hanna became aware of the rain. She produced a plastic hood from her bag. Tying it around her head, she set off towards the Avenue. Ellie wished, fiercely, that she could have helped Mrs Hanna. As usual she felt totally inadequate.

The driver of the Saab had kept the engine running, so that he could use the windscreen wipers now and again. It was necessary to report on what the two women were doing. The boss would be interested to hear that they had met and talked. When Mrs Hanna left, the car followed her.

Returning home, Ellie fell over something wet on the back doorstep. It turned out to be a ragged bunch of chrysanthemums.

Ellie glanced around, but there was no light on in the shed at the bottom of the garden and no sign of the boy.

Nine-year-old Tod lived three doors along the alleyway. His mother worked, his father wasn't around and Tod was a solitary soul who preferred making himself a den in her garden shed to playing football or mucking around with computers as most of his friends did.

Ellie liked Tod, and Tod liked her. She supplied him with biscuits, squash and the occasional battery for his camping torch. In exchange he sometimes helped her with the weeding in the garden. Frank never lifted a finger in the garden.

Tod didn't like his own garden, most of which was under concrete. Tod liked spiders, stray cats and swimming. Tod's mother had probably told him 'not to go bothering Ellie at the moment', and he wouldn't. Tod was a nice boy. But he'd obviously been thinking about her and had picked a bunch of chrysanthemums – from Ellie's own garden by the look of it – to lay on her back doorstep.

A nice thought, even though it looked as if he'd broken off the stems by hand. What would Mrs Dawes say to that!

Ellie began to laugh. She laughed until she cried. She told herself that having hysterics was no way to get the flowers in water, and set herself to finding a suitable vase for them.

The Saab followed Mrs Hanna as she crossed the main road by the pedestrian crossing and turned into the Avenue. The driver pulled in to the side of the road and watched as Mrs Hanna found her key and opened the door leading to the flats above the shops. A light went on in the corridor. After an interval that light went out, and another went on in the top flat.

The fat man extracted himself from his car with some difficulty and walked across the road to check on the names beside each bell-push.

Ellie was dozing in front of the television when the doorbell rang. Some door-to-door salesman, probably.

Archie Benjamin, churchwarden and something hot in the financial field; smallish, roundish, swarthy and six o'clock-shadowed. He had the good sense not to sit in Frank's chair, but arranged himself on the settee.

Ellie turned off the television. As she went to sit down, he captured one of her hands in both of his, and patted it.

'My dear Ellie, how are you?'

Despite her resolution not to cry in front of others, she felt a rush of tears coming. She managed to hold them off with a steady, 'Quite well, thank you.'

She liked Archie Benjamin in a tepid sort of way. He'd been one of Frank's best friends. The two men had always had their heads together on church affairs and together they'd backed the vicar in his crusade to rebuild the decrepit church hall.

Archie had a gold-glinting smile. 'You must ring me night or day, if ever there is the slightest thing I can do. Promise?'

She nodded, withdrawing her hand from his and wishing she'd taken out her supper tray before he came.

'Not too distressed with all the hoo-hah?' He gestured in the direction of the church.

She shook her head. She didn't like to think of poor Mrs Hanna. Or about Ferdy, who might have been a tearaway but who certainly hadn't deserved to end up dead in front of the altar.

'A terrible affair. Of course you're upset. Coming so soon after ... what a loss! Frank and I must have worked together for, oh, five years? Six?'

She nodded.

'You must feel bereft. Heartbroken.'

He's overdoing it, isn't he? said a little voice at the back of Ellie's head.

He laid his warm hand on top of hers. 'I meant it when I said you must ring me, if there's any little thing I can do for you ...'

The little voice in Ellie's head completed the sentence, '... in your time of trial.' It was awful to feel so ungrateful for his kind wishes, but he made her want to laugh. She stuffed her handkerchief against her mouth and kept her eyes down on her lap. Hysteria, of course.

He thought she was stifling tears.

'There, there!' he said.

She blew her nose, put her hankie away and said, 'I'm all right now, thank you.'

He cleared his throat. 'We shan't want to lose you, but I suppose you will be selling up, moving near your daughter in ... where is it? ... Birmingham? Leeds? Houses like this go for a bomb nowadays. Or do you want to sell up and buy a small flat somewhere nearby? I don't want to see you cheated. I know a good estate agent, and could contact him for you if you like.'

'I'm not sure what I want to do yet. My solicitor said not to do anything for a while. Diana does want me to move up there but I've lived here all my married life, my roots are here, I help out in the charity shop ... oh, not since the funeral of course, but I do plan to go back soon.'

He was nothing if not gallant. 'You do more than just help out, I hear. That place would collapse without you. I always said to my dear wife when she was with me ...'

His dear wife had upped and gone off with a wealthy businessman two years ago.

'... that behind every successful man, there is a mighty fine woman and let's face it, where would Frank have been without you, eh?'

Ellie's eyes rounded in surprise. Was Archie Benjamin making a pass at her? She was afraid she was going to get the giggles.

She said, 'You wanted to see me about something?'

He shuffled back in his seat. 'No, no. I wanted to see you, of course, to see how you were, offer to help in any way ... and I didn't plan to bother you about the other matter yet, but as you've raised the subject ... the fact is that there's the PCC meeting at church coming up and we're stuck for the minutes of the last one, which Frank took. He doesn't seem to have sent them out before he ...

'Now I don't want you to bother your head looking for them, but before I go, if you'd allow me, I could just take a shufti around in his study and see if I can find them. Frank was always so efficient, they're probably in a pile somewhere, all run off and waiting to be delivered.'

Ellie disliked the thought of rooting around in Frank's study, but on the other hand, she really did not want this tacky little man going in there by himself. She wondered how she'd gone so quickly from tepid liking to active dislike.

'I'll look for them tomorrow and if I find them, I'll drop them in to your house.'

She expected him to go now but instead he leaned back and laced his fingers across his waistcoat, ready for a gossip.

'A little bird told me Mrs Dawes came to you for tea and sympathy when she found the body in the church. I said to my secretary, "It sounds as if young Ferdy was seeking sanctuary in the church."' He laughed, fatly. 'Sanctuary from his sins. Get it?'

Ellie inclined her head, wondering not why his wife had left him, but why it had taken her so long to do so.

'Mustn't speak ill of the dead, I suppose. I saw him, you know, just after he'd had words with the vicar. Quite a lively exchange. About that van of his, of course. He'd parked it right across the church hall entrance with the stereo going full blast. I said to him – to the vicar, I mean – it was lucky I happened to come along straight after, gave him an alibi, what?'

'Why should the vicar need an alibi? Wasn't it a hit and run accident?'

'That's what we all thought, wasn't it? Hit and run and then dump the body. But the police came round doing house-to-house enquiries and they were very interested in what I had to say.'

He leaned forward, all confidentiality. 'I happened to see young Ferdy standing by his van as I drove back from work. He was looking after the vicar with such a wicked expression on his face. If looks could kill, you know? The vicar saw me and came across the road to ask about the missing PCC notes. Then as I was putting the car in the garage I noticed Ferdy quarrelling with that girl who's just moved in next door to you … what's her name? Kate something.'

Ellie's eyes went to the door leading to the hall. These houses were semi-detached. The previous owners had been very quiet, but since Kate and her husband had moved in Ellie had heard disturbing noises through the party wall. Shouting. Banging of doors. The odd scream.

Ellie had even had a nightmare in which Kate had been running along the alley, weeping.

Ellie frowned. Was that what she'd been trying to remember while she was talking to Mrs Hanna? Kate running along the alley … not towards her own house, but away from it? Crying?

The more Ellie homed in on the memory, the more she wondered if it had really happened or just been one of the awful dreams she'd been having lately. She'd been sleeping so badly that in addition to the pills the doctor had given her for daytime use, she'd resorted to sleeping pills. Nothing very strong, just herbal ones. They'd not been all that efficient, though. Several nights since Frank died she'd wandered around the house and thought she'd gone back to bed only to wake up in her armchair downstairs instead.

She was feeling a little better since she'd stopped taking the pills in the daytime.

She really could not be sure whether it had been a dream or not. Anyway, it was none of her business what Kate did.

Archie hadn't noticed her temporary abstraction.

'... so I told the police they'd better check that young woman out. Local girl married well, isn't she? Husband got a good job somewhere? Must be doing well, to have bought the house next door. I don't suppose you've had much to do with them?'

'They only moved in a month ago, just before Frank ...'

'... you won't have had time to get to know her, then. Best keep it that way, in case. It rather looks as if she quarrelled with the lad, hit him over the head with something ... she's a tall girl, isn't she? Well-built, always frowning, got a nasty temper, I wouldn't wonder. And that boy Ferdy wasn't tall. She could have killed him and then run over him with his own van to make it look like a hit and run accident.'

Archie was enjoying himself, relishing his reconstruction of the death. Ellie felt slightly sick.

She stood up. 'It's getting late and I mustn't keep you. I'll be in touch as soon as I can find your minutes.'

Flustered, he got to his feet. 'Feeling a bit tired, are we? Thought you might like it if I prayed with you for a while ... consolation, and so on.'

The skin crawled down Ellie's back. 'That's kind of you, but perhaps another time.'

She saw him out, promising that yes, she'd call him whenever she felt she needed someone to talk to. And not meaning it.

The lights stayed on in Mrs Hanna's flat until two o'clock in the morning. Soon after they were switched off, a car drove away.

Ellie woke at four in the morning, wept till five, went down to make herself a cuppa and finished the night off in the big chair in the lounge. She woke from another bad dream, but that was the usual one about looking for Frank through a series of hospital doors. Not about Kate.

If her 'dream' about Kate in the alley had been a true memory, then why had the girl been running away from her house, and not towards it? It worried Ellie. She wondered whether Mrs Hanna had heard Archie's story about Kate, and if the police had taken it seriously. She would not think about it. It was none of her business, despite Mrs Hanna's demand for help.

Ellie put the radio on for company.

Another day.

She would make a list of all the difficult things she had to do, and try to do one each day. She supposed she ought to ring Aunt Drusilla.

If the opportunity arose, she would also talk to Kate next door, not because Mrs Hanna wished her to make enquiries, but because Ellie was uneasy about the girl.

Archie Benjamin had assumed Ellie didn't know Kate but they had met in the alley once or twice and had talked over the hedge. Commonplace observations, nothing important, but laying the building blocks for a good relationship with her neighbour in the future.

Ellie had liked the girl and was disturbed to think Kate might be mixed up in Ferdy's death.

Could Kate actually have killed him? Instinct said no.

True, the girl's face in repose did have a brooding look, probably due to her rather heavy dark eyebrows and strong chin, but she lit up when she smiled. Her hair was always well groomed, her clothes unobtrusive but high quality, and she had an excellent figure.

Of course, thought Ellie with a sigh, the girl did have the height and the broad shoulders to carry off designer clothing. At five foot two, Ellie usually had to shorten her skirts to keep them off the ground. She remembered that Frank had once called her a pocket Venus. But that was way back when ...

Ellie made herself a cup of tea and resolutely thought about the couple next door. Her kitchen and front downstairs room – Frank's study – adjoined Kate's, but there was no sound of life today from the other side of the wall. Of course, Kate went off to work early, as did her husband. Had Kate said he taught at the high school?

Ellie thought about the noises they'd been making next door. Banging doors, screams, feet pounding up the stairs. Noises to be expected when a teasing newly married wife was being chased up the stairs by an amorous husband. Ellie had been slightly amused by the noises until she'd been so distracted by Frank's sudden illness that she'd forgotten about them.

Ellie thought, I must take Frank up his cup of tea.

And remembered.

She did not cry but turned to look out over the garden. It had rained hard all night, which would make the job of clearing up the leaves more difficult. The Michaelmas daisies were making a fine show and the chrysanths were coming along nicely. The pyracantha berries had turned bright red, and as the leaves dropped away from the viburnum fragrans, its dark pink flower buds opened, glowing in the dark November day. She would deal with the leaves on the lawn today.

First things first. She must be practical. She got a plastic bag and emptied the bathroom cabinet of Frank's shaving things, his aftershave, soap, pills …

Pills hadn't helped him. He'd prided himself on keeping fit, taking vitamin supplements, brisk walks.

She was not going to cry. She'd cried enough for one day.

She tied the bag up firmly, and dumped it in the dustbin with last week's *Radio Times* and free local newspaper, still unread. Should she cancel the daily papers? She hadn't read them for days.

Frank had taken a keen interest in all forms of the media. The Internet. The *Independent*. Watching the news.

She set out for the shops. She must buy lots of fresh fruit and vegetables. Perhaps a little fish. It was too far to go to the supermarket, but luckily most things could be found in the Avenue.

Most people, too.

Everyone she met wanted to talk about Ferdy's death. Only a few mentioned Frank, saying the usual things; how sorry they were to hear about him, what a shock it had been, how much she must miss him. Some of them meant it. Some crossed the road rather than speak to her.

It takes all sorts.

A cold day. The leaves stirred damply under her feet as she walked back from the shops with her purchases.

Spiderman was waiting outside her front door, shifting from one foot to the other while searching through his pockets. Their vicar, the Reverend Gilbert Adams.

'Dear Ellie, I was going to leave you a note.'

Tall, ungainly, bespectacled, concerned for her. He held her shoulders, kissed her cheek and stood back to take a good look. 'I can see you're coping. You're one of the strong ones.'

'Hmph!' said Ellie. 'I bet you say that to all the widows.'

'I do, and occasionally I mean it.'

She laughed. 'Tea, coffee, or a sherry? I think there was some sherry left in a bottle after ...' She swallowed.

Gilbert nodded. He knew all about wakes and sherry and how much alcohol might be left afterwards.

Sherry, the best chair. Frank's chair. Well, she had to get used to other people sitting in that.

She hadn't meant to complain, but the words burst out of her. 'Sometimes I get so angry with him for dying like that. And I cry a lot, don't sleep well.'

'To be expected. Better than denying it.' He leant forward to put his hand on her knee. 'Don't let anyone tell you to keep a stiff upper lip. Cry all you want ...'

'... but not in public?'

He laughed. 'You'll do. I hear you handled Mrs Dawes brilliantly.'

'She just needed to talk. It was a shock.'

'Yes, it was. I'm sorry for Mrs Hanna. If you've got a moment, perhaps you'd like to drop by her place. She lives in one of the flats above the shops in the Avenue. I've got the number somewhere ...' Again he started to search his pockets.

'I saw her yesterday. She practically accused me of having seen the murder and ignoring it. No, I exaggerate, but she did think I ought to have seen something. She asked me to help her find out ... Of course it's ridiculous. The police will deal with it. I'm sorry for her, but ... someone said you identified the body. Was he badly marked?'

'No. The back of his head was a mess. I suppose he hit the kerb when he was knocked down and then got dumped in the church to delay pursuit. His van's missing, you know. I'd told him off about leaving it across the entrance to the church hall that very evening. I suppose whoever knocked him down had a passenger who drove the van away ... who knows?'

Ellie thought of Archie and his tale about Kate. 'It's not murder, then?'

The vicar stared. 'Not that I've heard, no.' So much for Archie's gossip.

Gilbert finished his drink. 'Well, to business. Frank was a great guy, and we're all going to miss him. He and Archie Benjamin were the driving force behind so much that we're doing in the parish. I know Frank relied on you to help him in everything he did and I'm hoping that a bit later on, when you're feeling more settled, you'll perhaps take on one or two of his jobs for us?'

'Oh, I couldn't possibly. I mean, I did help Frank out with some typing sometimes, but that was all.'

'You underrate yourself, Ellie. I've never known anyone as cool as you in a crisis.'

She was amused. He didn't half know how to lay it on!

'I know it's too soon for you to make any major decisions, but ...' with a comical look, 'if you can spare a thought for our next crisis ...'

31

'The notes for the PCC meeting? I looked last night but couldn't find them. I suppose Frank must have put them on his word processor because he always did that straight after the meetings, but he can't have run them off yet.'

'Well, you can run them off for us, can't you?'

'I'm sorry, but I don't know how. The computer was Frank's toy and I never touched it. He was afraid I might erase an important document or damage it in some way. I must admit, I'm rather frightened of it. I used my old electric typewriter if he wanted me to type anything up.'

He frowned. In her fragile state she interpreted this as a criticism of her inadequacy. She hadn't meant to cry. She jumped up and went to stand in the window overlooking the garden. He put his arm about her, and pulled her close.

'Sorry. I'm being stupid.'

He kissed her cheek. 'Ellie, you know I was very fond of Frank, but he did tend to underrate you. Believe in yourself, my dear. You're a great girl.'

She sniffed. To be called a 'girl' twice that week was too much. Still, it was nice to be appreciated.

She said, 'Suppose I see if I can find the manual and work out how to run the notes off? But you'll have to give me time. It's all too much, too soon.'

'You should join the choir, take your mind off things.'

She tried to laugh. 'That would put the choir off singing for good! Frank always said I couldn't hold a tune to save my life!'

'Stand by someone with a loud voice, and no one will notice.'

He went off without even offering to pray with her. She didn't mind that. She knew he was praying for her at the moment. She couldn't pray for herself yet. But perhaps it would come.

She felt much comforted by his visit.

Only, later that day she remembered that the Reverend Gilbert Adams – though a delightfully caring pastor – did have a reputation for 'warm personal contact' with the widows of his parish. And, or so gossip reported, with their exceedingly plain but talented unmarried organist!

A nice man, she thought, but she wasn't going to take his winning ways at face value. Particularly since he had a delightful wife who understood him perfectly.

At the bakery they were short-handed. Where was Mrs Hanna? Was she ill?

She hadn't rung to say she was ill. But they were too busy to send anyone looking for her.

Ellie wondered if she should pop round and have a chat with Kate. But there was still no sound of movement next door.

She tried to work out what day of the week it was. The funeral had been on Tuesday. The house had been full of his friends and relatives. Some of them – particularly Aunt Drusilla – had lingered for hours. Diana and her wishy-washy husband Stewart had stayed over till Wednesday afternoon and then gone back north.

Mrs Dawes had found the body on Thursday. Ellie knew it must have been Thursday because Mrs Dawes had mentioned that she'd just come from her flower-arranging class. Therefore, Ferdy had been killed some time after Archie had come home from work on Wednesday. Ellie would have been alone in the house by then.

Mrs Hanna seemed to think that Ellie must have seen something of the murder. Now she came to think about it, it was odd that she hadn't because since Frank died, she'd stood at that window for hours on end, looking up at the church. She tried to think back, to imagine herself standing there the day after the funeral. Surely she would have seen if anything untoward had occurred up at the church?

No, it was a blank. She couldn't even remember if it had rained or not.

Yesterday she'd been shopping for herself and Mrs Dawes. Then Archie Benjamin had called. That would have been Friday.

So today was Saturday. Or was it? The shops had been open, so it couldn't have been Sunday. She scrabbled for the day's paper, but then wasn't sure whether it was today's or yesterday's. She found the new *Radio Times* and turned the television on to check on the programmes. Yes, it was Saturday.

It was a relief to have that straightened out in her mind.

What had she wanted to know for?

She'd wanted to talk to Kate. It was odd that neither of them were at home at a weekend. Ellie peered out of the front window on to the street, but couldn't see Kate's car. Or his. She wasn't good at remembering whose car was which, but she knew Kate's car number, because it had the letters FLU in it. They must have gone away for the weekend.

Very well, she'd go and see if she could find the manual for the word processor instead.

There was nothing so frustrating as trying to understand a manual if you didn't even know what language it was written in. This particular manual might as well have been written in Chinese for all the sense it made to Ellie. She tried to turn the machine on. Nothing happened. After a long wait she tried again with a firmer touch. This time she succeeded in conjuring up some incomprehensible language which to her horror disappeared before she could decipher it. A sort of brightly coloured flag. Then a whirligigging arrow and a clock on the picture of the inside of a station. It looked like Paddington station to her.

Superimposed on the station came some more, smaller pictures. She didn't know what she was supposed to do with them. She opened the manual and tried to find out.

When she looked up again, the screen had altered to present a blue sky with some clouds on it. Cartoon-style biplanes zoomed across in slow motion. How they had got there, she couldn't imagine.

Further recourse to the manual left her mind in a whirl. And still the biplanes swooped. Then suddenly the screen went blank. She'd been at it for what seemed like hours, was no nearer to finding out how to run off the PCC notes, and felt in need of a strong cup of tea. She switched off the computer and attempted to recover her wits.

Once fortified by tea, she decided to return to the study and sort out some bills to pay. She opened the front of Frank's bureau, and nearly dropped her cup.

Frank had inherited some valuable cufflinks and diamond studs from his father, which were kept in a leather case in the middle drawer of his bureau. It would have been more convenient to keep them in their bedroom, but the bureau – a cumbersome affair with many pigeonholes – had been one of the few items which Frank had managed to bring away from his old home, and it had come down to him with its contents intact. The bureau was where his father had kept his cufflinks, so that's where Frank had continued to keep them.

Only, the drawer in which they were kept was open. And empty. The key was still in the lock, but the leather case was gone.

She'd been burgled, on top of everything else!

3

Ellie hadn't seen any other sign that she'd been burgled, but the cufflinks were not there.

She told herself not to panic. To think back.

On the morning of the funeral there had been a phone call from one of Frank's cousins, needing directions to the church. The main phone was in the hall, with an extension in the study. Stewart had taken the call in the hall, saying he would get Ellie to ring the woman back. Ellie had gone into the study to look up the cousin's telephone number and make the call.

Aunt Drusilla had been in the study, too, picking up and reading the messages on Frank's get-well cards which had just been removed from the sitting-room. Ellie had supposed Aunt Drusilla was making notes to telephone anyone who had not sent a card, demanding to know why not.

Ellie remembered that she'd sat down at the bureau, taken out the address book, phoned the cousin and replaced the address book in its pigeonhole.

All the drawers had been shut when she last sat at the bureau. And the key? The key had been in the right-hand drawer, the one which held Frank's gold pen and pencil, his cheque book, their passports, and so on. She would have noticed if it had not been in its usual place.

She opened the right-hand drawer.

The chequebook and passports were still there, but Frank's gold pen and pencil had disappeared.

It was too much. She supposed she must call the police and report the burglary, but ... it was all so hopeless ... what could they do? She had no idea when the precious things had gone.

Since there were no other signs of breaking and entering, it must have been one of the people at the funeral who had taken the things. All Frank's friends and relatives would have to be questioned. Including Aunt Drusilla.

Ellie couldn't help laughing at the thought of Aunt Drusilla being questioned by the police. Ellie's money would be on the redoubtable old lady.

A couple of generations back, the Quicke family had made a lot of money in whalebone corsets. Of course, you never mentioned the word 'corsets' to Aunt Drusilla, who would have preferred that the money had come from owning land or property. Privately, Ellie thought Aunt Drusilla was a walking advertisement for whalebone corsets herself.

When old Mr Quicke died, he had left the corset business and large Victorian house to his son, while his money went to his only daughter Drusilla. 'Young' Mr Quicke – Frank's father – had been no great businessman, the market in corsets had declined and by the time his only son had been born and his wife had died, he had been struggling to keep the business going.

It must have seemed providential to the widower when his sister Drusilla offered to give up her own house and move in to look after her brother and his little boy. In time the corset business was sold and the proceeds invested in stocks which always seemed to go down and not up. Frank's father lingered on, an ineffectual man in the shadow of his more forceful sister.

Frank did eventually inherit the house when his father died, but Aunt Drusilla stayed on. As she said, where else was a poor old woman to go?

How could Frank turn her out, when Aunt Drusilla had sacrificed her life to bring him up? The least he could do was to see that she was undisturbed in her old age.

It went without saying that Aunt Drusilla had never liked Ellie. In turn, it had been difficult for Ellie not to imagine how much easier her early married life would have been if Aunt Drusilla had consented to move to a smaller place, so that the big house could have been sold. It was only after Frank got his first big promotion that life had become easier.

Worse still, when Ellie married Frank, Aunt Drusilla had assumed that Ellie would be available for all sorts of jobs which she would not entrust to hired help. Ellie's own mother had died a couple of years previously, so at first she had welcomed the opportunity to be of assistance to Frank's aunt. Until, that is, she discovered that services rendered were rewarded with criticism, not thanks or praise. Ellie had persevered, knowing how much Frank loved and respected his aunt, but it had been hard going.

Ellie put her head in her hands. She thought that Aunt Drusilla would have a field day when she heard of the loss of Frank's belongings. Ellie could hear her now ... 'such carelessness!' Why, she had even said loudly after the funeral that Ellie couldn't have been looking after Frank properly, or he would never have died.

Ellie felt her blood pressure rise at the thought of facing Aunt Drusilla's displeasure. But it would have to be done, wouldn't it?

She tried to be practical. If she were going to ring the police she must first discover what else – if anything – was missing.

Systematically she went through the house, checking. Frank's computer still sat smugly on its mat. Drat it! She wouldn't have grieved if that had gone missing! Her few bits and pieces of jewellery in the bedroom ... the silver salver on the sideboard ... the silver vase – with a wilted rose in it – on the glass cabinet ... the canteen of good silver ... the silver-framed photo of Diana and Stewart on their wedding day ...

The video was still there, and the television. Looking out of the window on to the street, Ellie averted her eyes from the space in the road where Frank had been accustomed to parking his car. Diana had driven away in it, when she and Stewart went back north again.

Ellie had never learned to drive. Frank had always said she would be the sort of driver who signalled left and turned right. Of course, it was only right and proper that Diana should have the car when Ellie couldn't drive, but ...

Diana might have asked nicely, instead of just assuming ...

Well, it seemed that nothing else was missing.

Glancing distractedly out of the French windows, Ellie thought she saw the boy Tod going into the garden shed, then realized that she was mistaken.

With an uncharacteristic surge of rage, Ellie told herself that she could guess where Frank's precious things had gone. Tod was a magpie, 'borrowing' the odd cup here and the odd Biro there to furnish his 'den'. If he'd 'borrowed' Frank's things ...!

But, no! No, Tod would never take anything as good as that. Would he?

While she hesitated, a large man in old but reasonably good clothes walked up the garden path next door. Ellie blinked.

Another burglar?

She put out her hand to telephone the police and then heard noises from beyond the party wall. One of her neighbours had returned. Not Kate. Armand, or some such fancy name.

She checked the street from the front window and saw that yes, his car was back. And another car was parked close up behind it. Very close.

A second man was walking down the path and knocking on the door. Ellie recognized him. It was the senior policeman who had been summoned to take Mrs Dawes' statement after she found Ferdy's body. Ellie couldn't remember his name. Inspector something. Mace? Brace? Middle-aged, hard faced.

Presumably they'd come to talk to Kate, who wasn't back yet.

Well, I can catch them on their way out and tell them about the thefts, Ellie thought. Or would they be too senior to bother about such a trivial thing as burglary?

In any case, if it were one of Frank's relations who ...

Ellie rubbed her forehead. She couldn't think straight.

She decided to go out and clear the leaves off the lawn. Armand must have let the two policemen into the house, for there was no sign of either of them in the garden.

She collected her rake and a garden bag from the shed – no sign of Tod, she'd speak to him later – and started work. The day was dull and unseasonably warm, the earth moist after the rain. The lawn could do with a good raking over, to get all the moss out. The lower part of the garden was always a little damp; perhaps some day she'd have a pond there.

'... what the hell's business it is of yours ...' a man was saying. Almost shouting.

She started. Armand had thrown one half of his French windows open. She could see part of their living-room through the gaps in the dividing hedge, and hear very well indeed.

Another voice murmured something.

'Nonsense!' Armand seemed angry. He was a foxy-looking man, not all that tall. He stepped out on to the patio and began wrenching a crust of bread into pieces and placing it on a bird table. Trying to ignore his visitors?

Ellie couldn't help overhearing. In fact, she found she was a little tired from all her exertions and sat down on the garden seat on her own patio to rest.

'... because we have reason to believe that your wife knew the dead man very well indeed ... school together ...' That wasn't the inspector speaking, so it must be his sergeant. She didn't know his name, either.

'She knew lots of people. She was brought up around here, went to school here. I suppose she did know him. So what? So did lots of other people.'

'I believe you haven't been married very long ...'

'Six weeks to the day, if you must know.'

'... yet your wife leaves you to go off for the weekend on her own?'

'She arranged to go to this conference long before we got married.'

'You expect her back ... when?'

'Tomorrow afternoon, early evening. Depends on the traffic.'

'I'm surprised you didn't go with her ...'

'What would I do at that sort of function? I'm a teacher, for heaven's sake, not a financial whizz-kid.'

'Your wife is a "financial whizz-kid"?'

'An accountant, yes. Works on computers, mostly.'

'A computer whizz-kid? Doing well?'

'I suppose.' Sulkily. 'I don't know anything about computers.' He turned back to the house. 'You should be asking her these questions, not me. And if that's all ... I've got a pile of marking to do and preparation for next week ...'

He picked up a broom that was leaning against the house and started to sweep the patio clear of leaves. He's trying to find something to occupy his hands with, Ellie thought, something that means he doesn't have to look at the policemen. He must be afraid of something, or he'd have told them to get out of his house.

Evidently the inspector agreed with Ellie, for he now took up the questioning.

'You've known your wife long?'

'Just over a year. Why are you asking all these questions?'

'How did you meet her?'

'At a party. She came with a friend. We left together, have been together ever since.'

'Was Ferdy Hanna at the party?'

'Is that why you're questioning me? Did I know Ferdy? No, I didn't. As far as I know, I've never set eyes on him. And if that's all ...'

'But your wife—'

'... then you can stuff it, and get the hell out of here ...'

'All we want to know is if—'

43

Armand threw down the broom with a clatter. 'You want to know if my wife was having an affair with him and I'm telling you, No, of course not!'

Startled, Ellie swivelled round in her seat and tried to peer through the hedge, but at that point the foliage was dense and she could see nothing either of Armand or the policemen.

'Since you've raised the subject—'

Armand swore and stamped back into the house. Ellie heard his feet scrape on the sill. The door banged to. Fortunately for Ellie, it creaked open again immediately. That door had always been difficult to shut. The previous owners had talked about replacing it but never got around to it.

Ellie imagined Armand busying himself, getting papers out of a briefcase, perhaps. Laying them out on the table in preparation for marking.

The door remained ajar but, maddeningly, the men inside had lowered their voices. After a while, though, Ellie could hear Armand's voice in snatches, as if he were striding around the room. She shifted on her seat, trying to line up with a gap in the hedge.

'... because she didn't tell me about him till ... and then I saw them together ... but she lied to me, saying she hadn't ... you can't believe anything women say ...'

The inspector – Mace? Stacy? Place? – came to stand by the door and look out over the garden. Ellie hardly dared to breathe but he didn't notice her. He turned back into the room while leaning on the door frame, to say, 'But you suspected that she was still seeing him, even after you got married?'

A mumbled 'Yes'.

'And you did nothing about it?'

Another mumble, the words indistinguishable.

'So what you're saying now is that in spite of everything you could do, she went on seeing Ferdy. What happened last Wednesday?'

Silence.

The inspector changed position slightly. 'What time did you get home from school?'

'I was late. There was a meeting. You don't know what it's like, being a teacher. You think we finish work at—'

'Just tell me what time you got home.'

The voices were both clearer now.

'About half five, I suppose. No sign of her. Obviously she was working late again. No supper ready, of course. Nothing in the fridge or the freezer. I had to go out and buy something in the Avenue. I don't know how long I was. Twenty minutes, thirty? When I got back, she'd been and gone again.'

'How do you know she'd been back to the house?'

'Her car was out front, her big coat and laptop were in the hall. The lights were on, but she'd gone straight out again.'

'To meet him, you think?'

'I ... don't know! I just can't ...! Leave me alone!'

'You think she went out again to meet him? By arrangement?'

Silence.

'She wouldn't have gone out again so quickly and without her big coat, if she were going far, would she? Perhaps he came and tapped on the window here, asked her to meet him at the church, where he'd parked his car. And then ... what happened then?'

Silence.

'I suggest that there was a quarrel, that she hit him and he fell over backwards, hit his head on the kerb. When she realized what she'd done, she panicked, spotted that the church was open, dragged him in there and left him.'

Armand sounded sulky. 'I thought it was supposed to be a hit and run accident.'

'He was killed by a single blow to the head, but not in front of the altar where he was found. Immediately after death, he was dragged to the altar and left there. Symbolic, don't you think? His being left at the altar. She was going to marry him before you came along, wasn't she?'

'No!'

'Are you sure?'

A long pause. 'Leave me alone! You're torturing me!'

Silence. The policeman at the window shivered, turned round and pulled the French windows to, shutting himself in with Armand and his colleague.

Ellie, too, shivered. The wind was getting up. She was stiff from sitting in an awkward position. Hastily she shovelled the leaves into a bag, dumped it at the back of the shed, and made her way up into the house for another cup of tea.

By the time she had drunk her tea, the policemen had gone and she hadn't done anything about the loss of Frank's precious things.

She lay back in her chair and put her feet up. Closing her eyes, she thought, I don't care about Frank's things. I don't care about anything. I just wish the day would stop right here, and not get any worse.

★   ★   ★

The fat man reported from his mobile.

'Yeah, all's well. She went shopping, didn't speak to anyone for long. The vicar came round later. I saw him in the window with her, him with his arm around her and all. The filth came round, but not to see her. To see her next-door neighbour. Yeah, it's a right laugh. The buzz in the neighbourhood is that it was some old flame of his that killed him. Even better, the girl lives next door to the old biddy. The filth came round to see the girlfriend and saw the husband instead. I saw them in the garden at the back. They were there about an hour … the old biddy was in her garden next door all the time … eavesdropping, it looked like.'

The phone quacked. 'Nah, doesn't look like she's said nothing, or the filth would have been on to her. Maybe she's just too dumb to realize what she saw …'

Sunday morning. Ellie got ready for church, doing all the little jobs that she usually did on a Sunday morning. She dusted the living-room, disposed of Saturday's newspapers, watered the houseplants and got a small joint out of the freezer for supper.

Then she rang Aunt Drusilla. Either she or Frank – usually Ellie – had always rung Aunt Drusilla on Sundays before church. Would she have the nerve to tell Aunt Drusilla about the loss of Frank's trinkets?

'You're late!' That was Aunt Drusilla's greeting.

Immediately Ellie was thrown on the defensive. 'Am I? I'm sorry. I didn't realize …'

'Do you think I have nothing better to do than sit around waiting for you to ring me? You never have had any consideration for me, have you!'

'Now you know that's not true …'

Sniff. 'Well, life has to go on, and if I can put the past behind me and look to the future then I expect you to do so, too. Are you going to church this morning?

'Yes, I—'

'Pity. There's a nasty smell in the larder. That woman of mine never does it properly and at least you can be trusted to use some disinfectant on the job.'

'I'm afraid—'

'I shall expect you tomorrow morning at nine o'clock. Don't be late!'

She put the phone down.

Ellie made faces at the receiver. She was not going to turn herself into a drudge for Aunt Drusilla. No way. She had never liked the old bat, and didn't see why she should put herself out for her now. Besides, she was planning to go into the charity shop tomorrow.

Feeling both guilty and elated, she rang Aunt Drusilla back.

'It's me again. I'm sorry, but I can't come round tomorrow. I'm due at the charity shop.'

Aunt Drusilla was not pleased. 'Is that really more important than—'

'Yes, I'm afraid it is. I'm sorry to disappoint you, but for the next few days I'm going to be rather tied up. I've got so behind-hand, you see ...'

'How like you! No, don't apologize! I'll get my woman to deal with it.'

She rang off, abrupt as ever.

Ellie wondered if Aunt Drusilla had ever really loved anyone, even Frank. She had never bothered to visit him in hospital. Frank would have left the big house to his aunt, of course ... how could he have done anything else? Though

48

what sort of life it was for Aunt Drusilla, rattling around in that great big place all alone, Ellie couldn't imagine.

Ellie had a dim memory of their solicitor being cornered by Aunt Drusilla after the funeral. No doubt she was asking if Frank had left her any money, as well.

With a feeling of having temporarily escaped a thunderstorm, Ellie slipped upstairs to put on some lipstick before leaving.

Another dull day.

As she leaned into the mirror to check her lipstick, she thought she saw ...

'Frank!'

It was only his green silk dressing-gown, hanging on the back of the door. She'd cleared out a lot of his clothes but had overlooked his dressing-gown. The bedroom door always swung gently open, unless you shut it with a firm hand.

Ellie took a deep breath. She told herself she was not going to faint, that it was all nonsense about people coming back from the grave and that she was merely suffering from a shortage of sleep.

It didn't work. She sat on the bed, rocking to and fro.

She didn't get to church.

She wept. Mopped up. Tried to make herself a cup of tea. Tried to read the newspaper, a book. Couldn't. Wept again.

Mid-afternoon there was a ring at the door. Ellie dragged herself to it, sniffing.

It was Liz Adams, the vicar's wife. Greying hair carefully blonded, the very picture of a horsey upper-class lady with a heart big enough to take in a whole diocese, never mind one miserable little widow.

Ellie dissolved into her arms. She hadn't known she had so many tears in her.

Liz sat and patted Ellie's shoulder and let her weep, listening while Ellie talked and talked and talked.

'... and all I've done these last few days is think nasty things about Frank, and really he was the sweetest ...'

'... I keep thinking and thinking how I might have stopped him killing himself by working so hard, but ...'

Later, Ellie couldn't remember that Liz had ever said anything but 'There, there!'

A very efficient comforter.

Liz coaxed Ellie up to bed, and sat with her till she slept.

Sunday afternoon. The fat man rang from his mobile, sitting in the Saab in the drive of the empty house.

He wheezed and used his inhaler.

'It's me. I'm back. She hasn't moved all day. I've driven round the front of the house a coupla times. She's been in bed most of the time. I could see a sidelight on in the front bedroom. Only one caller, came across from the vicarage, stayed a while. Ah, she's just got up again by the looks of it, lights going on downstairs, kitchen and living-room.'

The phone quacked at him.

'No, I can't see her front door, so I drive round that way every hour. But even if she goes out by the road she's got to come past this way if she wants to get a bus or something. It's quiet as the whatsit. The filth came round again this afternoon. This time they found the girlfriend in, had a long talk with her. Mister stormed out and left her to it. But even the filth didn't stay long.'

Quack, quack.

'Yeah, I know what he said, and he's right. If she was standing at the window, then she must of seen him up by the church. But the filth aren't showing any interest in her at all. I reckon we should act quick like, before she realizes—'

The quacking rose to a crescendo, and the phone was cut off.

Frustrated, the man in the car hit the dashboard with a large fist. It was costing him, this delay. Two old biddies, standing between him and what was rightly his. What was the point of playing pussy with them when pussies could be drowned, easy, no messing, end of aggro.

But the boss said there was a plan. 'Back off!' the boss said. Well, so he would. But there was no harm making a few plans, was there … contingency plans …

He knew where to find them, both of them.

Early that evening there was a hesitant ring at Ellie's front door.

At first she thought of pretending she wasn't in. She'd only just dragged herself out of bed with the intention of making herself some soup and going back to bed with it. But it might have been Liz returning for something, so she opened the door.

It was Kate from next door, holding a cardboard box in both hands. Now was she a murderess, or not?

She said, 'I'm sorry if I've disturbed you. I thought you might be lying down …'

She held up the box. 'Armand always goes out on a Sunday evening and I was by myself, feeling a bit blue. I'd bought myself a pizza for supper and then I thought you might not be up to cooking, and might like some, too.'

Ellie opened the door wide. 'Come in. I could do with the company.'

Kate stepped inside. She was indeed a tall, well-built girl, but today her usually glowing colour had faded. She was wearing an ancient brown baggy jumper over faded jeans. Her hair looked as if it could do with brushing, and she wore no makeup.

To Ellie's eyes, Kate looked as if she'd been crying. Well, that makes two of us, Ellie thought. 'Fancy a cuppa? Coffee or tea?'

Kate tried to smile. 'Anything stronger?'

Ellie didn't usually drink except for the occasional glass of sherry or wine at parties, but tonight she felt reckless. 'Why not?'

She got out the remains of the bottle of sherry and poured. 'Cheers!'

Kate was diffident. 'How are you coping?'

'Badly.'

'I thought so, because I hadn't seen you in the garden or heard you moving about. I didn't like to interfere. Then I was away at a conference, and when I got back, the police came round for a chat. Apparently they'd been chasing me up and down the country, thinking I was in Birmingham when I was down in Surrey. Armand must have got mixed up. It's Birmingham next month. They weren't very pleased, thought I'd misled Armand on purpose or something. They seemed to think that I ... oh, such a stupid idea. Eventually I had to tell them I wasn't answering any more questions until my solicitor was present and they left, saying that they'd be getting back to me soon. It's a nightmare.'

'I'm sorry.'

Kate glanced up, glanced away. 'It's me who should be saying I'm sorry. About your husband. It must be horrible for you.'

Ellie poured them both another drink. 'I sink into self-pity if I'm on my own and I've had my crying jag for today.'

The girl smiled, and her whole face lightened. 'We're a right pair. You're grieving for Frank and I'm so self-centred that all I can think about is poor Ferdy.'

'Did you know him well?'

'Yes, we go back a long way. We went to the same school, though he was a year ahead. We all used to look up to him because he was so streetwise, knew the best disco, learned how to drive early. He taught me how to drive. After I left school, we used to go around together. We all came from the same council block, you see. His mum and mine were mates, down the bingo. My mum still lives there, but Mrs Hanna moved to the Avenue when she got the job at the bakery.'

Ellie upturned the bottle over their glasses. 'Were you serious about him?'

'No, we really were just good friends. You see, I was good at maths, wanted to get on, while Ferdy hated school and dropped out as soon as he could. All he could think about was cars, buying old wrecks, doing them up, selling them. At one time we used to talk about the four of us setting up in a garage. Bob was going to be his right hand man, Joyce was going to run the office and I'd do the accounts. We even went around looking at possible sites.

'Then Joyce and I went on to college and Bob went in with his brother, window-cleaning. Ferdy let it all slide. I tackled him about it, once or twice. He used to say, "Give it a rest, girl. I'm doing all right as I am."'

'And was he?'

'Just about. He bought cars cheaply at auctions, did them up, sold them through his contacts locally and through adverts in the papers. He did the work in the road outside his flat at first, and when the people at the flats objected, he found space anywhere … up by the church here, as often as not. He could tackle most jobs, using that old van of his as a sort of portable garage, keeping spares in it, jump leads, batteries, you name it – he could do anything that didn't need a pit. He talked about renting a proper garage, but he never got round to it. It kept the overheads down, you see.'

'I thought he was on the dole.'

'No.' She bit her lip. 'Well, between you and me, I think that early on when the car business was slow, he did maybe have a stint on the dole. It's difficult when you're working for yourself, isn't it?'

Ellie was getting the picture. 'You mean, he never paid tax on anything?'

'Possibly not. And he did have a sideline, picking up bits and pieces here and there, selling them on at car boot sales. Anything for cash. He liked the freedom of it. He was fun. It's hard to realize I'll never see him again.'

4

The sherry had done its job. Kate was relaxed, lying back in the armchair, stretching out her long legs.

Suddenly Ellie remembered the pizza waiting to be eaten ... and the joint that she'd never cooked.

'Food? Shall we share your pizza?'

Kate jumped up. 'If I don't eat, I'll dissolve into tears again.'

They ate the pizza at the table in the kitchen. (Shades of Frank. What would he have said to such sloppy behaviour?) Ellie found a bottle of red wine and they both agreed that though they never normally indulged to this extent, tonight was definitely a night on which to drink oneself silly.

Ellie took some ice cream out of the freezer to finish with.

'Thanks,' said Kate, sighing and smiling both at once. 'I needed that.'

'The police ...' said Ellie, shaking her head in sympathy.

'Yes, I had to laugh when they said ... but it really isn't a laughing matter. Poor Ferdy. How could anyone do that to him! I can't help thinking that if I hadn't got so angry with him that night ... but it doesn't do any good to think if onlys, does it?'

'No,' said Ellie, thinking that if only Frank hadn't insisted on taking on that extra work ...

'Ferdy never wanted me to marry Armand. Said I'd regret it. I thought he was just jealous, but I wonder now ... we used to go round in a foursome, me with Ferdy, and Joyce with his mate Bob. Joyce was my best friend at school.'

'Is that Joyce McNally who helps with the Brownies at church?'

'Yeah. Odd how we turned out so different, isn't it? I mean, catch me going to church regularly and helping little girls on with their pinnies. But then, she's going out with the scoutmaster now, so she's not such a party girl any more. We used to joke that we both liked our tea dark and our men fair. Then I married Armand, she's going out with the scoutmaster, and they're both fair. Odd how things turn out, isn't it?'

'How did Ferdy and Armand get on?'

'I don't think they ever met. When you get married, some friends tend to drop away. When I saw Ferdy in the street or the pub, then of course I'd stop and we'd yak a bit. I wasn't going to cut him out of my life totally because Armand was, well ...' Kate's lips twisted, but not in a smile. 'Between you and me, he's a bit of a snob.'

Perhaps it's a good sign that she can see her husband clearly, thought Ellie. 'And the night of the murder? You don't mind talking about it, do you?'

'I can't think about anything else. I'd gone out to return a library book which was overdue and I saw Ferdy outside the church. He was in a temper already because the vicar had been on at him to move his van. Ferdy said something stupid about Armand, and I stormed off. End of story.'

'Whatever did he say?'

'I don't want to repeat it. It wasn't true, anyway.' She pressed her hand to her eyes.

'Did you tell the police what he said?'

Kate shook her head, without removing her hand.

Ellie said, quietly, 'Coffee?'

Kate nodded. They moved back into the living-room with their coffees.

'So you left Ferdy and ran down the alley, crying. I think I saw you.'

'Please, do tell the police. They think I clonked Ferdy on the head in a temper, and killed him.'

'You didn't, did you?'

Kate shook her head.

'Why didn't you go straight home when you left Ferdy?'

'I didn't want to let Armand see I was crying. He'd only have wanted to know why, and if I'd mentioned Ferdy's name ... Armand is – was – jealous of Ferdy. He has – had – no reason to be, but he was. I saw the lights were on in the house, and Armand moving around in the kitchen. I needed to be by myself for a while, so I ran over to the park and walked around. It wasn't raining, and it wasn't really cold.

'I went home in the end, of course. I told Armand there'd been a problem at work that I'd been trying to work out. He was furious that I'd been walking around the park in the dark, and of course he could see I'd been crying. I always look a wreck when I cry.'

Ellie said, 'That makes two of us.'

'No, you don't,' said Kate. 'You still look lovely, even though you say you've been crying. What I'd give for a skin like yours!'

'Flatterer.'

Kate rose, not quite steady on her feet. 'Whoops. Am I going to have a bad head tomorrow!'

'Worth it,' said Ellie, still feeling reckless.

Kate smiled. 'You remind me of my auntie. She was a lovely woman, and I still miss her.'

Ellie said, 'I must tell you about Frank's Aunt Drusilla some time. She is not lovely. She is a demanding old harridan.' She put her hand over her mouth. 'Oh, dear. I shouldn't have said that. It's just that I'm feeling guilty. She wanted me to clean her larder for her this week, and I refused. I still can't believe that I had the courage to do so. I suppose I ought to ring up and apologize. She is old, after all, and perhaps she doesn't realize how rude she is.'

'If she's been rude to you,' said Kate with tipsy earnestness, 'then you've every right to scut her ... cut her out. Relatives can't all be lovely. I've got an old nuncle – uncle! who's a real horror. Calls my mum up in the middle of the night to cut his t-toenails.'

They both laughed, then realized how late it was as the clock in the hall chimed the hour of twelve. Exaggeratedly putting her finger to her lips, Kate tiptoed up the path, wrestled the gate open, waved to Ellie and trod down the path to her own front door.

What would Diana say, Ellie thought, if she knew her mother was consorting with a murder suspect?

Monday. Wash day. Bother.

Changing the sheets on the king-size bed was always a chore. Frank liked pure cotton sheets, difficult to iron.

At least I don't have a hangover, Ellie thought. But I don't have to sleep in a double bed any more if I don't want to!

58

I don't have to iron another pure cotton sheet! Polycotton, here I come!

Smiling, she went to the bathroom.

A heavy thump shook the party wall, followed by the sound of an angry man's voice. Ellie nearly dropped her hairbrush. What on earth was going on?

She fetched her portable radio and turned the volume up high, placing it on the lavatory seat so that whoever was in the bathroom next door would be reminded that sound travelled through the party wall.

'Yes!' she said, wielding her hairbrush. 'Enough is enough. Frank's death was a shock, but if I'm being brutally honest ... well, my dear Ellie, we both know that life with Frank was not a bed of roses. He was a good man but he always thought he was right about everything. You and I know that he wasn't always right, was he? Mind you, it wasn't all his fault. His Aunt Drusilla is a narrow-minded, difficult woman and his father never took much interest in him.'

She opened the laundry basket to put her soiled clothes in, and winced to see how much had accumulated there. Including one of Frank's favourite shirts. She slammed the lid shut again.

'It wasn't all Frank's fault though. I let him have his own way far too much. At first because I loved him and thought the sun shone, et cetera. And then after Diana was born I was so tired ... and it was worse during those years when I was still working and we kept trying for another baby and all I had were miscarriages ...'

Not a good time to look back on. Especially with Aunt Drusilla openly making remarks about Ellie's inability to give Frank the big family he wanted. And Diana blaming

Ellie for being an only child. Something Aunt Drusilla or Frank had said to her …? Oh well, water under the bridge. No sense in blaming anyone, really.

She thought, Frank can … could … say what he liked, but his ideas about women were old-fashioned. Children, church, cooking.

'Fine as far as they went,' said Ellie, pulling on some comfortable, baggy clothes. It wasn't practical to wear good clothes when working in the charity shop, they only got filthy.

What would I have done if I hadn't got married so young? she thought. Been an explorer? Flown to the moon? Become a teacher?

She stripped the bed with vicious pleasure.

A nice single bed, she thought. Yes! With a really soft mattress. Frank would have thought I was going mad. But that's what I want, and I'll order one today. Luxury!

She fetched the radio from the bathroom – all was quiet next door now – and went downstairs as someone did the same on the other side of the party wall.

As she retrieved the newspaper from the letter-box she saw Armand leaving the house, stylish car coat swinging behind him, elbows angular, briefcase in hand. His car tyres squealed as he swung away from the pavement and tore off out of sight.

A moment later Kate appeared with a scarf around her head and shoulders. She walked stiffly up the garden path and swung herself into her car.

Has she just got a hangover, Ellie thought, or is it something worse? Am I imagining things? Yes, probably.

She had believed Kate last night when the girl had said she had had nothing to do with Ferdy's death, and had left him alive. But suppose Armand had seen them together and, driven by jealousy, had gone out to confront Ferdy? Had the police considered that?

Ellie knew Frank considered her to be naïve and unworldly, capable of being taken in by the simplest of conmen. But …?

Frank would have said Not To Interfere. He'd have said it was No Business of Theirs.

'But I'm not Frank!' said Ellie. 'And if I want to make a fool of myself by making some enquiries, then I shall!'

For a start, she would phone the police and tell them she'd seen Kate running away towards the park on the night of the murder. And today she would go into the shop. A pity, when the world was suddenly full of interesting things to do, but there would be time now to do them. Order a new bed. Buy some new bedlinen. Check how much money she had in her account.

Thank heavens Frank had insisted she have her own account for household expenses, even though he'd wanted to check the bank statements every month. Under his direction she was accustomed to paying all the household bills. And if she didn't know how to change a plug or operate his computer yet … well, give her time and she'd learn.

She must see the solicitor soon. She hadn't been able to take it in when he'd talked to her briefly after the funeral. She thought he'd said she'd be all right for money. He'd muttered something about Frank's life insurances, and said she mustn't worry about anything. He'd seen she was unable to concentrate, and asked her to make an appointment to see him when she felt better. She must do that.

Now what was it Kate had said last night while they were waiting for the pizza to be reheated? That Ellie should invest in a microwave oven? Frank wouldn't hear of them, but ...

Ellie smiled. Well, why not?

Kate had also said that if Ellie was having a problem with the computer, she could count on her for help.

Marvellous.

There was something else she could do. She'd been told that Kate's oldest friend was Joyce McNally, now going out with the scoutmaster at church. And Joyce's mother Rose was one of the volunteer helpers at the charity shop. So if Ellie were feeling inquisitive, she could make an opportunity to talk to Rose and find out what she knew of Kate and Ferdy. If anyone knew the background to that affair, it would be Rose.

Gossip. 'Oh dear,' said Ellie, grinning. 'How Frank would disapprove!'

He was only an errand boy, but he had ambitions to greater things.

The boss's instructions were clear, though they sounded daft to him. He parked by the wall, stowed the half-smoked butt of a cigarette behind his ear and waited till there was no one in particular around. Then he got out of the van, whistling. If you wore overalls and looked as if you knew what you were doing, no one ever challenged you.

Behind the wall there was a five-year-old estate of starter homes, flats and three-bedders. He thought they were pretty good, wouldn't have minded if someone had given him a key to one of them. Better than the council, any day.

But perhaps luck was swinging his way, and he'd be able to make the move upwards ... soon, very soon. He'd heard the field was wide open.

Course, you couldn't swing a cat in any of these tiddly little houses, but they were always in demand. Someone got a rise at work and moved up to the next size house. Someone died, or the children moved away, and the owners downsized.

So there were always houses for sale. At the moment there were six For Sale signs ranged along the wall that bounded this side of the housing estate. Some had the legend SOLD tacked over them. He checked the list. He was to choose one from an estate agent with an office some distance away.

He did so. There were two of them, so one wouldn't be missed. He took down one with a Sold sign on it, and heaved it into the back of the van. Still whistling, he drove the short distance to the Avenue. Turning left at the church, he parked in the driveway of the empty house.

Ellie let herself into the shop, and stifled a swearword. She didn't normally swear, but 'Oh, dear!' was not strong enough to express what she felt at that moment. Chaos reigned.

The charity shop was not open on Mondays. Staffing it on a Saturday was hard enough, so Mondays they were usually closed.

However, several key people were usually around on a Monday, putting in a couple of hours to deal with what had been handed in on Saturday, generally tidy up, redo the windows and so on.

No one had turned up to work today. The bookshelves were half empty. Garments had been dragged off the rails and left on the floor. Someone had smashed a rather fine teapot and left the pieces on the carpet.

Ellie considered closing her eyes, letting herself out of the shop and returning home. Or better still, going on a spending spree in one of the big department stores up town.

Someone tapped on the door behind her. A little bent brown mouse of a woman was making signs at her through the glass-paned door.

Mrs Rose McNally. Well, what a surprise! Rose never came in on a Monday if she could help it. But here she was, the answer to a maiden's – well, not so much of a maiden, actually – but definitely the answer to prayer.

'Dear Ellie, I know it isn't my day to come in, but when I saw you through the window, I thought … well, of course I was going to call around, see how you were bearing up, but then I thought you wouldn't want to be bothered with … and really there's no need to ask because I know how it is, the place seems so empty and you never do get over it really, do you?'

Ellie opened her mouth to reply that she thought she was doing pretty well, all things considered, but Rose was not to be diverted.

'… I can see you're wondering why everything's in such a mess here. We had such problems last week, you've no idea! Well, you probably do have an idea, because you know what Donna is like when she gets going and then Anita took offence and dear John had to go to the dentist – his plate, you know – and I told them we ought to try to get it sorted before you came back, but you can imagine how much notice they took of that!'

'Dear Rose, it's lovely to see you. I'm sure we can soon get this cleaned up between us …'

'Oh, I wasn't going to …'

Ellie put on her most appealing smile. 'You've no idea how much I've missed you all. I did want to come back last week, but well, you know how it is …'

One widow to another. Rose nodded. She knew, all right.

Ellie said, 'Thanks for your good wishes, dear. I do know it's not your usual day to help. But I thought while I was here, I'd try to clear up some of the mess. So, do you think you could spare a couple of minutes, and we can have a cup of coffee together while I tackle the worst of it?'

'Well, I …' Rose managed a lipless smile. 'I suppose I could.'

Ellie turned on all the lights, seized a dustpan and brush and set to work. 'And while the kettle's boiling, you can tell me what's happened to Madam.'

Each charity shop in the chain had a paid part-time supervisor, appointed by head office. Some were brilliant, some merely so-so. Their own particular supervisor was rather less than merely so-so. She was more often absent than present, and couldn't be bothered to stop the feuding among her volunteer helpers. She probably hadn't been in for a week.

'She hasn't been seen for a week!' Rose enjoyed a good gossip. Rose didn't serve in the shop, but was one of the invaluable ladies who patiently sorted through and priced the women's clothing as it came in.

Ellie fell over two large boxes of books which had been left under the men's clothes stand. Each helper had their own speciality, and John's was dealing with the books. Poor John suffered agonies with his few remaining teeth and his plate. He wouldn't have gone off and left the boxes like that if he hadn't been in pain. Ellie began to stack books, while listening with half her attention to Rose rambling on about the iniquities of Madam and what Anita had said to Donna, and what Donna had said to John, and ...

'... you wouldn't believe it, Ellie, but John actually swore at her!'

'Oh, dear ...' And how unlike John, who was usually brilliant at keeping the peace. He was also responsible for banking the money. John was indispensable. Pushing the last few paperbacks into place, Ellie turned her attention to the garments on the floor.

'A toddler broke that teapot and the childminder refused to pay for it. Donna said Anita should clear it up, and Anita said she was serving, thank you very much, and ...'

Ellie let Rose run on. Two mugs of coffee appeared, and they sat behind the counter, elbow-deep in black plastic sacks of unsorted clothes and bric-a-brac, which definitely should not have been left in the shop.

'... of course, Anita was worried about her grandson who's been ever so ill with a sweetie some man gave him. Then Mrs Hanna came in carrying that awful little dog of hers, and she wanted to talk about the murder, and of course we were all sympathetic, but Donna said Mrs Hanna was taking up Anita's time when she ought to be serving, and it's true the shop was full of people. Then Anita appealed to John, but he was being crucified with an abscess, and waiting to go to the dentist on an emergency appointment, so he wasn't really with it, if you know what I mean ...'

Ellie nodded, and thought that at this rate Rose would give her all the details she needed, without any need for prompting.

And so she did. After working her way through what the local paper had said about the murder ... not much, at such short notice, but there'd be a big spread this coming Friday, wouldn't there! ... and her opinion of Ferdy ... had it coming to him, I'd say ...

'Why do you say that?' asked Ellie. 'A bit of a layabout, I suppose, but ...'

Rose snorted, enjoying the drama of the situation. There was even a little colour in her cheeks for once. She had no one much to talk to at home, poor soul, now that her daughter had moved out.

Not that Ellie had now, come to think of it. Don't think of it.

'... well, everyone wondered how he managed because apart from taking a stall at car boot sales and being on the dole of course, he had that big car as well as his van, and they must have cost a bomb to run. And he was always going to clubs and raves and taking girls out. I pity his poor mother, I really do. Working her fingers to the bone and giving him handouts I shouldn't wonder. And as for fickle!'

'Didn't he go out with your Joyce at one time?'

'No, not our Joyce. It was her friend Kate he went out with, but that was ages back, just boy and girl stuff. They used to make up a foursome now and then, Joyce and that girl Kate, the one that did so well for herself up at the uni—'

'Joyce knew Ferdy quite well at one time, didn't she? What did she think about all this?'

'Terribly shocked. Well, we all were. Of course, she hadn't seen him to talk to properly for ages. You know she's going out with the scoutmaster up at the church now? Now he's much more like it.'

'You didn't approve of Joyce going out with Ferdy and his friend?'

'I can't say I liked it, but you know what girls are like nowadays. You tell them not to do something, and they go straight ahead and do it. It wasn't so much that Bob's father was black, as that he didn't have a proper job, and I don't say I wasn't worried at the time and so was her father before he passed over, but you can't put a wise head on young shoulders, and all's well that ends well is what I say. Those two girls did all right for themselves. Could have gone on the dole, like Ferdy. But they didn't, did they?'

Rose leaned closer and dropped her voice. 'To tell the truth, I think that come the summer we'll be booking the church for a very special occasion. And unlike some, I'll be really proud of my son-in-law.'

'Unlike some? You mean, unlike Kate?'

Rose refolded her lips, indicating that wild horses wouldn't make her divulge any more … unless she were pressed to do so.

'Oh, go on,' said Ellie. 'You can tell me.'

Rose looked around for eavesdroppers. A big, heavy-set man was peering in through the shop window. Both women started. He was so very large. Alarmingly so.

Ellie said, uneasily, 'The closed sign is up on the door, isn't it?'

The large man turned away from the window. Both women laughed.

'Poor man. I wonder what he wanted. I doubt if we have any clothing large enough for him. Go on, Rose. You were saying about Kate.'

'I thought that man was going to force the door open! Well, if you must know, Joyce never liked Armand. She didn't want to spoil Kate's fun, but she did feel she had the right to warn her. Kate wouldn't be told. Had to have him.

After all those years of being best friends, Kate and she broke up.'

'What's wrong with him?'

Rose pinched in her lips and raised her thin eyebrows. 'Mister Perfect. Mister going-to-be-headmaster. Mister don't want to know you. Bloody snob! Joyce told me she wasn't going to let herself be patronized by him.' Rose sighed. 'Joyce reminded me the other night, she'd always wanted Kate to be her bridesmaid when she got married. But Joyce doesn't think she can ask Kate now.'

'That's a shame. I think Kate's in need of a friend at the moment.'

Rose gave her a shrewd look. 'You think she's upset over Ferdy's death? Not her. No eyes for anyone but that stuck-up husband of hers. Didn't even ask Joyce to be her brides-maid. Sneaked off to the registry and did it one Saturday morning. I think he didn't want to invite her mother or Joyce. Chickens come home to roost, I say.'

Someone let themselves into the shop. John, looking drained and tired. 'Hello, there! Saw the lights. Sorry I couldn't stay on Friday. Emergency, abscess, you know. Ellie, lovely to see you back.'

'Just catching up on the gossip.'

'About Madam? Ah. If I could have a word?'

Rose picked up her coat and handbag. 'I'm just going ...'

'Thank you so much, Rose.'

'You're welcome.'

The shop door closed behind her. As she moved off, Ellie spotted the big man outside the greengrocers. He really was a very large man. But then – she reminded herself – big men were often surprisingly kind and gentle.

Ellie made another mug of coffee and pushed it towards

John. 'Dear John, sit down and before you say anything else, tell me how you are.'

John pulled a face. He had a rubbery face, which usually wore a kindly expression, but at the moment he looked lopsided.

'Oh, well. Abscess, you know. On antibiotics. Best not to think about it.'

'Same here. About Frank, I mean. Best to get on with things.'

'Mm. Did you put up the books for me? I don't suppose Rose was the good fairy. I was going to call round and see you, but then … the abscess. And I didn't want to bother you with our troubles here, when you have so much else on your plate.'

'It's Madam, isn't it?'

'Head office are catching on at long last. How long have we been covering up for her? Six months? Nine? Since before Christmas, when that married daughter of hers wanted free childcare. Spoilt little brat. Grandma dotes, but doesn't make him mind his Ps and Qs, I notice. We were doing all right till Frank got ill and you had to stop doing extra, but these last few weeks everything's gone to pot. The takings are down. We're at one another's throats all the time. When Madam is here, she doesn't take an interest. Head office sent a director down to our last committee meeting and she didn't even bother to turn up. So head office have said they're coming in again this week to talk to her. Between you and me, I think Madam's had enough of the job and might well resign. And if she doesn't resign, she'll be pushed.'

Ellie nodded. 'Yes, but who'd be able to take it on? You?'

'No, my dear. You. How would you feel about taking it on yourself?'

5

I didn't see that coming, Ellie thought. She didn't know what she felt about it. Bewildered? Frightened? No, she couldn't possibly ...

She stared through the window into the street. The big man was over at the newsagent's now. He turned and looked back at the charity shop, right through the front window and into her eyes. She wished he'd go away.

'Ellie?'

She fingered her wedding ring. 'I don't think I'd be up to it, John.'

'I think you'd be ideal. We all do.'

'You've actually discussed this with the others?'

'Exhaustively. It's about the only thing we can all agree on nowadays. You're good with people. You know what hard work means. You've practically been doing the job for Madam this last six months. You've always underestimated your capabilities. And now Frank's gone ...'

She got up with an abrupt movement. 'It's not that straightforward. I'm not sure yet how much I've got to live on. Suppose I have to get a job or sell the house? I'm just beginning to realize how much my life is going to change. Anyway, I'm sure head office can find someone much better than me to take over … and we don't even know if Madam really wants to go, yet.'

John took the used mugs to the basin at the back and washed them out. He said, 'I knew you'd say you couldn't do it, first off. Promise me one thing. Think about it seriously?'

'John, how could you put this on me just now? Haven't I got enough to worry about as it is?'

He patted her cheek and left. Ellie looked around her. She'd spent years of her life working here. It was another home to her. She knew the team, and they knew her. She'd miss it terribly if she left. But that wasn't enough reason to take on the responsibility of running it, was it?

A woman's voice on the phone. Businesslike.

'All fixed. You can move into the house today. Yes, of course get in through the back, but don't make it obvious. It's a perfect position for everything. There's some net curtains in the upstairs windows at the front. Keep watch from there. Get the garage open. We can use it to store the goods, but don't start moving them until I say so, right?'

Ellie was on her way home with a laden shopping basket when she noticed that a Sold notice had gone up outside the empty house. She wondered who had bought it. It would need a lot of work doing to it. She scanned the windows for signs of life, but there were none. They'd put builders in first, of course.

She made a mental note to call on the new people when they moved in. She'd be able to see any removal van from her back windows.

Nice to feel the old house was going to be lived in again. The old lady who had lived there before had been a bit of a tartar, wouldn't even let the children pick up the conkers from her driveway, never socialized. Ah well. Takes all sorts.

It was starting to drizzle with rain, so she hurried along the alley and up through the garden.

On her back doorstep sat a large open blue and white striped umbrella with one bent spoke. She recognized it as the one she kept in the garden shed.

'Tod?' she asked.

The umbrella lifted to reveal a young boy's peaky face under a ragged haircut. It was one of Tod's most attractive features – to Ellie, at any rate – that a tuft of his dusky-brown hair always stuck up at the back. He stood, banging the umbrella against the back door.

'Thought you'd never come.'

'I've been working at the shop today and then I did some shopping. Do you fancy a chocolate biscuit?'

'Mm. Mum's out till late. I wanted to come round before, but she told me not to. Said you'd enough to cope with, without my bothering you.'

She smiled at him, struggled to put the umbrella down, stowed it in a corner of the kitchen sink, dumped her shopping and put the kettle on. 'You're no bother.' Though perhaps she wouldn't have said so the previous day.

'You got my flowers?' He was looking over his shoulder into the hall. Nervous.

'It was a lovely thought. Thank you.'

'A course, in a way, they were your flowers, really. I 'spect you noticed that.'

'I was so pleased you'd thought of me.'

73

He sighed with relief. Confession over. But he was still not at ease. What on earth was the matter with the boy? It couldn't be the thefts …? No. He wouldn't have returned to see her if he'd stolen the things. Which reminded her that she still hadn't phoned the police about seeing Kate, and the burglary. And there was the ever-nagging question of whether she ought or ought not to phone Aunt Drusilla and apologize, offer to run whatever errands it was that the old lady wanted doing.

Tod ate three chocolate biscuits with concentration, not looking up from the plate. Then suddenly swung round and stared at the hall.

'Whatever's the matter, Tod?'

'Nothing.'

'Tell me.'

'A boy at school says he saw a ghost here.'

'Nonsense.'

'He did! By the church. Coming down to your gate, and then disappearing up the garden path. I thought it might be Mr Quicke, but my friend said it musta been the murdered man, wandering through the night, "seeking vengeance …"' His voice took on a doom-laden note. Although he was clearly frightened at the thought of a ghost, he was also enjoying the drama.

Ellie was overcome by giggles.

Tod stared at her, affronted. He liked Mrs Quicke, and he had thought she liked him, took him seriously, never made fun of him as his mum did.

'Don't laugh. It's true!' he insisted.

She remembered how she'd reacted when she'd thought she'd seen Frank at the bedroom door, when it was only his dressing-gown, after all.

She said, 'No, I shouldn't laugh. But really, Tod, my husband is not haunting this house, nor the Green.'

Bright eyes watched her from under his fringe. 'You sure?'

'Certain, positive. Another biscuit? An apple? Some baked beans?'

He took another biscuit. 'Maybe it's Ferdy who's haunting the place. Some of the boys in my class are daring one another to cross over by the church in the dark. Maybe his ghost is trying to get into other houses that back on to the Green.'

So that's why he hadn't gone home. He didn't want to be alone in his house if the ghost came tapping at his window.

'There's no ghost,' she said, 'but I'd be glad of your company for a while. Why don't you get out your homework and make a start on it? And when it's time for you to go back home, I'll walk along with you.'

He sat up straight and took out his homework.

She resisted the temptation to smooth down his hair at the back. He was a nice boy. It was stupid of her to have suspected him of theft, even for a minute. She would go and ring the police now, tell them about seeing Kate.

'It's prob'ly nothing,' he said. 'But I think the ghost – if there is a ghost – has been in your garden shed. When I went in for the umbrella – 'cause you were late coming back, and it started to rain – I put the torch on and must a knocked the lawnmower cable off its nail. Honest, I hardly touched it. But when I was picking it up off the floor, I noticed that the cable was all frayed where it goes into the plug. I 'spect the ghost was trying to warn you not to use it till it's been checked over.'

Ellie held herself back from repeating that there wasn't any such thing as a ghost. A *frisson* ran down her back. Had

75

Frank really returned from the grave to warn her about a frayed cable? Nonsense.

'Never mind,' she said. 'I won't need to use the lawn-mower again till the spring.'

She went into the sitting-room to draw the curtains. The sky was overcast and it was drizzling again. She could hardly see the church spire and a wind was getting up. She ducked her head to the right to see if there were a light on in the house that had just been sold. It had a name ... Endene ... something like that. She wasn't sure, but she fancied she could see a faint light upstairs.

Goodness, were the new people camping out there? She hoped they'd managed to put the water and electricity on. She must ask in the shop tomorrow, see if anyone knew who they were.

She rang the local police station. She'd thought they would leap into one of their crime cars and come rushing round to question her about seeing Kate on the night of the murder, but they just said they'd make a note of it, and was she prepared to go into the incident room at the church hall tomorrow to make a statement.

Rather blankly, she said she would. After she'd put the phone down, she scolded herself for having thought what she had to say was so important. Obviously they had checked Kate's statement already, and found people who had seen her in the park. So what Ellie had had to say was quite beside the point.

As she drew the curtains at the front of the house, she noticed that Kate was not back, though Armand's car was there. That couple puzzled her. She thought that tomorrow she might well ask around about Armand. And order a new bed. She'd have to go further than the Avenue for it. She'd go in the afternoon, after putting in a morning at the charity shop … and the more she thought about taking the shop over, the less she liked the thought of it.

Everything was happening at once. What was she going to do about Aunt Drusilla? She ducked the thought, but did ring the solicitor to make an appointment. She'd known him for ever. Perhaps he could give her some advice about dealing with Aunt Drusilla.

She went back into the kitchen to start her supper, and see to Tod.

The fat man had introduced a large folding chair into the master bedroom and made use of a rickety card table that he'd found in a cupboard. The owners had cleared the house of all but a few broken pieces of furniture. There were no carpets, only some old lino tacked to the floor-boards.

No lights. No electricity yet. No water.

He'd brought a large pizza, some tins of lager, plus a plastic sack to put the debris in. He'd thought of bringing his portable TV, but hadn't quite dared in case the boss caught him.

He'd got into the house courtesy of a faulty catch on the rotting French windows. The back garden was a meadow now. He supposed it had once been a lawn. The Saab was in the garage. It was a big double garage. Plenty of room for Ferdy's Bentley if they brought it back here. And for supplies.

The kitchen door downstairs was unlocked, ready for a quick getaway if needed. The previous owners had left a back door key hanging on a nail just inside the scullery. Thoughtful of them.

He munched and watched lights go on. Schoolchildren skittered across the Green, playing some game of Last Across, or Dare.

Commuters began to return from work, walking slowly, burdened by laptops, briefcases, shopping bags. A gap.

He huddled into an enormous leather coat, feeling the cold.

The target came out of her house, escorting a small boy … how did he get there? A golfing umbrella was erected with some difficulty. They went down the garden path together, past the garden shed – he hoped she'd remember to mow the lawn tomorrow – and along the path away from him.

Binoculars up.

They went up another garden. Knocked on a back door. He would check tomorrow which number it was. Boy deposited. Target returning under the big umbrella. Up the garden path. Into the house with the umbrella, which was still causing trouble. Light off in the kitchen. Light on in the living-room downstairs.

That flickering light behind the curtains would be the telly. He wondered what she was watching.

It was getting cold. He could leave soon, surely.

Lights off downstairs.

Landing light turned on upstairs … and in the bathroom … and out of the bathroom … and after a short while, the landing light was turned out. And so to bed.

Tuesday morning. Time to get up, have breakfast, go to work at the shop. Ellie felt tired and drab but forced a smile and thanked everyone when they asked if she were sure she wasn't coming back to work too soon?

By lunchtime she was exhausted. When Madam swept into the shop, ordering them all about and quite failing to say anything to Ellie about Frank's death … why, that was when she decided enough was enough!

One last customer … someone coming to pay the balance of a children's game she'd put down a deposit for on Saturday. Ellie knew the woman slightly.

As she put the game into a bag and took the money for it Ellie asked, 'You live somewhere near the big department store where they have good bedding, don't you? Do you happen to know if they've got a sale on at the moment? I was thinking of popping over there this afternoon, but it's two buses and I'm a bit rushed for time.'

'They do have a sale on, but it finishes on Saturday. I can give you a lift over there now if you like but you'll have to hurry. I'm due back at school.'

What a piece of luck. Ellie rushed to get her coat and bag and inserted herself into the passenger seat of a shiny new red Mini. They roared off into the traffic.

'This is very kind of you,' said Ellie. 'Which school are you at? Do you happen to know someone called Armand? A history teacher, I think. He and his wife have recently moved next door to me.'

The woman was a demon driver, taking roundabouts at top speed. Ellie found something to hang on to, and sent up a prayer that they would arrive safely.

'Oh, him.' Dismissive tone. 'He moved from my daughter's old school when he got the head of department job at the high school.'

'Not a particular favourite of yours?'

A half laugh. 'Too short a fuse for my liking. But I shouldn't tell tales out of school.'

'The reason I asked is that being next door to me … well, I like his wife enormously, but …'

'He won't bother you, I expect. Got his eye on higher things. Determined to make head well before he's forty.'

'Too short a fuse? With the children?'

'N-no. He doesn't have any trouble keeping order, I'll say that for him. Gets through the work OK. Got a good Ofsted report.'

Ellie said, 'I think I know what you're trying to say. He's smarmy to the head and the parents, but treats everyone else like dirt?'

The teacher laughed till she hiccuped, and didn't deny it. She signalled to turn right and then stood on her brakes. Ellie was jolted forwards and felt her neck muscles snap. She was glad they were wearing seatbelts.

The teacher grinned, looking in her wing mirror. 'Nearly gave him cardiac arrest! I hate men who drive big cars right up to your bumper.'

Ellie twisted in her seat, and saw a large green car inches behind them. In the driver's seat was the big fat man.

'Why, it's that man again. He's been hanging around the shop but never comes in. Trying to pluck up courage to ask if we've got anything his size, I expect.'

They both laughed at that. The teacher looked at her watch and made a cross noise. 'Look, I'm a bit late. Would you mind if I dropped you this side of the railway line instead of taking you all the way round by road? It's only a hop, skip and a jump over the bridge … but look out for workmen. They're doing something to the handrails. It's taking for ever.'

Ellie knew the shortcut well. She thanked the teacher for the lift, got out of the car and uncricked her neck. No real damage, thank goodness. What on earth would Frank have said about that sort of driving? Waving the Mini off, she looked around for the fat man in the green car. He had parked some way back, and appeared to be communing with a nearby tree. Swearing, she supposed. What a laugh!

The entrance to the footbridge over the railway was only a few yards away. She had always loved this bridge. When Diana had been young, they had often come this way so that they could see the 'choo-choos'. They'd stand for ages on the bridge, waiting for the next train to rush by beneath them … happy days. She sighed.

Climbing the steps, she saw warning notices of work being done on the bridge. There was plentiful evidence that the workmen were still repairing sections of the handrails, but no workmen to be seen at the moment. Lunchtime, of course. She kept well away from the left side of the bridge, where scaffolding poles, wooden barriers, and new lengths of railing were piled. There was plenty of room for one person to walk along it at a time. Even a woman with a pushchair.

In the middle, Ellie paused and leaned on the newly finished railing, smiling to think how good Frank had been, knowing which trains went to which part of the country. 'That's an express going into Paddington,' he'd say. 'Come up from Cornwall, maybe.'

Ellie felt in her pockets for a handkerchief. She hoped she hadn't come out without one. Just her luck …

The fat man couldn't believe his luck.

She was alone. Something on her mind, by the look of it. A deserted bridge, scaffolding poles and balks of timber to hand. No need to wait for the frayed cord on the lawnmower to do its work. One quick swipe with a pole and she'd be over the bridge and crash down on to the rails far below.

What a weepie-wailie she was. And she didn't seem to have a hankie with her. Bother. She sniffed and considered wiping her nose on her sleeve, as children do. No, she wouldn't do that.

Just by the steps up to the bridge there was a tiny newsagent's and tobacconist's. They would sell her some paper tissues, wouldn't they? She must hurry, though. She was wasting time …

She turned on her heel and bumped into the fat man. He tried to sidestep as she rebounded off his chest. Caught off balance and burdened by the uneven weight of the scaffolding pole he was clutching, he fell across a wooden barrier, bringing it smashing to the ground with him.

He screamed. A horrible, animal scream that raised the hairs on the back of her neck. She saw that he had one thick leg doubled up under him.

Frightened, both hands to her face, she cried, 'Oh, you startled me!'

He tried to get up, his face twisting. Grunting, furious.

She was worried about him. 'Don't try to move!' She looked around for someone to help him.

Incredibly, he tried to inch his way along towards her, still dragging the scaffolding pole … obviously he wanted her to help him get up. But she knew that with his weight, she would not be able to manage it.

A youth came cycling slowly along the bridge. He wasn't supposed to cycle on the bridge, but Ellie was not about to tell him off for that.

The fat man groaned and fell back, releasing his grasp on the scaffolding bar which had so treacherously let him down.

Ellie stopped the cyclist. 'Please, we need help. This poor man slipped and fell. He may have broken his ankle.'

'Got no mobile, have I!' said the youth, barely curious enough to get off his bike.

'Oi!' Two workmen, returning from lunch. 'What you lot doing?'

Ellie explained again. The workmen and the youth argued as to who should go to the nearest phone and call for an ambulance.

In the end the fat man produced his own mobile phone and with an angry flourish punched in the code to fetch an ambulance. Ellie hovered, so did the cyclist. The workmen were angry that the fat man had disturbed their scaffolding.

The fat man declared, 'It's all her fault.'

'I'm afraid it is,' said Ellie. 'Or partly so.' She turned on the workmen. 'I want to know why you left the scaffolding so carelessly stacked that an innocent passer-by could fall and hurt himself. Don't you realize that he could claim against the council for your carelessness, if he ends up in hospital with a broken leg?'

The workmen tried to justify themselves. They had left everything perfectly safe, properly tidied away. There were enough notices around, for heaven's sake. The fat man said nothing at all. He hadn't spoken except to ask for an ambulance on the phone.

The ambulancemen arrived and, after considering how best to remove such a large, heavy man from the middle of a footbridge, they piled him into a chair and bore him away. Ellie didn't envy him being bumped down the stairs at the end. She walked off the bridge with the cyclist, explaining how she'd first noticed that poor man outside the charity shop. She was angry with herself for having forgotten to ask him if there was anyone he would like her to contact about the accident.

The youth chewed gum and shrugged. She wondered if he were playing truant, or if he were old enough to be out on the streets doing nothing in particular. Well, that was none of her business.

But she did feel concerned about the fat man.

'I'll phone the hospital later, see how he's doing.'

It was almost enough to put her off the original purpose of her visit to this part of the world. But she remembered that the department store had a pleasant coffee shop and restaurant on the top floor and that she hadn't had any lunch. After some fish and chips and a good cup of tea, she'd feel able to choose a bed.

It was rather exciting to think of having a new bed after all these years. Something with a soft, comfortable mattress. And new bedlinen, too. On the way back, she'd pop into the incident room in the church hall, just to confirm her statement … and then home.

Smiling, she hastened towards the department store.

Ellie walked out of the church hall wishing that she had never gone there in the first place. She did not understand what was going on.

She put up her umbrella, and then put it down again. It really wasn't raining enough to justify having it up. Schoolchildren crowded around the bus stop, chattering, pushing and shoving, lively, bright … noisy. She looked to see if Tod were among them, but couldn't spot him.

She was so close to the Avenue, she wondered if she ought to pop along to the shops and buy some food, but recollected the joint defrosting in the fridge.

She really did not want to think about Kate. Or murder.

As she crossed the Green she met the vicar, striding along with his head in the air, no coat on, in a hurry as usual. She would have passed him with a wave but he stopped.

'Everything all right, Ellie?'

She made herself smile. 'Yes, of course. Well ...' seeing that he was not to be put off with a cliché, 'Just the usual. You know.'

He stooped to peer into her eyes. 'You look tired.'

'I've just come from the incident room.' She hadn't meant to mention it, but it was hard to keep quiet when he was showing an interest. 'The police suspect Kate of having murdered Ferdy.'

'Really?' He looked thoughtful but not surprised.

'Well, I for one don't believe she did it.'

The vicar raised his eyebrows.

Ellie felt tears threaten. 'I like her so much, and ... oh, I know that doesn't mean anything, but ... that husband of hers strikes me as ... take no notice! I'm making no sense at all.'

He pressed her arm, his eyes warm and bright.

'Take it easy. It's early days yet, Ellie.'

'I'm all right, really. Just a little tired.'

'Good girl.'

If anyone else calls me 'girl', Ellie thought, I'll ... I'll swear!

The Reverend Adams made as if to move off, then veered back to her side.

'Look, I'm late for a meeting, but ... did you get to see Mrs Hanna? I called there just now but she wasn't answering the door. I looked in the bakery but she wasn't there, either. I'm a little worried about her, to tell the truth.'

Ellie shrugged. 'I haven't seen her since last Friday. I'll pop around to see her tomorrow if you like. I expect she needs some time off.'

'I'd like you – or someone – to go to the inquest with her. She shouldn't have to go by herself. Then when the police release the body, we'll have to think about the funeral arrangements.'

Ellie nodded, and he started off again. Only to hit his head with the heel of his hand and return to her.

'I'll forget my own head next. Have you had any luck getting the minutes off the computer?'

'No, not yet. Kate promised to help me but that may not work out now …'

He pursed his lips as if to say something, shook his head, and steamed off towards the vicarage. Ellie went past the church, down to the alley and up through her garden to the back door. She needed to be quiet. And to think.

6

The errand boy was enjoying himself. 'You blew it, didn't you!'

The fat man flicked his eyes up to the hospital ceiling. He had been lying on a trolley in the corridor for four hours, waiting to go down to the operating theatre.

'A nice little fracture!' the doctor had said.

The fat man didn't think there was anything nice about it at all.

The errand boy tapped out a cigarette. The fat man pointed to a 'No Smoking' notice.

'That's all right,' said the errand boy. 'I'm not staying. I just came to give you the bad news. She says you're out of it, and I'm taking your place. So give me the back door key. She said you'd got it on you. Oh yes, and the mobile phone. You won't need that in here.'

The fat man's eyes almost disappeared in a poisonous stare. 'I'll be outa here in a tick. They'll set and plaster it. No problem. Tell her I'll be back on the job tomorrow.'

'You ain't listening, mate,' said the errand boy, smugly cheerful. 'You blew it and she don't give no second chances. Fancy having the target helpless on a bridge, and she walks away without a scratch while you end up in hospital. What a laugh! Wait till I tell them down the pub!'

The fat man's blood pressure climbed to danger point. 'She bumped into me just as I was about to do the job!'

'She bumped into you!' mocked the errand boy. 'That's what comes of employing labour what's thick in the head. Now me, I'm a technician. What I don't know about electricity and gas and plumbing, you can forget. I fancy a nice little accident with the gas. It's always happening. Just read the papers in a couple days time, right?'

He held out his hand. 'Key, please.'

The fat man made a grab for his jacket but the errand boy got there first. Delving into one pocket after another he fished out bunches of keys, a single old-fashioned key and the mobile phone.

The fat man knew he couldn't argue with Herself while he was flat on his back in the hospital but in a few hours' time … a day or two at most, he'd be out of here, and then he'd give them a good sorting out.

'Tarra, then!' said the errand boy. Whistling, he made his way out of the ward. He thought he might as well pick up the fat man's car while he was about it. He knew where he could stash it away for a few days, maybe take the girlfriend out in it at the weekend, big car, would impress her … and then he'd flog it. And the fat man wouldn't be able to do nothing about it.

Ellie sat in the kitchen, drinking cup after cup of tea. The joint was sizzling quietly in the oven, together with roast potatoes and parsnips. She was determined to eat properly. She knew by the looseness of her skirts that she'd lost weight recently. The next thing she knew, she'd be ill down the hospital, like that poor man on the bridge today.

The problem was that there were too many problems and

she didn't know how to cope with any of them.

There'd been a horrible message from Aunt Drusilla on the answerphone when Ellie returned. She kept replaying it in her mind. Perhaps what Aunt Drusilla had said was true and Ellie really was selfish, only thinking of herself and never considering for a minute what her husband would have wanted her to do.

It was partly true. Ellie was thinking for herself, and gut reaction to Aunt Drusilla's demands was that for the moment at least, Ellie could not cope.

She thought that if she even tried to cope, she'd break down and cry. And in any case – said a nasty snide voice deep inside her head – why should she walk twenty minutes just to help a spry old woman summon a taxi to take her to the dentist, sit in the waiting room for her to have her bridge seen to, and ditto back again?

As for those barbed remarks about Frank's not being sound of mind when he made his will and it being clear that Ellie had exacted undue influence … Ellie did not under-stand what the old – dear – was talking about.

For the umpteenth time she went to the front window and looked out. Kate's car was still there. Ellie could tell, by the drift of leaves on the windscreen and roof, that it hadn't moved since that morning.

Armand had come back, very quiet. Within the hour he'd gone out again. Ellie hoped he'd gone across to the incident room to support his wife. Well, you could always hope. She didn't really think he had. She was beginning to get a nasty feeling about that marriage.

She went back over her own interview with the police again. They had been pleased she'd gone in. They'd even offered her a cup of tea. The inspector whom she'd met before – his name was Clay, she discovered – had listened while she told them about seeing Kate run down the alley towards the park in the dusk. It must have been about tea-time. She couldn't place it any closer. She really hadn't been attending to the time.

But surely, they said. Any movement up at the church must have caught your eye?

No, she couldn't remember having seen anything else, though she'd thought about it a lot. No, she couldn't remember having seen Ferdy, nor the confrontation with the vicar, nor Ferdy's quarrel with Kate.

She hadn't seen any activity at all, but then she'd hardly been looking for it. It sounded silly, she knew, but she'd had her mind on other things. She was sorry she couldn't help them more.

No, of course she hadn't been standing there all the time. Yes, she supposed she had gone to the bathroom. Had she gone to get herself a cuppa? Make a meal? No, she didn't think so. She hadn't felt like it.

At what time had she drawn the curtains? She didn't think she had that evening.

But she'd turned on the lights inside when it got dark? Well, no. She hadn't bothered. There was a side lamp which came on at dusk, on a time switch. She supposed that had been on. She really hadn't noticed.

So she had been standing at the window, looking out, all that time? Yes, she thought she had. And hadn't seen anyone else but Kate?

At that point, Ellie became aware of where this was leading. If she hadn't seen anyone but Kate then far from confirming Kate's alibi, she was putting Kate firmly on the spot as murderer.

She'd hastily reviewed everything she'd said. And was appalled.

'I don't believe Kate did it!'

The inspector smiled, forgivingly. Asked her to sign her statement. Well, she had to sign it. It was the truth, and nothing but the truth.

But she wasn't happy about it.

Suppose Kate was even now being charged with Ferdy's murder? It seemed more than likely.

With an abrupt movement, Ellie went to check on Kate's car. Still there. Still no sound from next door.

Put it out of your mind, girl, she thought. If Kate did it – though I still don't think she did – then you shouldn't interfere. If she didn't do it, then I'm sure she'll be cleared.

Although perfect in its way, this line of reasoning failed to soothe. So Ellie decided to tackle some of the difficult jobs still hanging around the house. First she would phone the hospital and find out how that poor man was doing. She rang and explained that even though she was not a relative and therefore perhaps not entitled to news of the patient, she had been on the bridge when it happened … in fact, she was afraid she'd almost caused the accident. The nurse was sympathetic and found out for her that the leg had been set, was now in plaster, and that the patient would probably be discharged that evening. Ellie sent him her best.

She was glad he would be released today. She supposed he would take a cab home from the hospital, to be cosseted by his wife …

With that job out of the way, Ellie sat at the computer and switched on, remembering to give the buttons a firm push.

The screen came alight with a brightly coloured sort of flag advertising Microsoft Windows 98. She'd seen this bit before. Then came a threatening message about not having turned the computer off properly before. She had to wait like a chidden child while it went through the motions of checking that everything was OK before it proceeded. Now she got some clouds before Paddington station arrived with a whirring propeller in the middle. The propeller settled down and transformed itself into an orange arrow, rather a pleasant apricot colour. Some pretty pictures appeared on the screen on the left. She knew enough now to ignore nearly all of these.

Ellie concentrated on positioning the arrow on the Microsoft Word picture. Two clicks, she remembered. Nothing happened.

Another click. Nothing.

A double click, rather faster. A blank screen, waiting to be written on.

The manual said she should go through the button START. That seemed appropriate. She winced as a flag-like box jumped up from the bottom of the screen. Just like a Jack-in-the-box. Ellie stared at a number of options that appeared on this pop-up screen. What on earth did they all mean? And what about all those little pictures now spread across the top of the screen?

She remembered seeing Frank using the mouse, zizzing around the screen up and down, left and right, clicking away. Modern-day magic, she'd thought. She'd never wanted anything to do with it, herself.

She started playing around with the mouse – 'mouse' indeed! She watched the arrow zoom up the screen, then sent it left and right, making zigzags. Fun, if spectacularly unhelpful. Oh where, oh where has my little dog gone?

She reached for the manual and must have brushed against some important key, for the flag disappeared.

She centred the arrow on one of the pretty little pictures at the top of the screen, and another flag dropped down. Help, what did it all mean?

The telephone rang. Reaching across for it, by accident she hit the key marked Esc, and found that the new flag disappeared. Was this the key she'd hit before?

Archie Benjamin, the plump little steward. 'My dear Ellie, how are you getting on? I know what it's like to be on your own when you're used to having someone around. So how about I pick up a bottle of something and bring it round to keep you company?'

Engrossed in the screen, Ellie got the mouse to hit another pretty picture, made another flag drop down, and then hit the Esc button. To her delight, it disappeared.

She said, 'Thanks, Archie, but really I'm perfectly all right.'

'Oh. Well, would it be in order to ask gracious madam if she's had time to find the minutes for the PCC meeting yet?'

She replied with perfect truth, 'As a matter of fact, I'm working on it at the moment. Thanks for ringing. I do appreciate it. Perhaps some other time …'

She put the phone down and repeated her previous actions. Bravo! She could make something happen on the computer, all by herself! She did it again, just to make sure she had got the hang of it.

Unproductive, though.

Trained to start reading at the top left-hand corner, she homed in on the picture top left, marked File. The F was underlined for some obscure reason. She tried Shift and F, as you might on an ordinary keyboard. Nothing happened. Oh well, you couldn't win them all.

Try the mouse again. Bingo. A cartouche containing a lot of names in alphabetical order. Presumably each one was a file. There seemed to be an awful lot of them, but she hadn't a clue what was in them. She tried the one marked 'Business'. Another list of names turned up. Experimentally, she clicked the mouse on a name she thought she recognized.

The screen cleared and a letter to their local garage came up. Frank had been writing to complain about an incomplete service that had been done on the car.

Daringly she explored the keyboard, and found that the Delete key got rid of some of the words on the screen. Wow! She held the Delete key down till she had got rid of several lines of type.

She tried typing something … anything … on the screen, and as she typed, so more characters on Frank's letter disappeared.

What should she write? The quick brown fox jumped over the lazy dog? Those were the words they had used to try out a new typewriter in the old days, because they included all the letters of the alphabet. It worked! Well, sort of. The words were so tiny she could barely see them.

She couldn't write a letter yet, but she had put some words on the screen. She played about with it idly. Her name and age. The date of her birth. Frank's …

Then she found herself writing …

    I do not believe that Kate killed Ferdy!

                ★   ★   ★

She stared at the words, then got up to look out of the window. It was dark now, but the street lights showed her that Kate's car was still there, and Armand's wasn't. Oh dear. Well, she'd make herself a cup of tea while she'd stopped. While the kettle boiled, she went to the kitchen window to draw down the blind. An old woman was plodding along the Green, head down, walking with the stolid gait of the refugee.

The woman reached the alley, turned right and opened the gate into the garden next door. It was Kate.

Ellie caught her breath. What had they done at the incident room, to turn Kate into an old woman?

Ellie waved, but Kate didn't look up as she let herself into her house. A cold, empty, dark house. Ellie hovered, indecisive. Should she interfere? Go round to Kate's, offer food and comfort? A shoulder to cry on?

She had a joint cooking in the oven. She could offer to share it with Kate.

Yes, she would do that. But first she had to turn off the computer.

The screen had gone blank. Why? How? Was it sulking because she'd left it unattended?

She addressed some words of reproof to the screen. It failed to respond. She considered hitting it. That had always worked with her old wireless set, but it would probably upset this box of tricks for good.

Frustrated, she joggled the mouse up and down. Slowly the screen lit up again. Ah, now to close. The manual said that to close she had to put the mouse on X. Up to the 'X'. Yes. But what else was it she ought to be doing before she turned off the machinery? The screen had gone blank. Now she could turn it off. Couldn't she?

Her finger hesitated over the 'off' button. That was the way she'd turned it off before but for some reason the machine hadn't thought that correct, and had sent her an impolite message about not having turned it off properly. There was nothing for it. She had to consult the manual again.

Such a time-wasting operation. She wondered who had written the manual. An alien from outer space, or a man? No woman would have set it out like that. It must have been someone who ate and slept and dreamed of nothing but computers. A nerd.

With incredulity she learned that to stop the machine, you had to activate the button marked START again. Surely it couldn't mean what it said?

Wondering if she were giving the signal to blow the whole caboodle up, she set the mouse on START, and jumped as the Jack-in-the-box file came up from the bottom again. Her eyes went to a line near the bottom. It said, Log Off Frank Quicke.

That made her laugh, though it really wasn't very funny. He'd logged off, all right.

The bottom line of all said something about Shutting Down. Click that. Another message, this time in the middle of the screen, asking if she really meant it. She did. The screen went blank and then put up in enormous letters that even she could not miss,

It's now safe to turn off your computer.

So she did. And the button on the works unit as well. Peace and quiet.

She flopped back in the chair, quite worn out, then heard

the pinger in the kitchen. The joint was ready. She must quickly cook some frozen peas, and eat. She was hungry.

She couldn't hear any sound from next door. She would just ask Kate if she'd like some food. She didn't like to think of that poor girl alone after having been with the police so long.

But there were no lights on downstairs next door and the curtains were still open. The upstairs curtains had been drawn, and there was a light on in the front bedroom. Evidently Kate had gone straight to bed.

Probably the best place for her, if she were that tired.

Ellie closed her front door on the night.

The errand boy put his feet up on an old box he'd found in the scullery, and lit himself a cigarette, flicking ash onto the floor. His Walkman was pounding out some heavy metal, a Chinese takeaway tray lay discarded on the floor, and a six-pack of beer was now down to four. He whistled along to the music on the Walkman, thinking about gas, and pipes, and getting some passable ID to fool the target into letting him into the house. Tomorrow.

Ellie slept better than she had done for days. She only woke when she heard Armand's car drive off. She lay in bed, watching the digital display on the clock radio, tick-ticking the minutes off. She remembered that Frank had gone. She knew that there were a lot of problems to be solved, but she felt surprisingly calm.

That's what a good roast and two veg does for you, she thought. Calms the stomach. Helps you to cope.

She dressed, put a load of dirty washing in the machine and had a good solid breakfast. 'Go to work on an egg,' she thought, while knowing that lots of people thought eggs were bad for you nowadays. Or was it that too many eggs were bad for you? If you listened to the pundits, everything seemed to be bad for you. Perhaps they all sat around a table and took it in turns. This week, the media can say that beef is bad for you. Next week it's the turn of butter. Then eggs. Or red wine.

Or was red wine always supposed to be good for you?

She couldn't remember. She couldn't care less.

She decided that from now on she was going to eat what she wanted, when she wanted, and not read any more scare-mongering articles about this or that being bad for you. If she wanted an egg for breakfast, then she would have it. So there!

Kate's car was still outside. Her bedroom curtains were still drawn. Ellie rang the doorbell and waited. No reply. Not even a twitch on the curtains. Ellie went through to her back garden and looked up at Kate's house. The back bedroom curtains were drawn, too. Was Kate not sleeping in the same bedroom as Armand, then?

As she watched, the curtains were drawn back and Kate was revealed, wearing a flimsy nightie.

Ellie cried, 'Kate!' and waved.

Kate saw Ellie – she could not have overlooked her – but she stepped back into the room. A moment later the curtains were closed again.

The message was clear. Kate was at home, but didn't want to talk. Oh, well.

Wednesday was not one of the days Ellie put in at the charity shop. She could go in, if she wanted to. There were always plenty of black plastic bags to clear. She had to see her solicitor later on.

She decided that she really didn't want to go into the shop. Every time she thought of it, she remembered John's suggestion that she take it over. She didn't know how she felt about it. Partly scared, and partly excited.

More scared than excited, though.

The postman dropped some letters through the letter-box. Letters of condolence, bills, pleas for subscriptions to this and that. A reminder from the dentist that Frank's six-monthly check-up was due. A note from Aunt Drusilla on embossed, very thick paper. Ellie stared at it in awe. Did Aunt Drusilla use such expensive notepaper still? She was impressed.

So what had the old dear to say?

Ellie read it in increasing bewilderment.

'My dear Ellie … Needless to say, I am extremely disappointed … I had expected better of … after all I have done for … Naturally, I am consulting my solicitor … Yours truly.'

Whatever did Aunt Drusilla want to consult her solicitor about? And why? She didn't say.

Ellie put Aunt Drusilla's letter to one side. She would deal with that later when she felt stronger. Meanwhile, she really must get down to writing to thank some of the people who had written to her after Frank's death and sent flowers to the funeral.

A nasty job. But yesterday she had bought some pretty little cards with a 'Thank you' message on them. The beauty of these was that they were so small you didn't have to write much on them, and the recipient would appreciate them enough to stick them on the mantelpiece for a while.

She squared up to the task with resignation. Sitting at the

bureau, she thought fleetingly of Frank's missing pen and cufflinks.

She wondered if Aunt Drusilla had taken them. Aunt Drusilla could convince herself that black was blue, if it were to her advantage. She could easily have convinced herself that Frank would have wished her to have them. Although what she would want with them …

Well, if that was where they'd gone, Ellie was not going to do anything about getting them back. Warfare with the formidable Aunt Drusilla was not an option for pacifists.

Surfacing at noon, Ellie remembered that the vicar had asked her to look in on Mrs Hanna, who hadn't been to work yesterday. She would get some bread and fresh salad stuff in the Avenue and call in on Mrs Hanna on the way.

The entrance to Mrs Hanna's flat lay between the bakery and the launderette. Ellie rang the bell beside Mrs Hanna's name. No reply.

A woman popped her head out of the bakery. One of the shop assistants, the one with the thin, over-permed hair. 'You wanting Mrs Hanna? We think something's happened to her. Hasn't been in all week. We've been up and knocked. No reply. The boss has phoned the police, reported her missing …'

A police car drew up outside, and two policemen got out. Ellie didn't recognize either of them.

The shop assistant was joined by her boss, whose darker skin proclaimed an Asian background. He bustled to the doorway, brandishing a bunch of keys.

'You come for Mrs Hanna, no? She rents the top flat from Mr Patel, who is owner of this bakery, too. Mrs Hanna reliable, very conscientious woman, always punctual. Very clean, you know. She hasn't been in this week, all wrong, no message. I worry something is wrong, yes? With her son being killed, yes? Has something bad happened to her? Last night I rang Mr Patel and asked him what to do about Mrs Hanna. He has sent round the keys for me to investigate into her flat, but said I must wait for the police first. So, please … I lead the way?'

Still talking, he unlocked the front door and let himself in. The police followed. As did Ellie, at a distance.

Up the narrow stairs they went, hitting light switches on the way. On each landing there were two front doors, leading to flats above the shops. Up. And up again. A television set blared out the news from one of the flats, a local radio station announced a special offer at a mobile phone shop and a dog barked somewhere. On the top floor there were two doors, as before.

The larger of the two policemen knocked. 'Mrs Hanna?'

No reply. He unlocked the front door. The air inside the flat smelt stale, not quite clean. Unstirred, as if it had been empty for some time.

Ellie sniffed, thinking she recognized a particular odour. The manager of the shop stayed at the front door, looking worried. Ellie stepped past him with an excuse-me smile.

The larger policeman walked along a short corridor and threw open the door at the end. His colleague followed. Ellie ducked to one side, trying to see into the sitting-room from where she stood in the hall. The first policeman called Mrs Hanna's name. No reply. Ellie could see part of a three-piece suite, a television set, a cupboard with a glass front holding ornaments of the kind you could pick up at the charity shop.

Ellie peered at the floor in the hallway, a carpet runner on lino. There was dust on the lino, and the carpet was rucked up where something heavy had been dragged along.

The second policeman pushed open another door, into a bedroom. Ellie craned her neck to see. Another matching suite, probably second-hand. The bed was neatly made up, but clothes had been tossed on a chair and some drawers were half open. The wardrobe door was swinging wide. There was no sign of Mrs Hanna.

An open door to the left led on to the kitchen. Ellie took a pace towards it and sniffed, trying to locate the origin of the odour that had intrigued her from the moment the front door was opened. The acid smell intensified.

Inside the kitchen a chair had been knocked over on its side. A washed saucepan, some crockery and cutlery had been left to dry on the draining board. A couple of cloths were on the floor, tangled with an overturned vegetable basket and stand. A cupboard door stood open, pans and lids scattered on the floor.

'Uh-oh!' said the second policeman, pushing past Ellie. He got out his mobile. 'Back-up needed. Looks like trouble.' Turning to Ellie he said, 'You – out!' and pushed both Ellie and the bakery shop manager back to stand on the landing outside the flat.

The manager had been watching television. 'We must not touch, eh? Fingerprints, yes? Something terrible has happened to Mrs Hanna?'

'We don't know anything yet.'

The manager was sweating.

Why was he so uneasy, wondered Ellie. The thought popped into her head that he might be an illegal immigrant who didn't want his papers looked at by the police. She dismissed this thought as soon as it took shape in her mind. She had known him for years. His wife often bought clothes for their three small children from the charity shop. No, that was not it.

Ellie recollected that it was he who had instigated the search for Mrs Hanna and obtained the key. It was very close on the landing, and he was feeling it. That was all.

As for that particular smell … it was fading fast. She peered round the edge of the door, and sniffed again.

The policeman spoke into his mobile. '… no, no sign of her. Looks as if there's been some kind of struggle in here. Bedroom and kitchen, both. In view of … yes, we'll wait.'

The policeman politely but firmly suggested that the manager wait downstairs. He looked at Ellie properly for the first time.

'Who are you?'

'Ellie Quicke. The vicar asked me to call to see if Mrs Hanna were all right.'

The policeman shrugged. 'Please wait downstairs.'

Ellie obediently went down the stairs, as did the manager.

Of course, she thought, it does look as if Mrs Hanna has been abducted, perhaps even killed after a struggle in her kitchen. And that was a terrifying thought.

But whatever that smell had been in the kitchen, it had not been stale food. Moreover, she could have sworn that the fridge was empty and the door ajar, with a tea towel folded over it to keep it from closing.

Something was knocking at the back of her mind. Some sound. Something not quite right. Something someone had said? She was developing a headache. The air was indeed very close on the stairs.

As she stood on the pavement outside the shops, a car drove up with Inspector Clay and another policeman in it whom she recognized. Ellie turned her back and walked away. She really did not want to face them again. They believed Kate had murdered her ex-boyfriend and Ellie didn't. She hadn't anything more to say to them.

Except that now the investigation into Ferdy's murder was bound to take a different direction, with his mother going missing under suspicious circumstances. Ellie could see the line the police were going to take. They would think Mrs Hanna must have known something about her son's murder and been killed because of it. They might even start dragging the river locally.

Ellie could see the logic of this, but ... oh well, it was no business of hers.

She glanced at her watch and quickened her pace. She hated being late for appointments and she was due to see her solicitor ... in five minutes' time.

The errand boy reported from his van, which he'd parked in the Avenue.

'Looks like the old woman's gone missing. You know anything about that? Yep, the Old Bill all over the place. The target? She's set off at a cracking pace. Down the far end of the Avenue. Yep, I can still see her. Going into a shop. No, I can't see inside. There's no way I can park near here. I'll have to park down a side street and hope to keep her in sight.'

The phone quacked at him.

'Yep, got all the stuff to do the gas. Soon as she gets back, I'll drop round to see to it. Tell her a gas leak has been reported and I have to check on her supply. Yep, I'll set it for tonight. No probs.'

The phone quacked some more.

The errand boy began to laugh. He had to put the phone

down, he was laughing too much to talk and steer round the corner. He loved it! The fat man had got out of hospital only to find his car gone! And of course he didn't dare ring the police!

It made the errand boy's day.

He was lucky with the parking. He broke out another can of beer and sat there, waiting. Hoping she wouldn't be too long.

7

Ellie came out of the solicitor's office feeling dazed. She almost walked under a bus as she crossed the road.

This would never do. She must sit down somewhere, have a cuppa. She realized she hadn't had any lunch. No wonder she was feeling a little strange. Well, the unexpected news hadn't helped, of course.

She hesitated outside the new Sunflowers café. She hadn't been in there before but she seemed to remember that someone's granddaughter worked there. Of course, Chloe. Mrs. Dawes' granddaughter. Ellie remembered young Chloe from when she was eight and had fallen off her bike and grazed her knees outside the church. Ellie had taken the child in to clean her up and calm her down. Why, that must be a good ten years ago now.

The café looked clean and tidy with a fine stand of cakes at the back and one of those splendid Gaggia machines to make coffee. There was a reproduction of Van Gogh's 'Sunflowers' on the wall. Naturally.

There were still some customers eating lunch. Cottage pie? Something on rice, with suspiciously bright peas? Ellie's stomach grumbled, and she went in. She recognized Chloe at once, even though she had shot up into a beanpole. The girl was model-thin now with smooth dark hair tied back in a ponytail, wearing jeans and a top which exposed her navel, neatly pierced with a gold ring. She was chewing gum, but smiled at Ellie and brought her the menu.

'Hi, Mrs Quicke. Nice to see you. Gran says she doesn't know what she would have done if you'd been out, the day she found Ferdy. What a thing, eh! I haven't got over it, for one. If you're eating, I'd suggest the sausages or the chilli.'

Ellie chose sausages, which had always been one of Frank's favourite dishes. She sat back in her chair and closed her eyes to replay the recent interview at the solicitor's.

Frank and Ellie had known Bill Weatherspoon the solicitor for many years. A handsome man in his sixties, he showed no inclination to retire. Indeed, he seemed to be sitting on the boards of more charities now than when the Quickes had first known him. He was a member of their church and had been on the PCC with Frank and Archie. When his wife had been having treatment for cancer, Ellie had helped out, looking after the teenage girls as best she could, seeing to their laundry and masterminding the big weekly shop. Frank had joked about that, calling it Ellie's 'Lady Bountiful' act.

After his wife died and the girls had left for university the two families had drifted apart. Ellie had been pleased to find he was to be Frank's executor. She was particularly pleased that he was to be sole executor. For some reason she had been afraid that Diana, or perhaps Aunt Drusilla ... no, she would not complete that thought.

After the first pleasantries were over, Ellie said, 'Put me out of my misery. Will I have enough to live on? Will I have to sell the house and take a small flat somewhere? I dread the thought of losing my garden.'

Bill Weatherspoon looked startled. 'No, of course you don't have to sell up – unless you want. My dear Ellie, I did try to reassure you after the funeral, though I realized you weren't taking it in.'

'I'm afraid I'm still not functioning very well. There's so much to think about, so many people to consider. Indulge me. Tell me in words of one syllable how I'm fixed.'

'I'll give you a copy of the will to take away with you. Ellie, you are going to be very comfortably off. You don't have to sell the house or the car or anything that you don't choose to get rid of. There are a few bequests; to your daughter Diana, to the church rebuilding fund, and so on. You are the residuary legatee, which means you get the rest of the estate including both houses, though there is a string attached to—'

'Both houses? You mean – Frank's family house as well? The one Aunt Drusilla lives in?'

'That's right. The house presently occupied by Miss Quicke is left to you.'

Ellie stared at him, open-mouthed. What was Aunt Drusilla going to say to that?

'There will be death duties to pay, of course, but Frank made provision for that, too. Now about your own house; I believe it has always been in your joint names?'

'Yes, because when my mother died, not long before we got married – my father died when I was a child – I used the money I got from selling her flat as deposit for our present house. Frank didn't have any capital, you see. So he put the house in our joint names.'

'In simple terms this means that in law you already own half the house, and can do with it what you wish. Frank has left his half of the house to you for life, with the proviso that it goes to Diana after your death. If you wish to stay where you are …'

'Oh, I do!'

'… then there's no problem. If you wish to sell up and buy another house somewhere, then there might have to be some adjustment of money … which you'd have to discuss with Diana.'

'Yes, yes. But will I be able to afford to go on living there?'

'Certainly you will. For a start, as Frank's widow you receive a pension from his firm. Then there's various insurances which will wipe out anything that remains of the mortgage, plus giving you a lump sum which Frank suggested you invest to give you a comfortable income. In addition, Frank himself invested in various companies from time to time. His portfolio of stocks and shares looks healthy.'

Ellie felt rather faint. She had had no idea. 'How much, roughly?'

He handed her a piece of paper. 'Frank worked it out for you. That's only a rough estimate, of course …' The amount consisted of noughts which seemed to go on for ever. Ellie blinked, and hardly took in what he said next.

'Now what would you like to do about the old family house? Do you wish to live there, or will you want to put it up for sale?'

'I don't understand. Frank can't have left it to me. Surely he meant to leave it to his aunt. Why, she's just sent me a note saying she's going to be in touch with a solicitor …'

Mr Weatherspoon grinned. He had rather large, handsome teeth, and Ellie was reminded of the fairy tale of Little Red Riding Hood. What big teeth you have, Grandma!

'Your husband's aunt Miss Quicke came to see me last

week, demanding a copy of the will which I was happy to provide her with. As you know, Frank only made a will after he became seriously ill. Naturally he had expected to outlive his aunt and yes, he had always considered that she had a right to live out her days in the old house. But something happened recently which led him to reconsider. I can assure you – as indeed I assured Miss Quicke – that he was in sound mind when he made this will.'

'Why did he change his mind?'

'He told me he'd discovered she was much better off than he'd been led to believe, and that she could perfectly well afford either to buy the house from you, or to buy something else for herself.'

'But she's always been so hard up! That's why we scrimped and saved to buy our own place, and why I had to go on working so long after we got married …'

Bill Weatherspoon got to his feet and went to stand looking out of the window. 'Forgive me if this is a sore subject, but I wonder if your health would have been better … all those miscarriages … if you had not had to work for so many years after you got married.'

Ellie blinked. How very kind of him to think of that. 'Oh, I expect they would have happened anyway.'

'Frank made some enquiries and was satisfied that he was doing the right thing by leaving the old house to you. Do what you like with it. Turn Miss Quicke out, make her buy it off you … all right?'

He returned to his chair. 'Listen, Ellie. Frank asked me to look after you, and I will. He was afraid you'd be unable to cope, that you might fall prey to some conman or other. I told him he underestimated you. But if you need help in dealing with Miss Quicke …?'

Ellie was silent. She thought she might very well appreciate some back-up in that quarter. 'I don't suppose she will want to move at her age.'

'It's a beautiful house with a big garden. You might wish to live in it yourself?'

'I wouldn't wish to turn her out … yes, I would! I would like to turn her out on to the streets tonight! To think how hard Frank had to work to …' She felt for a hankie, and failed to find one.

Mr Weatherspoon fished a box of tissues out of a drawer and put it beside her.

Ellie mopped and blew. 'Oh, how could she!' And then, 'Why didn't Frank tell me?'

'He said – forgive me – that you had always been a little afraid of her. He wanted to make things easy for you, so he asked me to keep quiet until he'd had a chance to talk to her direct about it, persuade her to give up the house and go quickly and quietly. He felt he owed her that much for bringing him up.'

'I don't think,' Ellie said, 'that woman has ever given up anything she ever wanted, the whole of her life. As far as I know, she never once troubled to visit him when he was in hospital, so I suppose she wouldn't have realized he'd willed the house away from her until she asked you for a copy of the will. To think of the way she made Frank dance attendance on her all these years, claiming she was too poor to take taxis …'

'Do you plan to continue acting as lady-in-waiting to her?'

Ellie coloured up. 'I hope you don't think too badly of me, but she never put herself out to help me once during all these years. Not when Diana was little and I suffered those miscarriages … not even when Frank fell ill and it was obvious that … I can't remember her ever saying a kind word to me. And I know she used to tell Diana that I was a bad mother … oh, I have a hard place inside me when I think about her!'

'So you'll put the house on the market as soon as probate is granted? That will give Miss Quicke plenty of time to move.'

'I'll have to think about it. Now may I ask how much Frank left to Diana?'

'He left her five thousand pounds to buy a new car.'

Ellie gaped. She looked at the figures on the piece of paper she was holding, and compared the two amounts. Frank couldn't have left Diana only five thousand. No, it wasn't possible. Or was it?

Bill Weatherspoon was giving her a quizzical look.

Ellie said, 'Frank had a – a difference of opinion with Diana …' In fact, it hadn't been a difference of opinion; it had been a blazing row. 'He'd given them a lot of money to buy a small house. Stewart is very sweet but he doesn't earn much. Anyway, Diana went for something bigger and wanted Frank to double what he'd given her. He refused. He said she ought to cut her coat to fit her cloth. Oh dear! I hope she hasn't got herself into a mess financially. I'll have to talk to her, work something out.'

But Diana took Frank's car after the funeral, thought Ellie then. She said she needed it. That was … sneaky! But perhaps she didn't know then that Frank had left her money for a new car? She said, 'About Frank's car …?'

'Right. Now I know you don't drive, and you won't want to be responsible for car tax, et cetera. I know someone who would like to buy the car off you. It's only a year old, isn't it? Suppose you have the RAC give it the once-over …'

'Diana took it. She didn't realize, I suppose.'

His eyebrows rose. 'My dear Ellie, Diana – like Miss Quicke – came to see me the day after the funeral and demanded a copy of the will. Which I gave her. She knew that her father had left her money for a new car, and she knew that Frank's car was yours.'

Ellie said, feebly trying to defend Diana, 'I didn't mind letting her have it, really.'

He steepled his hands and frowned, indicating displeasure at this irregularity. 'You realize she has removed valuable property from the estate?'

'It doesn't matter. I don't mind.'

His expression indicated that he thought she should mind.

Well, actually, Ellie did mind, rather. She'd had fantasies about learning to drive herself, one day. But as things were … no, it was all right for Diana to have taken the car. She had asked permission. No, she hadn't. She'd assumed permission.

Bill gave her a warm smile. 'Take your time, Ellie. I can see you haven't taken it all in yet. You are going to be very comfortably off. Having known you all these years, I can truthfully say that it couldn't happen to a nicer woman. Give yourself a good holiday. Go round the world. Go on a cruise. Buy yourself some clothes in Paris. Just see me first if you want to set up as a diamond trader …'

He laughed. Ellie relaxed enough to smile back.

He said, 'One piece of advice. All this is very new to you. People will ask how you're fixed. I advise you not to tell anyone – not anyone! – how much you have inherited. You don't need people asking you for loans, or capital to start up a business, do you? Maybe later on, when you've found your feet, yes. But do nothing in a hurry, Ellie. The will is simple, probate should not be delayed unduly. Have you sufficient funds in your own account to pay outstanding bills? Yes? Because if not …'

The solicitor rose. 'Ring me any time, if ever you are in any difficulty.'

The sausages and mash came, plus two kinds of mustard. Really the Sunflowers café was a pleasant place. Most of the other diners had departed. Chloe cleared tables, humming to herself. There was some background muzak on, but it was not obtrusive. Ellie thought, I could have dined at the Ritz today, if I'd wanted to.

The sausages and mash were excellent, and so was the treacle sponge which followed. The custard was good and hot. And then a pot of tea.

Ellie felt better. A lot better. She thought, I can afford to go on a cruise … fly on Concorde … visit the Great Wall of China. She smiled at this. She didn't really want to do anything like that. She just wanted to sit in this pleasant café, be waited on by a charming girl and drink strong tea in peace and quiet.

From where she sat, she could see that the police were still at Mrs Hanna's. Curious passers-by kept peering at the open front door – guarded by a policewoman. The bakery was doing a great trade, and the charity shop was thronged, too. Everyone would want to know what was going on.

Chloe asked Ellie if she'd like some more hot water.

'No, thanks, dear.' Ellie indicated the activity across the road. 'Do you happen to know …?'

'Mm. Mrs Hanna, her that works in the bakery … it was Ferdy, her son who got himself killed last week … and now she's disappeared. Not a trace. Murdered, they think. My friend who was in here earlier says he reckons her body will be under the new development up the High Road … under six foot of concrete, you know. But me, I don't reckon it. That sort of thing, gangsters and that, it doesn't happen much around here.'

'Gangsters?' said Ellie. 'You don't really think …?'

'Nah. Stands to reason. Not around here. Got a big imag-ination, my bloke. He thinks the ex-girlfriend did it, and so do I.'

Some new customers came in and Chloe drifted over to serve them. A man and a woman, elderly churchgoers whom Ellie knew by sight. They waved at her and she waved back.

'Exciting, isn't it?' the woman said to Ellie, indicating the bustle over the road. 'We saw her in the shop only last week, just before her son was murdered. It looks as if she found out something she shouldn't.'

Ellie smiled but didn't comment. She wanted to say that she'd seen Mrs Hanna after the murder had been discovered and that Mrs Hanna hadn't known anything then, because she had been putting pressure on Ellie to find out what had happened.

Perhaps someone thought Mrs Hanna did know some-thing – perhaps something that she didn't know she knew …

A nasty thought. Poor Mrs Hanna.

Ellie thought of all the useful things she could be doing but inertia held her in her seat. Besides, Chloe was busy serving more and more customers. People all wanted to discuss the latest developments. Sandwiches, bacon and eggs, tea and more tea were dispensed by the ever-efficient Chloe.

Suppose, thought Ellie, Ferdy had indeed been part of a gang … no, it was absurd to think that. Ferdy had been a loner, working on his cars, taking stalls at car boot sales.

Well, she only had Kate's word for that.

Well, just let's suppose for a minute that Ferdy had been part of a gang. What sort of gang would it have been? Drugs? Spare car parts?

Stealing cars and getting them out of the country?

Ellie had heard of all these things but had difficulty in fitting them into what she knew about their pleasant neighbourhood.

Chloe came and hovered, writing out Ellie's bill.

Ellie said, 'I suppose it could have been some sort of gang warfare … although what could have happened without us noticing?'

'Not drugs, that's for sure,' said Chloe, slapping down the bill. 'Not Ferdy. He didn't believe in doing drugs. My friend says it would have been a lot simpler if it had been drugs. No, it's the girlfriend, believe me.'

Ellie wondered if they could find out when Mrs Hanna disappeared, and where Kate was at the time. No, it was quite ridiculous. Kate couldn't possibly have done it. Clonking someone on the head and dragging them up the church to the altar was one thing. Killing Mrs Hanna and disposing of her body was another. Mrs Hanna must have weighed thirteen or fourteen stone.

Of course, there had been those drag marks along the carpet runner in Mrs Hanna's flat …

Ellie paid, left a generous tip and made her way out of the café. The police were still keeping guard over Mrs Hanna's place.

Someone hailed her from across the street. John, exiting the charity shop on his way home for the day.

He caught her arm. 'Just the person I wanted to see. I was going to come round by your place on my way home. The thing is …' his rubbery face expressed anguish. '… well, I didn't want you walking in tomorrow and finding … the truth is that the director came down and Madam told him she was turning over a new leaf and staying on. Apparently her daughter's moving away and putting the child in a nursery. So Madam's going to hang on to her job here and there's not much we can do about it.'

Ellie found that she was relieved … and then annoyed. Relief dominated. She thought.

'I'm pleased for her,' she said.

'Really? We aren't.' Gloom settled on John's shoulders. 'She'll be all right for a while, no doubt, and then revert to her old ways. She never has been able to soothe awkward customers either on the shop floor or behind the till. You should have seen our faces when she announced what was going to happen. Didn't know where to look. Most of us were counting the days till you could take over.'

'Now, John, you know I only promised to think about it. I never said I would do it, and the more I did think about it, the more problems I could see.'

'Hmph. Bet you don't say that in a couple of weeks' time when you're landed with sorting out yet another of her messes. But I'm holding you up. Are you on your way home? I'm going that way, too.'

As they walked along, John told Ellie that the antibiotics

were finally kicking in and he was feeling a lot better. She opened her mouth to tell him what the solicitor had just said, then closed it again. Perhaps if she boasted about it, it would all vanish into thin air.

No, she didn't really think it would vanish. But perhaps it would be better not to speak about it to too many people. Mr Weatherspoon's warning came to her mind. He knew someone who had been pestered for money in the street, at home, on the phone, by letter, just because she'd come into a little inheritance.

Not that John was going to ask her for a loan, of course. Ellie felt dizzy with plans for what she could do with the money … she would sort things out with Diana, of course. Her favourite charities would benefit, she would treat all her friends to a slap-up lunch somewhere, or a day out in a minibus, or perhaps a matinee at the theatre. Then all the small children she knew would have extra-special Christmas presents … and for herself? Well, she didn't really need much. Perhaps, if she were to be really self-indulgent, she might install a small greenhouse and replace the curtains in the sitting-room, which were getting rather frayed at the edges …

Waving goodbye to John, Ellie crossed the church grounds to the rambling late Victorian vicarage. Built of red brick, it had imposing gables and a semi-circular gravel driveway.

Inside the tiled porch were a number of bell-pushes. Press One for the vicar, Two for the curate and Three for the office. She pressed One and was almost knocked over as the Reverend Gilbert careered out of the front door, hair awry, with his arms full of sheet music.

'Ellie, my dear!'

Ellie stepped back. 'I can see you're busy! Another time.'

He freed an arm to put it through hers, and swept her out and across the road.

'Just the girl we need. Carol singing. Practice. Short of sopranos, would you believe? You can give us a couple of hours, can't you? Monday evenings, 6.30.'

'No, no!' Ellie began to laugh. 'You know I told you I can't hold a tune—'

'Doesn't matter, carol singing. Do you good. Hold these.' Dumping the music in her arms, he started feeling for something in his pockets. Then stopped. 'Meant to ask. Did you see Mrs Hanna? I've just come out of a meeting and someone was saying something about her but I wasn't attending, I'm afraid.'

'She's gone missing. They think murdered, but—'

'Murdered!' His glance switched to the side door of the church, and then over the alley towards the house in which Kate was hiding behind drawn curtains.

'No, it wasn't her, I'm sure of it,' said Ellie.

His eyebrows danced a tango, indicating scepticism. 'Then … who?' He set himself in motion again, finally producing a vestry key from a waistcoat pocket. Unlocking the door, he led the way into a cold, dusty-smelling room lined with clergy and choir robes.

Ellie followed him because he was expecting her to do so, and because she was still holding the pile of sheet music. 'It's a mystery, I know. There are all sorts of rumours …'

'Shouldn't listen to rumours.'

He led the way into the main body of the church, took the music from her and dumped it in a choir pew. Ellie's eyes went to the altar. The red carpet which had covered the area in front of the altar was gone, exposing the original black and white tiles. It was only her imagination that there was a dark stain where she supposed the body must have lain.

The vicar saw where she was looking. 'Yes, poor fellow. He lay just there. Gave me a fright. Mrs Dawes, too. But Mrs Dawes seems all right now. Bullying everyone as usual on Sunday. How about you?'

He seated himself in a pew, patting the padded cushion beside him. He seemed to have all the time in the world to talk. It was one of his greatest strengths, that he could do this. He was probably due at another meeting, thought Ellie. He'd be late for it, but perhaps he had his priorities right. Weren't people more important than meetings?

The bereaved think so, anyway.

She sat beside him. She wanted to tell him how confused she was by the provisions of Frank's will, and Diana's behaviour. She thought he'd sympathize, tell her to be tough with Diana, make her refund the value of the car. But did she really want to do that? No, of course not.

She must talk to Diana, see how much money she needed to get straight again and arrange for it to be given her.

She said, 'I've just been to see my solicitor. He says I shall have enough to stay where I am. If I'm careful.' Now why did she have to add the rider? The vicar wasn't going to ask her for money, was he? How horrid of her to deceive him.

'Now Ellie, I've been thinking about this, and I don't like the thought of your scrimping and saving to make ends meet. I'm glad you can stay in the house because I know you love it, but when the bills start coming in, and there's no one to pay them … well, that's where friends come in.'

Did he mean he'd lend her money? Oh, the embarrassment!

'Oh, no!' she said, reddening. 'I didn't, couldn't … there's really no need! I'm going to be quite comfortably off, it seems.'

'Bless you, my dear! I hope you are. But just in case, would you consider taking a lodger? I don't have anyone special in mind at the moment, but …'

'That's kind of you, very kind. But at the moment …'

'…you don't know whether you're on your head or your heels.'

'No, I don't. And you know, I really must be going. I want to ring Diana tonight.'

She stood up, to indicate that she really must go. He hauled himself to his feet – awkwardly, his arthritis must be playing up again – and kissed her on both cheeks. 'You'll do,' he said.

Going up the path to her own house, Ellie looked up at the back bedroom of Kate's house. The curtains were still drawn. It was dusk now, not raining for once. A vicious cold wind was lifting her skirt and crawling down her neck. She let herself into the house.

Cold. Dark. No Tod. No Frank.

Don't give way to self-pity.

Unpack your shopping.

Lay out some salad for supper. She could really do with something hot to eat, even though she had had such a good lunch at the Sunflower. Someone had put a note through the front door. Mrs Dawes, reminding Ellie about coming to her flower class on Thursdays. Nice of her, though of course Ellie couldn't go because she'd be at the charity shop.

The house felt like a cold shroud, settling around her shoulders.

She bumped up the central heating, made herself a cup of Bovril.

Put the radio on.

Sat down at Frank's desk in Frank's chair to ring Diana.

Diana very rarely rang home, expecting her parents to bear the cost of the phone bills. As Diana said, they could afford it, couldn't they? Ellie found she was gripping the phone so tightly that she began to shake. Of course she loved Diana. She was her only daughter. But how dared she take the car when she knew her father had left her enough money to buy another one! Was she so much in debt that she couldn't wait for her legacy to come through? Couldn't she have explained it to Ellie?

Just because Frank had always doted on her … never criticizing her, even when Diana had been rude to him …

… and always criticizing Ellie, even in front of Diana …

She let the phone crash back on to its base. Anger didn't help anyone.

She must be calm. Be reasonable.

Diana had asked permission to take the car, and Ellie had given it. She hadn't really been thinking straight at the time. No. But that didn't alter the facts.

Blowing her nose, Ellie considered not phoning her daughter that night. But finally did it. She would be very calm and understanding about Diana's money situation and they would work something out together. Diana had been so sweet, so caring about her since the funeral, Ellie was sure they had begun a new and better relationship.

Unfortunately, Diana seemed to have lost all her sweetness and light since they last spoke. For starters, she was surprised to get the call.

'Mother? Anything wrong? You usually ring on

Thursdays … this is only Wednesday, isn't it? Has something happened?'

Ellie thought of everything that had been happening to her: the murder, Kate's visit, the possibility of taking over the charity shop, the accident to that poor man on the bridge, buying a new bed; finding Mrs Hanna missing, visiting the solicitor … then John saying that Madam was staying on at the shop, and everyone blaming Kate …

'I just wanted to talk to you, dear, if you can spare a moment.'

'Well, if it's really important … you know I have to go out on Wednesday nights. Oh, didn't I tell you? We've been invited to play bridge with some neighbours, very nice people, got one of those new top executive detached houses up by the bridge … oh yes, and I'm putting some details of flats around here into the post for you. Stewart and I spent ages last weekend going around them.'

Ellie clutched at her sanity. 'I didn't know you were planning to move, dear.'

'No, of course not. Really mother, you are the end. It's for you, of course. Something not too far away, where you can get to the shops easily and come here to babysit. Perhaps one bus stop away. We found just the thing for you in—'

'But I don't want to move.'

Diana sighed. Ellie could just imagine her raising her eyes to heaven in annoyance.

'Don't be silly, mother. You can't possibly stay where you are now. As I said, I've popped some details in the post and you can pick the ones you like best at your leisure. I know you don't like being rushed into things. So I thought you could come up next week, Tuesday perhaps, and have a look at the best of the flats. Stay till Thursday …'

Yes, thought Ellie, so that I can babysit for you on Wednesday?

She said, with a firmness that surprised her, 'I'm sorry, my dear, but that won't be possible. I have commitments here, you know. At the shop. To the vicar, and so on. I'm going to join the church choir. Did I tell you? No, I know I can't sing very well, but it's just Christmas carols. I'm sure I can manage that.'

Diana was not pleased. 'Really, mother, when we've been to all this trouble, telling the estate agent that you'll be up next week. We're going to look very foolish if you don't come …'

Ellie was beginning to get annoyed. 'Well, you shouldn't have done it, should you, dear? Not without asking me. I have a lot to do down here. In fact, you should be proud of me. I've even been trying to work your father's computer—'

'That's ridiculous, mother! You'll never be able to do that. In fact, I was only saying to Stewart yesterday that he must arrange to collect it from you some time, as we could do with a second one. It will be nice for the little one to play games on in a year or two—'

Ellie put the phone down with exaggerated care.

She was so angry she didn't know what to do with herself.

She clutched at her shoulders, shivering. She hoped she wasn't going down with anything. Widows often did, she had noticed. They developed abscesses, laryngitis, asthma, tummy troubles. They always seemed to be on antibiotics. She'd go and have a nice long hot bath. And pour lots of bubbly stuff in. And soak.

The phone rang again.

Ellie cast it a look of dislike and turned her back on it. If it was Diana, well, she could wait. The answerphone was on. Diana could talk to that. Ellie could hear a message being recorded as she went upstairs. It only went quiet when she ran the bath water. Good. Diana had given up because she would have to get ready for her date with her new high-flying friends.

Ellie set her radio on the toilet seat, turned the dial to some soothing music, poured in a generous amount of bubble bath, slipped into the water and lay there, unwinding.

She thought, I really am enjoying this!

It surprised her that she could enjoy something so soon after Frank's death. Of course, she would never have been able to take a hot bath at such an early hour of the day if he were still around. At this time of day he would have been bustling back from work, fussing about having a cooked supper on time, worrying away at his papers for whatever meeting he was going out to that evening …

Ah well, there were compensations in being a widow. You could go out for lunch to the Sunflowers café, and not cook in the evening.

Fancy him trying to protect her from Aunt Drusilla like that! He had been a lovely man, in so many ways. And she would not cry. No.

Ellie let herself sink under the water completely, and blew bubbles.

As she surfaced, she thought she heard the phone ringing. It couldn't be Diana. Well, she couldn't be bothered to get out of the bath now.

Then the doorbell rang.

Drat!

Ellie climbed out of the bath, hoping that whoever it was would go away again. They didn't. They rang again. She towelled herself roughly dry, and reached for her old dressing-gown and fluffy slippers.

'Hold on! I'm coming!'

She descended the stairs in a warm cloud of scented steam. Two people stood outside the front door, a workman with a badge dangling from his breast pocket, carrying a large toolbox, and Kate, looking pinched and cold, huddled into a big black coat.

Kate said, 'I was just going out to get some fish and chips, and wondered if you'd like some. Oh, and the gas man says there's a leak been reported, wants to check your supply.'

8

'I haven't reported any leak,' said Ellie. 'Kate, do come in for a minute. I've been wanting to speak to you.' And to the workman, 'Sorry you've been troubled.'

The man mounted the doorstep and pushed at the front door which Ellie was holding, trying to keep the cold weather out.

'Listen, missus, I've got to check it out. Once a leak is reported, it's as much as my job's worth to skip a house.'

Kate said, 'Oh, do you want to do mine as well? My husband's just come back and he can show you where everything is.'

Armand was just getting out of his car. Kate turned to Ellie with a ravishing smile. 'Yes, I'd love to come in for a few minutes, if I may.'

The workman looked thunderous.

'What's this?' asked Armand, storming down the path. His eyes were on Kate even though the question seemed directed at the workman. He was evidently in a shocking temper.

'Gas leak somewhere,' said Kate, smiling vaguely in his direction but not at him. 'Will you let him check out our place? I'm just going to spend a little time with Ellie.'

'Hurry up,' said Ellie, beginning to shiver. 'I've just got

out of a hot bath.' Then to the workman, 'Look, you can come in and check if you're quick. My husband installed one of those gadgets which show if there's a gas leak, but it hasn't gone off so there can't be anything wrong with our supply.'

At that point Ellie noticed something. 'Oh! May I see your identification papers, please?'

By this time Kate had joined Ellie in the hall. 'What?'

Ellie held out her hand, meeting the workman's eyes with what he afterwards described as a steely glare. He didn't realize he was catching the tail end of Typhoon Diana.

He took a step back. 'Who d'you think I am?'

'Possibly not who you say you are,' said Ellie. 'Are gas board employees allowed to smoke on the job? You've got the butt end of a cigarette lodged behind your right ear. Householders are always being told to be careful, ask for ID. So where's your papers?'

The man looked around for inspiration and found all three of them looking at him with suspicion.

Armand grimaced, showing fine white teeth. 'Shall I phone the police?'

The workman backed away. 'It's true I got no ID on me. I left it in the van. But it's getting late …'

'Yes, that's another thing,' said Ellie. 'It's well after six o'clock. I'm sure you shouldn't be working this late.'

'You're right. I'll be off then. Be back tomorrow some-time.' He walked back to the road and turned left. They watched him out of sight.

Armand spoke to Kate, rather than Ellie. 'Do you think we ought to phone the police anyway? Suppose you'd been on your own, and let him in … who knows what he'd have got away with?' He spoke with a subdued violence. Ellie noticed with a shiver that his eyes had gone small and bright.

Kate seemed to be taking it lightly. 'I'm not very fond of the police at the moment. Don't let me keep you, Armand.'

Ellie was shivering. 'You won't mind if I shut the door? I've just had a bath.'

'Bye bye, Armand!' Kate waved goodbye to her husband with a laugh, and closed the front door on him. There was an edge to the way she spoke that worried Ellie. A husband and wife on good terms don't speak to one another like that.

Ellie led the way into the kitchen and looked at the cold meal with disfavour. 'That's all I've got to eat, I'm afraid. Tell you what, I'll make some home-made soup to start with. Unless you still want to go out for some fish and chips. And what about Armand's meal?'

Kate threw her big coat over the chair in the hall and slumped on to a kitchen stool. 'He always goes out on Wednesday nights. Chess club. He'll eat out. I didn't expect him back so soon, or I'd have gone out sooner … and no, I don't want to talk about it.'

Ellie opened her mouth to pursue the subject, and Kate got in first.

'No, I don't want to talk about Ferdy, either.'

Ellie chopped onions and mushrooms and threw them into a pan to sizzle in oil. Salt, pepper. A chicken stock cube, some boiling water. She turned the gas flame down and put the lid on.

'Smells good,' said Kate, closing her eyes and stretching out her legs.

'When did you eat last? Or is that another of the questions you don't want to answer?'

Kate leaned forward, and laid her head on folded arms on the table. 'What would you do in my place?'

That was when Ellie shocked both herself and Kate. 'Leave him, of course!'

'Leave him? After only six weeks of marriage?' Kate laughed. 'Am I such a poor creature as to give up so quickly?'

'Marry in haste …'

'But I didn't. I thought about nothing else for three solid months. Shall I, shan't I? Will he give up and look for someone else? Why don't my friends like him? Does that matter, when the sun and moon and stars shine out of his eyes? Why do I shake with fear if he so much as looks at another girl? Why can't my mother see that if I don't have him, I'll die? What's wrong with me?'

'Nothing.' Ellie stirred the cooked mixture, emptied it into the liquidizer, whizzed it up with some cornflour and returned it to the pan to reheat and thicken.

Kate spoke to the table. 'If there's nothing wrong with me, then why—'

'Why does he hit you?'

Kate sat so still that Ellie wondered if she'd fallen asleep.

Ellie stirred the thickened soup, tasted it for seasoning and poured it into two large mugs. Setting one on the table before Kate, she sat opposite her. 'Drink up.'

Kate lifted her head. 'How did you know?'

'I've got eyes and ears. Sound travels through the wall.'

'He's only done it once.'

'No, he hasn't.'

Kate sipped her soup, eyes down. 'It was only a slap at first.'

'How soon after you married?'

'The second day. I got a rise at work, you see. I hadn't told him about it before because I thought what a marvellous surprise it would be. His face, when I told him …'

'Envy.'

Kate sighed. 'I don't understand it. He's got a good job. He's doing well. He can expect a deputy headship within a couple of years …'

'But he hasn't got it now and you're probably earning a lot more than he is.'

'What does that matter when you love someone?'

Ellie didn't bother to answer. Kate could work that out herself. Kate, of course, did not know how Armand had spoken of her to the police. Ellie considered telling her but refrained. The poor girl had enough to worry her as it was.

Ellie dished up cold meat and salad. To wash it down, she found a bottle of red wine at the back of the store cupboard. Frank would probably have told her it was an insult to the wine to drink it with cold meat and salad, but she considered that both she and Kate could do with it. It went down a treat. They ate all the meat and salad. And some of the home-made cakes Ellie had bought at the Sunflowers café.

'What am I going to do?' Kate asked. She spoke so softly that Ellie thought it was a rhetorical question, not requiring any reply.

However she did say, 'You could try lashing out with the frying-pan if he hits you again.' She poured the last of the wine into their glasses. She felt warm and well insulated against the world's troubles.

Kate grimaced. 'You don't understand. I love him, but he frightens me. When he loses his temper the skin round his mouth goes white, his eyes go small and dark, and even before he hits me I can feel him hating me … oh, I don't mean that he really hates me. Well, perhaps for just a second or two. He loves me, really. He's so sorry afterwards. So sad that I've made him do it.'

Ellie waved her wine glass about. 'Nonsense, Kate. He's nothing but a plain, common or garden wife beater.'

'He says he got a lot worse than that when he was growing up. The problem is that he switches moods so quickly. I never know how he'll react. But I can't give up on him because at bottom he loves me, I know he does.'

Ellie opened her mouth to object, but Kate got there first. 'I don't want to talk about it any more, Ellie. Please. You've been very kind, but it's not your husband we're talking about here and I've got to work it out my own way. Now tell me how you've been getting on.'

Ellie thought of all the things that had been happening to her: the talk with the solicitor, Aunt Drusilla's peculiar behaviour, the accident on the bridge, Diana taking the car, the struggle with the computer …

She found she was still extremely angry with Diana. But she started off on a less emotional note.

'All right, my turn to moan. The computer's driving me insane.'

'I'll give you a few lessons on it at the weekend, if you like.'

'Would you? You're an angel. I can't tell you how frustrated I get with it. What's more, it's just occurred to me that there's probably some e-mail on it, because Frank loved getting e-mail and there's bound to be some there, only I don't know how to get at it.'

Kate laughed. 'Leave that to me. Anything else?'

Ellie hadn't meant to say it, but it just burst out of her. 'My daughter Diana took Frank's car after the funeral even though he's left her money to buy one for herself. For years

I've been thinking how convenient it would be if I learned to drive. Frank was always against my learning because he thought I'd be a menace on the roads. But I would have liked to have tried. I mean, if I'd been so awful then I'd never have been able to pass a driving test ... but now Diana's taken the car and I'll never know.'

Ellie sought for a hankie and failed to find one, but made do with a square of kitchen towel. 'Diana just picked up the keys, and told me she was taking the car. She said that was all right, wasn't it? I was so bogged down with the funeral and taking those awful pills and everything that I let her. I mean, it did cross my mind that yes, I did mind her taking the car, but then I thought that probably Frank would have wanted her to have it. I let her take it and now I'm so angry because the solicitor told me that Diana knew Frank had left her money to buy a car and I could spit!'

Kate patted Ellie's hand. 'Tell you what, I'll give you a driving lesson in my car. It's easy to drive because it's an automatic and that's probably what you ought to have, anyway. Why don't you put some warm clothes on? It looks as if there's going to be a frost tonight. We'll sit in my car and go over the controls. We might even drive up and down the road here. If that feels OK, you can book yourself some official driving lessons.'

'I couldn't take up your time like—'

'Of course you could. What would I have done these last few days without you to prop me up? Get dressed while I check to see if you've got any e-mail.'

Ellie floated upstairs and climbed into a warm pullover, jogging trousers and a pair of trainers. A padded waistcoat and dark woollen hat would help to keep out the cold. It was a very cold night.

'Eureka!' Kate waved a clutch of papers at her as she emerged from the study.

'Not much here for you to worry about. I've deleted all the junk mail.'

Giggling a little at their daring, the two women went out to Kate's car. Kate tossed the keys to Ellie.

'You unlock it, and get into the driver's seat.'

'Oughtn't we to have L-plates on?'

'Sure, but we're not going far, are we? Just to the end of the road and back.'

'I think I'm a little drunk.'

'No, you're not. You're just nicely relaxed. Get in, woman. Fit the key in the ignition — that's it. Turn it. Seatbelts on. It's a good old car, this. Reliable even in cold weather. Now let's see what you make of all these dials on the dashboard.'

Kate gave Ellie a swift rundown of everything she needed to know before they set off. She knew most of it already, of course, having been a passenger for so many years while Frank drove.

'Now,' said Kate. 'Turn on some lights. Side lights are here. Indicators you do like this.'

'No gears?'

'No, you just put your foot down on the accelerator when you want to move. The harder you press down, the faster you move and it changes gear automatically. That's the brake pedal. This is the handbrake.'

Ellie repeated, 'Accelerator, brake and handbrake. Right.'

'Before you move out into the road, look in your mirrors to see if the road is clear … it is? Then take off the handbrake gently and press the accelerator pedal, while turning the steering wheel to move out into the road …'

Biting her lower lip hard, Ellie moved out into the road at a snail's pace.

Kate corrected the angle of the steering wheel, saying Ellie would soon learn how wide the car was. There was, luckily, no other traffic on that quiet little road. Just some residents' cars and the odd white van.

'Now when we come to the corner, take your foot off the accelerator – gently – and put the handbrake on.'

Ellie was gripping the steering wheel so hard she could hardly move her hand off it.

'Look right, left and right again. Indicate that you're turning right, even if there's nothing in sight. Turn the wheel to the right ... we'll make a circle round by the park and back into our road again.'

'Is it safe? Am I all right?'

'You're doing very well. Don't worry about that white van behind us. It's going as slowly as we are. He's probably looking for a house number. Watch it. You're steering slightly to the left again.' Kate touched the wheel to return the car to the centre of the road.

'Suppose we meet another car?'

'Then you'll draw into the side and park. There's nothing much on the road tonight, though. That's right, slow down at the park gates. Look both ways, indicate, put your foot down gently ... and here's the turning back to our own road. That's it. Pause, look, indicate, and off we go again. Now when we get back home, indicate, slow down, and turn the wheel to the left. Don't panic, there's plenty of space to park and it doesn't matter if you do take a few yards more to park. And don't worry if the back of the car sticks out a bit, there's so little traffic on this road. Now put the brake on, handbrake as well. Lights off. Ignition off. Well done, Ellie! Of course you'll be able to learn to drive!'

Ellie unstuck herself from the driver's seat, and stepped out into the road. 'I'm trembling all over.' But she was laughing, too.

'You'll be just fine.' Kate was laughing, too. 'Now remember … whoops, mind the kerb!'

Ellie straightened up with the aid of Kate's hand under her elbow. 'Sorry. Disorientated. Getting a bit tired.'

'Time for bed.' Kate collected her big coat and handbag from Ellie's hall, retrieved her car keys and returned to her own house.

Silent house.

Waiting for Armand to return.

Oh, the poor thing, thought Ellie as she turned out lights, bolted the doors and climbed the stairs to bed. The poor, poor girl …

Tired as she was, she lay awake until she heard Armand's return. A car drew up on the frosty road outside. Then came the sharp bang of a front door. She hoped for silence after that. She prayed for it. Please don't let him hit her again. Please.

The party wall was lined on her side with built-in cupboards. They muffled sound. Ellie buried her head in her pillows, telling herself that even if it were thumps and shouting that she heard, she could do nothing about it.

The errand boy was using the mobile phone, sitting in his white van.

'… that's right, they must have been at the old vino, both of them. Lurching around all over the place, giggling fit to burst. And her driving! You'd have thought she'd never driven in her life before … yeah, I thought they'd spotted me, because she just drove round the block and parked back in front of her house again. But she couldn't have spotted me, 'cause I parked way back down the road. Yeah, I'll do her car, right away. Trust me, I can fix any car you like. Nah, she won't notice nothing. She'll have such a thick head in the morning, she won't be looking for trouble, will she?'

Ellie woke to the sound of car windows being scraped clean of frost. She couldn't think what day it was at first, but she did remember that something extremely important had happened to her.

The driving lesson!

'Wonderful!' She jumped out of bed and peered out of the window to see if it was Kate working on her car. If so, Ellie decided she'd run downstairs and tell her how marvellous it was to know that driving lessons were on the menu.

But it was only Armand, chipping away at his car windows with a scraper. Frank had always used a can of de-icer. Ellie turned away from the window and pulled on some clothes. What day was it? Thursday? Yes, Thursday. She must put in an appearance at the charity shop, and perhaps drop Mrs Dawes a note saying she was sorry not to make the flower-arranging classes.

And then … she remembered about the money, and what the solicitor had said. It took some getting used to.

Washed, dressed, brushed and lipsticked, Ellie made her way downstairs, collected the newspaper from the front door, and heard next door bang as Kate left for work. Opening her own front door, Ellie stepped outside and met the chill of the morning full on. Her breath hung like cigarette smoke on the air before her.

Kate, huddled into her big coat, was shoving her handbag, laptop and briefcase up on to the top of the car with gloved hands while she fiddled with the lock on the car door.

'Hi!' cried Ellie, hugging herself against the cold. 'Just wanted to say thank you!'

Kate turned her head. She was wearing dark glasses and an all-enveloping scarf. Hiding who knew what injuries. Ellie's prayers seemed to have gone unanswered.

'That's all right,' said Kate, attempting to smile. 'Say, have you got the kettle boiling? The lock's frozen, and I have a nasty feeling Armand's got our only scraper.'

'Just a tick.' Ellie rushed into the kitchen, switched on the kettle, said 'Come on!' to it several times and dashed out of the front door with it in her hand.

'Ta,' said Kate, dribbling the hot water gently over the lock. The key now turned, so she handed the kettle back to Ellie. 'I'll just start the engine and wait till it defrosts the windows.'

'I think Frank's aerosol of de-icer is still under the stairs. I'll fetch it, shall I?'

Ellie went back towards the house as Kate leaned into the car to turn the key in the ignition.

There was a muffled whumpf! The bonnet of the car burst open. The whole car seemed to lift off the road. Kate was thrown backwards out of the car and Ellie was thrown forwards into the gutter. The handbag and laptop landed in the road. Kate's briefcase erupted, sending papers everywhere.

For a moment Ellie could not even breathe. Looking at her right hand, which was still holding the handle, she noticed that the kettle had broken apart on impact with the

138

kerb. She wriggled her arms, and then her legs. Nothing broken.

Lifting her head, she tried to call out for Kate, but no sound came out of her mouth. She was also deaf.

Kate wasn't listening, anyway. She was standing in the middle of the road, her dark glasses both starred. The left arm of her coat was in rags. There was a nasty cut on her chin.

Kate opened her mouth and screamed. And screamed. And screamed. Ellie could see her scream, but not hear it.

Doors opened up and down the street. Ellie's hearing began to clear as anxious voices called out to know what was the matter, what was that noise.

Flames began to lick around the edges of the bonnet.

Kate looked as if she'd been blinded, because of the stars on her glasses. If they'd broken, and the glass had been thrust into her eyes …

Shock caught up with Ellie. Sobbing, she abandoned the kettle and inched painfully to her feet. The heels of her hands and her legs were grazed, and her left hip felt sore.

Neighbours in varying states of undress opened doors and windows. The boy Tod came hurtling out of his house, screaming. His mother ran after him, keying numbers into her mobile.

'Fire! Ambulance! Police!'

Tod sent Ellie staggering as he rushed into her arms. 'I'm all right, I'm all right,' said Ellie, trying to reassure him. His grip on her was that of a python.

Kate stopped screaming. The silence was as unnerving as her screams had been.

Ellie found herself looking at the papers which strewed the road. Those need picking up, she thought. But it's too far to reach down to the road …

Kate yanked off her glasses and turned her head to look at the fiery wreck of her car. At least she had not been blinded.

Tod's mother was an anorexic-looking bottle blonde. She caught Kate's arm. 'Come away! Petrol … the car might explode! Tod, what do you think you're doing?'

'It's all right,' said Ellie, soothing the instant jealousy in the eyes of the boy's mother. 'He thinks of me as a sort of grandmother, I think …'

'Yes, of course.' Tod's mother accepted the explanation at face value, burying the knowledge that Ellie was dearer to Tod than herself.

Without a word, without seeming to see or hear them, Kate retrieved her handbag and limped past them, down the pathway to her front door.

'Kate!' cried Ellie.

Kate took no notice, but let herself into the house.

The car was burning fiercely and it took little urging for Tod and his mother to get Ellie to retreat. Mercifully her own front door had not blown shut and locked her out of the house.

Tod's mother said, 'I've phoned for the police. Tod, what are you doing here? You ought to be getting ready for school.'

Tod shook his head. He helped Ellie over her doorstep and into the kitchen.

He said, 'You're bleeding.'

'Tod!' screeched his mother. 'You've got blood on your sweater! Go back home and change at once and put that sweater in cold water, do you hear?' Then to Ellie, 'The police and the ambulance will be here in a minute. Tod, go home! What was it, a bomb? You hear of these things, but never expect … ohmigod, will you look at the time! I ought to be ... Tod, go back to the house this instant, and get your things ready for school.'

Ellie agreed that Tod ought not to be on the scene, but his grip on her arm was as strong as ever and he showed no sign of hearing what his mother was saying. She tried to say that she was all right, but in fact she was very far from all right. She thought, 'Does Armand hate her that much?'

Another neighbour came in. They had left the front door open, of course. The house was desperately chilly. Ellie ground her teeth together in an effort to stop them clattering.

'Tea! Hot, sweet tea!' said the newcomer.

Ellie began to laugh. Her kettle lay smashed to pieces on the road, together with Kate's laptop and briefcase.

'Hysteria, poor thing!' said the newcomer in an undertone to Tod's mother. 'Who'd have thought of such a thing, in this neighbourhood. First that boy was found in the church, then his mother gets dragged out of the river, and now this!'

Ellie made a gigantic effort to still the shakes. 'Would someone make me a cup of tea, please? My kettle's broken.'

Tod's mother said she had to get off to work and took Tod away, but the newcomer – a friendly, busty plain Jane who lived a couple of doors away with her sickly brother – said she'd make a pot of tea in her own house and bring it over. Never fear, she said, she'd look after Ellie.

Ellie would have liked to object, knowing that plain Jane's middle name was Gossip, but she hadn't the energy. Plain Jane left to fetch the tea and no doubt to regale all the neighbours en route about how well Ellie was taking it, and what a thing to happen, my dear!

Left to herself, Ellie saw that she was dripping blood on to her clothes and the lino. Painfully she made her way to the sink and ran water over her hands. A movement outside made her look up.

Through the screening hedge next door she could see a tall dark figure walking rapidly down the garden path. A woman in a long black coat and large, enveloping headscarf, also black. Kate, carrying a suitcase and with her handbag over her shoulder. Ellie tapped on the window, but Kate didn't turn.

Out into the alley, across into the churchyard, and up … over the church grounds to the main road, where a loaded bus took on just a few extra passengers – including Kate.

Dressed like that, Kate could easily be taken for a Muslim woman. Nothing could be seen of her except gloved hands and face.

Making her escape?

Probably.

She wasn't waiting around to see if Armand would be blamed for the explosion. Ellie didn't blame her in the least. She decided that unless directly asked – and even if directly asked, come to think of it – she would not tell anyone what she'd seen.

She might well have been mistaken, anyway. Some movement of branches, seen through the wintry hedge …

She knew she was in shock. She dabbed at her grazed legs with a wet kitchen towel, and heard sirens outside. She went on dabbing. Plain Jane returned, breathless with haste, plus a large pot of tea. This was making her day. Police, firemen, the car being sprayed … didn't Ellie want to see?

Then the ambulancemen, cheery and kind but firm.

'Got your handbag, dear? And a nice warm coat? That's it, let's just strap you into this chair and get you looked over in the hospital.'

The police didn't get a look-in on this one. Ellie closed her eyes as she was wheeled up the drive to the ambulance ramp. A policewoman did try to question her, but the ambulancemen waved them aside.

Ellie rather wished she hadn't woken up so early that morning. In which case, she wouldn't have been out in the road when the car exploded. But then, Kate might have got into the car to turn on the ignition, instead of just leaning in as she talked to Ellie. And in that case, Kate would now very probably be dead.

Ellie turned her mind away from all of that. Her hands hurt, and so did her legs. And her head. She decided that she would rather like to take a short nap, till matters improved …

The errand boy watched proceedings from the other side of the road. He was the very picture of a workman on his way to mend a leaking pipe, taking time out to gawp at fire engine, police and ambulance. After a while he retreated up the driveway of a house whose occupants had driven off to work earlier. He got out the mobile phone.

'Bingo!' he announced. 'She's just been loaded into the ambulance. Unconscious. They wouldn't even let the police talk to her. And the car's totalled.'

The phone quacked at him. He shifted from one foot to the other, uneasily.

'I don't give a damn who left by the back door. I tell you I got a good look at her, and she's no longer with us, period!'

'No, she wasn't stretchered out in a body bag. I could see her face clearly. Yeah, OK. I'll check with the hospital later. And yeah, yeah. I'll move the van away. I'm bored with it, anyway. I've got another car I can drive for a bit. See ya.'

He snapped off the phone and walked away.

The fat man lowered his binoculars to answer the phone. His plastered leg was propped up on a gaping hassock he'd found in the same cupboard that had provided the table. The chair sagged and creaked under his weight.

His new mobile was trickier to operate than the previous one; but cheaper. Emergency calls only. And this was an emergency.

'I told you. I saw that tall bint, the one that used to go around with Ferdy, come out of her own house, dressed like the black widow and carrying a case. She goes across the Green and catches a bus. Where does the bus go? To the tube station first and then on to Shepherd's Bush. No, she didn't look like she'd been in an accident. Walked down the path cool as you please, and got on the bus. Off to work, I suppose.'

9

Ellie alighted from the minicab with due care for her cuts and bruises. Walking down the path to her front door felt like descending a mountain. She was relieved to see that the burned-out remains of Kate's car had been removed.

Once in, Ellie dropped her coat and bag and surveyed herself in the hall mirror. She thought she looked ancient. Her hair was all over the place, she had a bruise on her chin and the blood was never going to wash out of that jumper and skirt.

She gave only a passing glance at the winking light on the answerphone, ignored the post lying on the floor and went into the kitchen. No kettle. That was a major disaster. She ought to have got the minicab driver to stop on the way from the hospital, to buy another kettle. How did you cope in an emergency without a kettle?

The answer came slickly to mind. You bought a microwave.

Well, she would do so as soon as she could get around to it. In the meantime she simply had to have a cup of tea ... if not three. And some carbohydrates. Biscuits, cake, anything. She'd just have to boil water in a saucepan, that was all.

You could always improvise ... as she had done when the police had interviewed her at the hospital. Waiting in a corridor, waiting to be assessed, waiting for the doctor … for the nurse … for the all clear …

Waiting, as she'd waited for Frank to die.

Don't be morbid.

You've got to get a grip on yourself, girl, or you'll go under.

So some bad things have been happening to you, and to Kate … to Ferdy and Mrs Hanna … but there was no point sitting down under it. You had to get moving again. Do something to solve the mysteries. Clear Kate of suspicion of murder.

The water boiled, and Ellie inhaled the aroma of strong Darjeeling as she poured the water into the teapot.

Fetched milk and a mug. Sat at the kitchen table.

Thought about things.

The policewoman had been – more or less – sympathetic. Could Ellie tell them what had happened that morning?

Ellie had told them. Clearly. Calmly. The shakes had left her. She supposed one of the injections she'd been given was responsible for that. She'd been given a tetanus injection, too. What for? Did they think the kettle had been lethal?

Anyway, she could tell the police about the explosion without having to pick and choose her words.

Did Ellie have any idea why the car had exploded?

Ellie was silent for a while, wondering if it were right to point the finger at Armand. She decided it was. 'All I can say is that Armand was very jealous of his wife's successful business career and the friends she had made prior to their marriage. And I know he used to hit her.'

The policewoman blinked. She hadn't expected this. She asked Ellie to substantiate her theory and Ellie gave her chapter and verse. Ellie then had a rather brilliant idea; at least, she thought at the time it was brilliant. In order to deflect questioning about Kate's escape, she asked the policewoman if Kate had been brought into the hospital, too. Was she all right?

Again the policewoman blinked.

Ellie repeated the question.

The policewoman said, with reluctance, that Kate seemed to have disappeared.

Ellie thought she'd registered astonishment rather well. In any event, the policewoman left her alone after that. They'd probably drag Armand away from school to grill him. A good job, too! thought Ellie.

A second and third cup of tea. All the biscuits remaining in the packet. Half a bar of chocolate. The phone rang. Ellie ignored it.

She dragged herself upstairs, divested herself of her bloodstained clothing and fell into bed.

She awoke to hear someone leaning on the doorbell. Twilight had settled on the room, and street lamps glowed cherry red outside. She pulled on her dressing-gown and made her way downstairs, hoping the caller would give up and go away. But they didn't.

To her immense surprise, it was Madam from the shop on the doorstep.

'I've been ringing for hours!' she complained, stepping past Ellie into the hall. 'Really, Ellie, have you no consideration for others? If you were not well today, you ought to have telephoned. How do you expect me to keep the shop running and meet our targets if the helpers don't turn up?'

This is unreal, thought Ellie.

Madam marched into the sitting-room and seated herself in Frank's big armchair. She looked around with disfavour, not caring for Ellie's colour scheme and furniture. She frowned at the coffee table. She's actually going to run her finger along the surface to see if there is any dust there, Ellie thought.

'I'm sorry I didn't phone,' said Ellie, thinking that in a moment Madam would notice Ellie's cuts and bruises and express sympathy.

'I dare say.' Madam put out a forefinger and ran it along the surface of the coffee table. Ellie stifled hysteria.

Ellie said, 'I'd offer you a cup of tea, but the kettle's broken.'

'Indeed!' Madam was not interested. She gave the impression that Ellie was a feckless sort of person who broke kettles every day of the week. 'Well, I'm not here on a social call. I was going to have a word with you at the shop today but since you didn't bother to come in, I thought I'd call on my way home. Head office have asked me to tighten up the rules where volunteers have been taking advantage of us, taking time off without good reason. They want doctor's notes if anyone phones in sick in future ...'

Would forced attendance at the hospital count? thought Ellie. But she didn't say it. She was also thinking, The nerve of the woman! After all the time she missed this year, and all the extra hours I put in to cover for her ...

'... and I've noticed that you've been very slack just lately. Oh, I know your husband was ill and then you took time off afterwards. But today you didn't even bother to phone in! You must appreciate my position. I can't possibly run the shop with volunteers who don't turn up. Now as it happens, a very dear old friend of mine has volunteered to come in and help on Tuesdays and Thursdays in future. Naturally I have accepted her offer. I know that I can rely on her …'

This can't be happening! thought Ellie. The woman's actually giving me the push!

'… and I expect you will like some time to reorganize your life now that your husband is gone. So perhaps it would be best – in fact I'm sure it will be best – if you don't bother to come in again. I'll get someone to pack up any belongings that you may have left at the shop, and drop them in to you. Naturally we appreciate all the hard work you have put into the shop in the past, but well … we all have to move on, don't we?'

And she looked down at the dust on the coffee table.

Ellie just gazed at her. It would sink in, soon.

Rejection, she thought. And then, No, this is not about my not being up to the job, but about her never having liked me, and possibly being jealous of me because the other workers in the shop preferred me to her … and maybe she's even got wind of the idea that they wanted me to take her place. And that's why she's making an opportunity to get rid of me.

And then, I wonder what John and the others will say to this …

But then, she is the boss, and volunteers do tend to come and go.

Ouch.

I never really liked Madam, did I? It will be a relief not to have to be polite to her any longer.

HOW DARE SHE!

Madam stood up, spotted her reflection in the mirror and put her hand to her hair, smirking.

Ellie got to her feet, too, her aches and pains catching up with her. She showed the woman to the front door.

Madam held out her hand, smiling in triumph. 'No hard feelings?'

Ellie shook her head, but ignored the proffered hand. She was tempted to bang the door after Madam's back, but refrained. Instead she put her own back to the door and closed her eyes. What a thing!

After all those years.

What would Frank have said …?

She was not going to cry. A clean break with the past, that was it. It was what she needed. The past was gone and she had to get on with her new life. She looked at the phone. She'd rather like to talk to Bill Weatherspoon about this. Such a nice man. She'd known him for years. He'd been so sympathetic.

But no. She must stand on her own two feet … even if she did feel rather rocky at the moment. She must take a grip. Cook something. A pity she hadn't got a microwave yet. That would be marvellous for the odd frozen meal.

She stooped – with surprising difficulty – to pick up the letters from the mat. Bills. Circulars. Two more letters of condolence. A letter from Frank's firm, confirming that she would be in receipt of a good pension … another nice lot of noughts. She'd need a financial adviser soon. A pity that Kate had disappeared. She'd have been able to help, advise …

A letter from the insurance company, enclosing a cheque. More noughts. Ellie thought, I'm getting blasé about all these noughts.

But it does take the sting out of having been sacked!

Of course, I could send Madam a nice fat cheque for the charity shop. That would show her … no, I wouldn't do that. That would be cheap. If I do send the charity a cheque, then it will be anonymously. I wonder how you send a cheque anonymously.

The doorbell rang again. As did the telephone.

Ellie opened the door to face a complete stranger, a woman with a flushed, excited expression. Behind her was a man holding what looked like a large blue cat on a stick.

'We're from the *Gazette* …'

'She's in!'

Another man joined the first. 'Mrs Quicke, I represent the—'

'Evening news bulletin—'

She gave them one unbelieving stare and shut the door on them. Whatever next!

She began to giggle. What a turn-up … Getting the sack one minute and then on the front page of the *Sun* the next. Well, not the *Sun*, precisely. She wasn't exactly page three material.

They continued to bang on the door and ring the doorbell. Over that noise Ellie could hear someone on the telephone, trying to leave a message for her. It was Diana. But was it Diana? Diana never rang her. It was always Ellie who rang Diana. But it was Diana's voice.

Ellie tried to concentrate. The voice was threatening, saying something about being with Ellie at half past six, latest. Then came 'I've still—' and the voice was cut off in mid-word.

The answerphone tape must be full. Ellie eyed it with dread. Then fetched a pencil and paper and sat down to play back her messages.

The first two messages were calm enough. Mrs Dawes had rung to ask why Ellie had not been at the flower-arranging class. The vicar had rung to ask how Ellie was and to enquire if she'd located the PCC minutes yet. The third message was from Aunt Drusilla. Peremptory, to say the least.

'... I am amazed not to have heard from you. I need to see you at once. I shall expect you at four p.m. prompt. Don't be late. Oh, and you can bring me a couple of chocolate buns from that new café in the Avenue while you're at it.'

Ellie glanced at the clock. It was after five now. Aunt Drusilla must be hopping mad. Tough.

The next two signals showed that people had rung but not bothered to leave a message. Then one from the police. Would she call them as soon as she got back from the hospital?

And then the one Ellie had been waiting for. Softly spoken, but clear.

'It's me; Kate. Just to tell you I'm perfectly all right. Hardly a scratch on me, but I thought I'd make myself scarce for a few days. I won't give you my address and I'm not telling Armand where I'm going, either. I need some space. Bless you. I'll be in touch.'

Ellie smiled to herself. Good for Kate.

Then Diana. Very agitated. 'Mother, what's going on? I've just had Aunt Drusilla on the phone with some incredible story about your being blown up, or something. I told her it can't be true, but she said she got it from one of your neighbours who knows her and went round to see if she'd got any news. If you have been involved in an accident, you might at least have let me know. Give me a ring, soonest ...'

Then a loud man's voice. 'Mrs Quicke, we'd like your story ...'

Another two hang-ups.

Then Aunt Drusilla again. 'Ellie, I would like you to ring me—'

Ellie fast forwarded. Another newspaper. Then Diana again, 'Mother, it's on the evening news. I knew I shouldn't have left you by yourself. I've rung the office and told them what's happened and I'm coming straight down, as soon as Stewart gets back from work. With any luck, I'll be with you about half six. I've still—'

And that's where the tape finished. Ellie cancelled the messages, wondering if Madam would come rushing back to reinstate her now that she was famous. Well, sort of famous.

But there was an immediate threat which must be averted at all costs. Ellie did not wish Diana to come rushing down. It might even now be possible to stop her.

She dialled, and Stewart picked up the phone. That was bad news. Stewart must have left work early to look after their little boy.

'Oh, Stewart. Ellie here. I've just had a message from Diana …'

'Are you all right? Diana's been worried sick about you.'

'Cuts and bruises. Honestly, I'm just fine and there's absolutely no need for Diana to come down. I know how busy you both are.'

'She's well on her way by now. She left, oh, about half an hour ago.'

'In my car?' Ellie could not prevent the acid creeping into her voice.

Pause. 'In her car, yes. Why?'

'Oh, I just wondered.' Ellie was feeling a trifle light-headed. She knew it wasn't fair to take it out on poor easy-going Stewart. She suspected that she was going to regret being so tough, but for once she felt she might as well assert herself. 'If she is coming down, then I'll get the garage to assess what the car is worth and you can let me have a cheque in due course, right?'

'But I thought …' Some heavy breathing.

'That's all,' said Ellie, and put the phone down. It rang again immediately.

'Mrs Quicke, I represent—'

She broke the connection and took the phone off the hook. Someone was still banging on the front door and ringing the doorbell. She was getting a headache with all that banging. She thought of going into the sitting-room to see if she could catch some news on television, but then she realized the curtains weren't drawn in there, and she was still in her dressing-gown, with her hair all over the place.

Right. Into the kitchen. Someone was peering in through the back door. The nerve! She pulled the blinds down as a flash went off in her face.

How dare they!

She turned on the wireless, loudly, to cut out the interference from outside, while she investigated the contents of the fridge. Not much there. She cooked some onions, threw in a small tin of corned beef. Rice. Some frozen peas. It didn't take long. She sat at the kitchen table, thinking that after taking a couple of aspirins she would go to bed.

Except that she supposed Diana was on her way. Luckily she hadn't stripped the beds in the spare room since Diana and Stewart were here last. And if Diana expected a meal, she would have to think of something to give her … eggs, perhaps?

Humming a little hum, she went upstairs – her left knee and hip were still sore – and going into the dark front bedroom, looked down on what was happening outside her house. Several strange cars were lined up outside. Waiting for her to emerge?

Journalists, she assumed. No sign of Diana yet. She drew the curtains and put on the lights.

The knocking from the back door had ceased.

Good.

She felt very tired, but knew that if she lay down on the bed she'd fall asleep, and Diana would soon be arriving. So Ellie had a good wash, brushed her hair and dressed in casual, warm clothing just as the banging started up on the front door again. Peeping through the curtains, she saw Armand standing below. He looked frenzied. Some of the journalists were leaving their cars to converge on him. For pity's sake, Ellie felt she must let him in before they ate him alive.

As she opened the door Armand fell in, gasping. Ellie just managed to close the door behind him against the invasive horde. Her eye fell on the phone, still off the hook. She'd forgotten something – what was it?

Armand looked dishevelled, a lock of carroty hair fraying over his forehead, his tie pulled down. His top shirt button had been wrenched open, and he was breathing rapidly. He started to speak but she picked up the phone, motioning him into the kitchen. He bared his teeth at her, and didn't move.

'Leave that!' he said, trying to take the phone off her. 'Where's my wife!' He was very angry.

Ellie was getting tired of being pushed around. 'Let go of me or I'll scream and bring the press in. You don't want that, do you! I've a message to ring—'

He wrested the phone off her and slammed it down. It immediately rang. She put out her hand to pick it up. He swung at her, open handed, but she managed to duck it in time and pick up the receiver.

'Ellie, my dear. Are you all right?' She couldn't place the voice for the moment.

Holding Armand off with her other hand she said, 'Who is it?'

'Your old friend Archie, of course.'

Archie? Archie Benjamin, Frank's friend from the PCC.

'Oh, Archie. Good of you to call. I have someone here at the moment. Armand. My next door neighbour, you know…'

Armand was seething, taking two short steps down the hall and two back.

'… And I'm expecting my daughter Diana to arrive any minute …' It wasn't a bad idea to let Armand know that she was expecting friends.

'I was worried about you. Someone said you'd been blown up, taken to hospital …'

'Reports of my death have been grossly exaggerated.'

'What?'

Of course, she'd forgotten that he'd no sense of humour.

'I'm all right. Just bruised. If you don't mind, Archie, I have to ring the police right away … yes, yes, really I'm quite all right. Thanks for calling.' She replaced the receiver and turned on Armand.

'Now, Armand, let's behave in a civilized manner, shall we? Why don't you go and draw the curtains in the front room so that the press can't see in, while I phone the police. After that I'll be happy to talk to you. If you don't, I shall open the door and call the press in. And I'm sure that's the last thing you want.'

He bared his teeth at her. His eyes had gone small and sparklingly black.

'Where's my wife? What have you done with her?'

The phone rang again. Armand reached a long arm and took it off its hook.

'Now!' he said. 'Answer me, woman!'

'The answer is that I don't know where she is. I told the police. I went out to help her unfreeze the lock on her car door. She hadn't got a scraper for the frost on the car windows. I said I thought I had some de-icer in the cupboard here, and started back to the house to fetch it. The next thing I knew I was in the gutter, deafened, unable to speak. Cut and bruised.'

'I don't give a damn about you! What about Kate?' He got her by the upper arms and shook her.

He projected violence like a force field. Ellie could understand why Kate had been so afraid of him. She was – almost – afraid of him herself.

'Kate screamed. Then she picked up her handbag and went back to the house.'

'She must have told you what she was going to do …'

'No. Not a word.'

'She's here, isn't she? Hiding upstairs!' Armand let go of Ellie and started up the stairs, shouting for his wife.

Ellie rubbed her arms where he'd gripped her and wondered what she should do next. Phone the police. Of course. Frank had the number of the local police station in the phone's memory. Number nine, if she remembered rightly.

She replaced the receiver and pressed the number nine.

'Kate, where are you! Come out!' Doors banged. He had gone into the front bedroom, was opening wardrobe doors.

'Police station, who's calling?'

'Mrs Ellie Quicke. I was involved in the incident this morning in which my neighbour's car was blown up. I've been at the hospital all day, and returned to find a message on the answerphone to ring the police.'

'Just a moment. I'll put you through to the incident room …'

Armand was coming down the stairs, taking them two at a time. His anger had intensified, if anything. He saw that Ellie was on the phone and assumed she was phoning for help.

'Bitch!' he said and, snatching the receiver out of her hands, threw it to the floor and pulled the telephone cord out of its socket.

'That was rather stupid of you!' said Ellie, trying to keep calm. 'I was through to the police. They'll be wondering now why I was so abruptly cut off in the middle of my call to them.'

'You shut up!' Armand threw open the door into the sitting-room with a bang and charged in. Switching on all the lights and seeing it uninhabited, he hurled a couple of chairs to the ground and kicked the coffee table over.

Ellie winced. She considered her options. It appeared to her that she stood between a homicidal maniac and the press. Which was worse? Lifting her big coat and handbag from the hall stand, she opened the front door just as the bell rang.

To a chorus of photoflashes, not one but two newcomers stood and gaped first at the press straggling down the path, and then at her.

10

Diana dumped her overnight bag in the hall. 'Mother! What is going on!'

Archie Benjamin hovered on the doorstep, holding a large pink-flowered azalea and a bottle of wine. He seemed lost for words.

'Come in, quick!' Ellie pulled Archie into the house and slammed the door shut in the face of the first journalist to reach them. She put on the chain, and leaned against the door.

'My dear Ellie!' Archie perspired, despite the chill wind that had blown in with them.

Diana glared at him, resenting his familiarity. At that moment Armand erupted from the living-room.

I am so tired I can't be bothered to be frightened any more, thought Ellie. She said, as if this were a normal, everyday event, 'May I introduce you? Gentlemen, this is my daughter Diana, whom you may or may not have met when she stayed with me for some days over the funeral. Diana, this is my next-door neighbour Armand, who has come here in search of his wife … whose car was blown up this morning and me with it. Diana, this is Archie Benjamin, a great friend of your father's, from the church. You probably did meet him at the funeral.'

Archie tried to find somewhere to put his plant down so that he could shake hands with Diana but she was past observing such civilities. 'I dare say, but …'

Armand was beyond observing the civilities, too. He had failed to find his wife but he did have just enough control left to realize that attacking Ellie physically in the presence of her daughter and Archie Benjamin was going to be counter-productive.

Approaching Ellie, he spat some words low into her ear. 'I'll be back!' He wrestled the chain off the door and flung himself outside. Ellie neither knew nor cared whether he was attacked by the waiting journalists. She thought him well able to take care of himself and indeed in a few seconds she heard his own front door bang. Perhaps the journalists would turn their attention to him now.

She had other problems to solve.

'Mother, ring the police and get rid of that rabble outside!'

'I can't, dear, unless I can get the telephone working again.' She pushed the telephone cord back into the socket, replaced the receiver and the phone rang at once. Somebody was making use of the latest technology to ring as soon as the line was free. So she couldn't get a line to ring out. She took the receiver off the hook.

Diana whipped off her coat and gave Archie a withering glance. 'Mother is perfectly all right now I'm here, so you needn't stay.'

Ellie wondered why Diana had to be so rude all the time. In her fatigue, she felt a distance growing between herself and the others. Little as she liked him, she didn't want Archie to go away feeling offended – as indeed he appeared to be at the moment, pursing his lips at Diana, and screwing up his eyes at her.

'Archie, Diana is right. I shall be quite safe with her here to look after me. But there is something you can do for me if you will. I was speaking to the police when Armand interrupted me and they'll be wondering if I've been the victim of another murder or something. When you get home, would you ring them for me? Tell them what's happened, say that I'm perfectly all right now but could they do something about the journalists out there?'

Archie preened himself. 'Of course, dear lady!' He darted at Ellie and kissed her cheek. Ellie was too tired to react quickly, but a second later she did recoil. Diana saw the kiss but not the recoil, and her eyebrows almost met in disgust.

Ellie let Archie out and replaced the chain on the door, saying to Diana, 'Darling, it's lovely to see you, though you really need not have hared down the motorway just for me. I really am all right, you know. Just a little tired. Would you like to go upstairs and dump your things? I'm afraid your bedroom is just as you left it last week, but I'm sure you won't mind that at such short notice …'

'Mother, who is that dreadful little man?'

'I told you, dear. A friend of your father's. He's the church treasurer and wants to retrieve some of the minutes your father put on his computer. He's very thoughtful, really. Lovely plant. I'll deal with it in the morning. Do you think you could draw the curtains in the living-room while I see what I can find you for supper?'

'I snatched a sandwich at a motorway stop. Mother, you can't possibly stay here. Pack an overnight bag, and we'll go to a hotel somewhere. You can pay by credit card—'

'I'm not going anywhere.'

Ellie wondered what it was about drawing curtains that was so unpopular. She'd asked Armand to draw the curtains, and Diana. Neither of them had done it. She went and did it herself, keeping behind the material so as not to be photographed by the journalists outside.

'Don't be silly, mother.' Diana had followed her in, and was at least righting the furniture. 'You can't stay on here, and that's flat. Stewart and I discussed it at length after the funeral. You've never lived alone and you can't be expected to cope now. We've found a nice little one-bedroom flat for you, fully furnished and at a reasonable rent. You can stay with us till you've recovered, and then move in. The flat's vacant at the moment, luckily. As for your furniture, well, if there's anything small that you particularly want to keep, I daresay that will be all right. Stewart and I will have Grandad's bureau, of course …'

Ellie sank into a chair, leaned back and closed her eyes. 'Diana, you are not listening. I'm not going anywhere. I like it here. I have all my friends here. Why should I move?'

Diana exhaled noisily. 'Mother, if you could see yourself, you wouldn't say that. Of course you don't want to leave this house, but there comes a time when common sense makes it necessary to do so. Now don't let's argue about it. Off you go to bed and I'll bring you up a nice hot drink.'

Ellie hated hot drinks last thing at night. She thought, I'm too tired to argue, about hot drinks or about moving. We can have it out in the morning. She inched herself to her feet, feeling all her bruises complain, and made her way to the stairs.

Diana said, 'I'd better ring Stewart, if I can get through. He always worries when I have to drive on the motorway.'

As Ellie reached the landing, she heard Diana jiggling the phone and finally managing to dial out.

'Stewart, it's me. Yes, a good journey but bedlam here,

with journalists camped outside and a horrid little man trying to pay court to my mother, yes, really! And the phone's been jammed, so I hope you haven't been trying to get through …'

A pause while she listened to Stewart. Ellie smiled to herself, feeling a little guilty but not very, knowing what was coming.

'She said what about the car? She's mad! She—'

Ellie shut her bedroom door on the outside world, grinning as she thought of the consternation Diana would now be feeling. Of course she wouldn't really take the car away from Diana, but she would make her ask for it nicely. Then she would go out and buy a nice new car of her very own, an automatic, and take driving lessons.

She decided against having a bath. She didn't think she could get in and out of the bath without help and she was certainly not going to ask Diana to help her. Besides which, she remembered now that the hospital had told her she must keep her grazes dry for a few days. So she washed, put on her prettiest nightie, took a couple of paracetamol and rolled into bed.

There was an excited babble of voices outside. Not another visitor! Followed by a peremptory two rings on the doorbell.

Oh, no! Ellie knew her own doorbell. You would think that one person ringing it would be just like another. But it wasn't true. Frank had always rung with three short pushes, Diana with one short and one long. Ellie didn't suppose they were aware of doing it, but that's what they did. Aunt Drusilla always rang twice, two long pushes.

Ellie did not, definitely not, feel up to coping with Aunt Drusilla that night.

She could hear a murmur of voices down below, and then Diana ran up the stairs to Ellie. 'It's Aunt Drusilla, just arrived in a taxi. She hasn't any money for the fare, of course. Where's your purse?'

Ellie turned off the bedside light, as a signal that she was not going to get up again. 'In my handbag in the hall somewhere, but don't be taken in by the old bat. She can well afford to pay her own fare.'

'Mother, really! You know she's only got her old age pension. Oh, I'll pay it for her. Don't you bother to come down again. I'll bring up your hot milk in a little while.'

Ellie hadn't the slightest intention of getting out of bed again. She had a nasty feeling that if Diana and Aunt Drusilla got together it would mean trouble, but she was too tired to care.

She was just drifting off to sleep when Diana came in with a mug of steaming hot milk. 'Drink up, now.'

Ellie touched the mug with her lips and set it down again. 'I'll just let it cool a bit.'

'Mind you drink it.'

Ellie smiled and didn't reply. She had no intention of drinking it. She supposed Diana would have put some more of those sleeping pills in it, just as she had done over the period of the funeral. They'd made Ellie feel woozy. No, she wouldn't drink the milk. She hated hot milk, anyway. That horrible skin that formed on it … ugh!

She went to sleep very quickly but woke, sitting upright, chest tight, heart pounding. Reliving the experience of being blown up. Two o'clock. Every movement hurt. She thought of taking the now cold milk, but didn't. A couple more paracetamol. Tip the milk down the sink. No sound from Diana's room. Back to bed.

It was painful to move, but then it would be after what she'd been through. She wondered where Kate was sleeping tonight.

She cried a little because Kate had been so kind to her and because her bruises hurt. Then the paracetamol began to take effect, and she slept again.

The errand boy reported in from the back seat of the fat man's Saab which he'd adopted for his own use.

'Gone to bed early. Reporters still outside. Two taxis brought women. One's staying the night, I think, because she hasn't come out again. The other – grandma type – she was there about an hour, then left in another taxi ... yeah, I tried to get in with the old rigmarole about the gas again, but the younger woman – daughter or something – she wouldn't let me in. She said, though, her mother wasn't staying, but moving up north with her. Yes, going up tomorrow. If she does ... well, we're in the clear, aren't we?'

The fat man also reported in, from the bedroom of the empty house. 'Yeah, there's someone staying in the back bedroom. All quiet, otherwise. No filth. Nothing ... well, if she's going north, we can forget about her, can't we?'

Ellie woke slowly. Very slowly. It was fully daylight, so she must have overslept. A bright morning, for once. Good.

She made to sit up. Not so good.

The door opened and Diana came in, bearing a breakfast tray.

Wonders would never cease!

'Don't bother to get up.' Diana was all smiles. 'I brought you your breakfast up, so you can have a nice long lie-in. Don't worry about a thing. I'm here to take care of everything for you.'

'Very thoughtful of you, dear. Thank you.'

Diana drew back the curtains. 'There's only one reporter outside now. The police must have had a word with them … or there's been another more important news story come up. Why don't you stay in bed this morning?'

Diana left, still smiling. Ellie suppressed a suspicion that Diana had been up to something she didn't want her mother to know about. There was a definite 'cat been at the cream' look about Diana that morning.

Ellie eyed the breakfast tray with dislike. If there was one thing she hated, it was having to eat toast in bed. The buttered side of the toast always ended up on the duvet, and the crumbs inside. And the tea spilt itself everywhere.

She couldn't possibly be so ungrateful as to tell Diana that. So Ellie sat on the dressing-table stool and ate her breakfast. Far more than she usually ate. Cereal, scrambled eggs – rather hard and cold – two pieces of toast. Diana had given her margarine instead of butter. Ugh! But Ellie wasn't looking gift horses in the mouth that morning. Two cups of tea, plus some more paracetamol.

Refreshed, she dressed and jerkily descended the stairs. Slowly. The phone was back on the hook. Good. The morning paper and the local paper had arrived. The local paper had given Ferdy's death a prominent spread, and reported Mrs Hanna's disappearance – which was giving rise to considerable concern – separately.

In other words, the paper thought Mrs Hanna had been done in, too. They also mentioned a body dragged out of the river, but did not put a name to it.

Hm, thought Ellie. I wonder if I ought to say something to the police about what I saw in Mrs Hanna's flat …

The doorbell rang. It was Diana, saying she'd forgotten her key. She looked pleased with herself. 'Down already, mother? Why don't you go back to bed, take it easy till this afternoon. Then you can just walk to the car and I'll whisk you up north. See, I bought another kettle so you can have your usual mid-morning cuppa. Just relax and leave everything to me.'

'Thank you dear. But I'm perfectly capable of managing my own affairs. I really do appreciate your coming down at such short notice, but …'

Diana continued to smile but not to meet Ellie's eyes.

Diana has certainly been up to something, thought Ellie. The explosion had taken more out of her than she had thought. She realized she simply did not feel up to dealing with Diana at the moment. The doorbell rang again.

This time it was Mrs Dawes, huffing and puffing, well wrapped up against the cold outside with a hairy woollen beret and scarf added to her padded green jacket.

'My dear Ellie, how are you? I was going to call round to see why you didn't come to my flower-arranging classes, but then someone told me – little Rose McNally, I think – that you'd been blown up, what a thing! How are you, my dear? And this is your daughter Diana? Quite grown up now, aren't you, dear? I remember you when you were so high and in Brownies at church …'

Diana showed her teeth again. 'Mother, do take Mrs Dawes into the sitting-room, and I'll bring you some coffee. I won't join you, if you don't mind. I have some phone calls to make.'

167

Ellie resigned herself to being bossed around and settled Mrs Dawes in the big armchair. But no sooner was the dear lady settled than she was leaning across to the coffee table to test the earth in the azalea pot which Archie Benjamin had given Ellie.

'A little too dry, dear. Syringe with warm water once a day in centrally heated rooms, stand on a basin and pour hot water into the sink around it twice a week, and never ever let the compost dry out or the leaves will fall and the flowers droop. So tell me, what exactly happened?'

Diana brought coffee for them both before Ellie had finished telling her tale. Ellie didn't much like the way Diana carefully closed the door behind herself. Who was she phoning and why? Aunt Drusilla, presumably. So why had Aunt Drusilla turned up late last night, and what was she plotting now?

But Mrs Dawes must be attended to.

No, Ellie didn't really think flower-arranging classes were quite her 'thing' but she had agreed to join the choir and was looking forward to that, although she was afraid that she wouldn't know what to do, and her voice was not brilliant.

'Nonsense, dear! You stand next to me at rehearsals, and I'll see you're all right.' Mrs Dawes was brisk, well upholstered against the vicissitudes of fortune. A woman comfortable in herself. Ellie found herself envying Mrs Dawes.

What on earth could Diana be doing, making all those phone calls? And who was she phoning?

Ellie wished Mrs Dawes would go. But Mrs Dawes wanted to gossip about Ferdy and Mrs Hanna's disappearance and speculate as to whether the body in the river had been Mrs Hanna or not. Most people thought it would be, but the police weren't saying. Did Ellie know anything about it? No? What a pity. Mrs Dawes had thought that if anyone had known anything it would have been Ellie, though why she had had to get mixed up with that no-good Kate next door, who everyone knew had been responsible for her ex-boyfriend's death, and it was probably all a gang killing, the gang trying to get back at Kate for Ferdy's death by bombing her car, didn't Ellie agree?

Ellie didn't agree, but didn't have any other suggestions to make. Her head was beginning to ache again, and she wished herself back in bed.

Finally Mrs Dawes heaved herself out of the chair and announced she must be making tracks. Ellie showed her to the door, still talking. A kindly woman, Mrs Dawes. Ellie noted that the door to the study was firmly shut and Diana still on the phone.

This required immediate investigation, thought Ellie, but as she let Mrs Dawes out, Inspector Clay plus henchman came down the path and asked if he might have a word.

Diana must have heard the man's voice for, finishing her phone call, she came out into the hall to say that her mother was not well enough to be interviewed.

'Of course I'm well enough,' said Ellie. At that moment the phone rang and Diana darted back into the study to take the call, this time leaving the door half open.

Inspector Clay looked enquiringly. 'My daughter,' explained Ellie. 'She's trying to cosset me. Thinks I need a nurse. But really, apart from various grazes and bruises and feeling tired, I'm perfectly all right. Would you like to come through to the living-room?'

'… she said WHAT?' Diana's voice rose in anger. 'But she agreed … yes, of course I realize it isn't really her fault, but … yes, of course you have to go in, I do see that. But I'm right in the middle of things here, and … yes … yes. Oh, all right, I'll just have to do the rest from home. Yes, I'll grab a sandwich and set off straight away. Yes, yes. Kiss, kiss. Bye.'

Diana erupted into the living-room, looking furious. 'That was Stewart. His boss wants him in this afternoon and the babysitter can't come, so I'll have to get back. And I haven't got you packed up yet. Do you think you could put some things into a bag and be ready in half an hour?'

'That's all right, dear. I'd rather stay put, you know. A bit shaky still.'

Diana nodded, accepting the situation for the time being.

Ellie felt a mixture of guilt and relief. But habits die hard and she said in reasonably convincing tones, 'It was good of you to come down to look after me. I shall miss you.'

'Well, it won't be for long. You'd better come up on the train tomorrow. I expect you can get someone to buy your ticket for you. Take a taxi to the station and get the twelve o'clock. I'll meet you at the other end. Bring just what you need for a few days.'

'Now Diana, I realize you mean it for the best, but—'

Glancing at her watch, Diana shrieked and fled up the stairs. 'I must go!'

Ellie explained to the policeman. 'A domestic emergency, you know. Coffee? Tea?'

'Nothing, thanks. I understand you were in the wars yesterday. I know you went through it with one of our people when you were at the hospital, but do you think we could just go over it again for me …?'

Ellie did so, being careful not to mention her last sighting of Kate leaving the house by the back door.

'Now you were asked yesterday if you knew of any reason why someone would wish to blow up your neighbour's car …' The policeman was not perhaps as stupid as he looked.

'… and I said – though perhaps I shouldn't have – that Kate and Armand had not been getting on well, that he had been using her as a punchbag. Yes, I did say that. But you know, I've been thinking and I don't feel that Armand would want to blow up his wife's car. He wants to hit her, to make her suffer, but to kill her? No.'

'If it wasn't the husband, it's only logical to look again at the murder of Kate's ex-boyfriend, isn't it?'

Ellie sighed. 'I realize that, but I don't believe Kate killed him. Ferdy was an old friend of hers from schooldays. That evening he upset her by denigrating her husband, and she ran away crying. That's when I saw her.'

'But you didn't report that when the body was found, did you? In fact I remember you made a statement to the effect that you hadn't seen anything at all.'

'I know, but when I thought about it, I remembered.' It sounded weak, even to her. She wasn't surprised that the inspector looked incredulous.

The inspector went to the back window. 'You saw her from this window?'

Ellie joined him. 'Yes. She ran down the path from the church, turned into the alley and ran along to the left, which is the quickest way to the park.'

'You get a good view of the church from here.'

'It's my favourite view. So peaceful usually. Mrs Dawes saw me standing in the window when she came out of the church after finding the body, and that's why she came here to report it.'

Diana popped her head around the door. 'I'm off, mother.'

'Take care of yourself, dear. I'll talk to you tonight on the phone. We have things to discuss, haven't we?'

'Kiss, kiss,' said Diana, disappearing.

Ellie reflected that when Diana had first started to say 'Kiss, kiss' as a child, it had been a charming gesture. Now, not so. The policeman was looking thoughtfully at her and then at the door behind which Diana had vanished.

'Giving you a hard time?'

'Over-protective. Thinks I can't cope. It was sweet of her to throw everything up and come down yesterday, and I appreciated it. I needed a spot of tender loving care, after being blown up like that.'

'I'm sure you did. Now let's get back to the night of the murder. You were standing here. Were the lights on?'

'The living-room lights?' She understood what he was getting at. If the centre light had been on, everything outside would have looked black and she wouldn't have been able to see Kate. 'It was dusk, not really dark but getting there. The lights would have been on in the church-yard, because they go on at dusk. That side lamp there is on a time switch, which comes on at dusk. I really can't remember whether it was on or not.'

'But you must have been able to see everything that happened up at the church if, as you say, you were standing here in the window.'

'Well, yes and no. You see …' She explained about Frank's funeral and the pills which had made her feel so strange. '… so I really can't be sure what I saw. For a while I wasn't even sure that seeing Kate was real. I thought it might have been part of the nightmares I'd been having.'

He pressed her hard on this, but she stuck to it. She had been standing in the window. She had seen Kate rush down from the church and run along the alley, crying. But that was all that she had seen. 'Perhaps,' she said, 'it would be helpful if I were hypnotized, or if we recreated events under the same conditions?'

She thought he would laugh at the suggestion, but he said thoughtfully that it might well come to that. 'And that's all you can remember?'

'I'm afraid so. I told Mrs Hanna—'

'When was this?' Sharply.

'The night after the body was discovered. She was sitting up there, on that bench next to the side door. I was so sorry for her. She showed me a picture of Ferdy when he was small. She thought I must have seen something, too. That's what jogged my memory about seeing Kate. Mrs Hanna – poor dear – she wanted me to find out what had happened to Ferdy for her.'

'I wish you'd told us about this earlier. Tell me exactly what she said, and you said.'

Ellie obliged to the best of her ability. '... and that's it. Just a short conversation. Was it that night that she ...?'

The inspector looked blank, giving nothing away.

'Tell me,' Ellie said. 'Was the body in the river ...?'

He relented. 'No. It was a psychiatric patient from the hospital over the other side of town.'

'Ah. Then ... I wonder, did you see Mrs Hanna's flat yourself? I only caught a quick glimpse, but I did wonder ...'

The policeman rose to his feet. 'No need for you to bother your head about that. You can safely leave the detection to the professionals, right?'

This made Ellie so cross that she didn't complete what she'd been going to say. Well, let them get on with it. She had plenty of other things to worry about.

11

Saturday morning. It was good to have the house to herself again. She wondered if she felt well enough to walk to the shops, but she still felt shaky and the sky was leaden. A nasty wind gusted through the trees, bending the smaller branches sideways. She had heard that Tesco's would deliver for a small fee. She found the number in the phone book but found to her annoyance that this service was only for Internet shoppers. Now what?

Ellie had no idea how to cope with the Internet and was too shattered to go out and shop in the usual way. Who could she ask to shop for her? Archie? She shuddered. No. This was ridiculous. She had all that money in the bank and could afford to ask someone to do it for her. She would ask Liz if one of her children would like to earn a fiver. Liz was not at home, but her teenage son said that he did all the family's food shopping on the Internet and if Ellie would give him a list and a fiver, he would have it delivered. She could pay Liz back later. What a blessing friends were!

Ellie decided that she would get on the Internet herself as soon as possible. She wouldn't have to trail around with heavy shopping any more. In future she would be Lady Muck and order everything in.

She made up a list of what she thought she might like,

including a few treats. And why not? As she was phoning her list through, the doorbell rang again. Archie Benjamin. Suppressing irritation, she motioned him to go through into the sitting-room, and finished her call.

'Dear Ellie, are you feeling better? Are you taking things easy? I know how you ladies are, never taking enough care of yourselves when you are ill.'

She decided not to offer him coffee, but thanked him for the beautiful azalea and the wine. Also for getting the police to move the reporters on.

'I'll call again in a couple of days and see if you're feeling stronger, eh?'

Ellie looked at her watch. Surely he'd take the hint and go?

'Well, I suppose I must be on my way. A bachelor's life is one long round of gaiety. I've just remembered I'm supposed to be meeting a friend for a drink at noon.'

She nodded and smiled, pretending to accept his newly remembered engagement. As she showed him out, she felt the first drops of rain. She was glad she wasn't having to leave the house.

Besides, there was something on her mind which couldn't wait.

She put the chain on the door and made for the study. Business first. The affair of the PCC minutes was weighing on her mind and the sooner she got rid of them, the sooner she could refuse to let Archie Benjamin into the house.

First to find Frank's notebook. It was lodged in one of the partitions in the bureau. Frank had always taken the minutes down in longhand, put them on to the computer and then torn out the pages he no longer needed. She had hoped that the minutes would still be there, waiting to be transcribed. In which case, she could type them out on her old electric typewriter and be done with it.

Blast. Nothing but the remnants of torn-out pages. So the only record of the minutes was on the computer and she was going to have to find them, somehow or other.

Switch on here and there. Wait. Point the mouse at File. Existing file, not new file. The screen threw up a number of names which presumably were files. She couldn't find 'Church' or 'PCC'. Now where would he have filed them?

Under Gilbert Adams, the vicar? No, there was nothing for that name.

It ought to be under 'Church'. Why wasn't it under 'Church'? Frank had had a logical but somewhat punning sense of humour. Think, Ellie! What would it have amused him to call the minutes of a PCC meeting? 'Boredom Incorporated'? 'God Talk'?

She didn't really expect to find either, and she didn't.

There were files for Personal, Home, Home and Away, Family, one under the name of his firm, Charities …

Would it be under 'Charities?' As in unpaid work for other people? Lots of names that she recognized, but no church minutes. She opened 'Personal', but it all seemed to be business: insurance, stockbroker, health records … that was a laugh, considering how he'd ended up …

She tried 'Home'. Again, dozens of names. Mostly business again. Builders, correspondence with. Queries on service contracts, quotes, complaints … it should have been labelled 'House', not 'Home'.

She was getting tired, but tried one more. 'Home and Away' looked promising at first, as there were lots of files here containing the names of friends and relations. Two names jumped out at her … 'Quicke Di', and 'Quicke Dr'. Aunt Drusilla was presumably 'Quicke Dr'?

Perhaps it would be advisable to find out what basis Frank had for disinheriting his aunt. Ellie still couldn't quite grasp the notion that Aunt Drusilla was comfortably off. It felt rather sneaky to go into someone else's files, but she would overcome her qualms in the name of common sense. Or of curiosity. Take your pick.

She could just press the Delete button. Her finger hovered over Delete. Then she removed it and opened the file. She had an unpleasant feeling that Diana and Aunt Drusilla were planning something together. That late-night visit and long conversation with Diana was disquieting, to say the least. So she had better find out what was going on.

Carefully Ellie positioned the mouse on 'Quicke Dr' and clicked. Nothing much happened. Again. Still nothing. She got cross with it. Then noticed that on the right-hand side there were a number of slots, one of which said 'Open'.

'Open Sesame,' said Ellie, and clicked on that. A letter shot on to the screen. A letter to some people of whom Ellie had never heard. Only the top part of the letter showed on the screen. Ellie inspected the keyboard and found some arrows which, when pressed, moved the letter up and down. Good. Now she could read what Frank had written to them.

The date was just after the doctors had diagnosed the fatal liver disease and given Frank a couple of weeks to live. They'd wanted him to go straight into hospital, but he'd stayed out for almost a week, practically living in the study, phoning people, writing letters, having visitors. He'd called it 'putting his house in order'.

Ellie felt a flood of tears threaten but refused to give in to them. She wished Frank had told her he'd been making these enquiries. But there … he'd always wanted to protect the 'little woman'. And possibly he'd also felt a bit of a fool if Aunt Drusilla really had been taking advantage of them all these years.

The letter had been written to a firm of enquiry agents. Gracious! Ellie hadn't known such people existed in their neighbourhood. Not so very far away, either. Frank had asked them to check on the ownership of flats in an exclusive block down by the river and to report back to him in an envelope marked 'Confidential'. Just so. Then there was a short letter enclosing a cheque for services rendered. And that was all.

There must be a report from these people somewhere here, thought Ellie. She started opening drawers and checking files. Frank was meticulous in keeping papers filed in the right place. She found the file marked 'Quicke Dr'. There was nothing in it. Not a single piece of paper.

Ellie sat back in the chair and thought about it. The letter to the enquiry agents must refer to Aunt Drusilla because it was in the 'Quicke Dr' file. It looked as if the old bat had somehow managed to buy a flat and rent it out while keeping quiet about it, so that Frank should not suspect. But why had the enquiry agents' report disappeared?

Had Frank destroyed it? Ellie considered another scenario. She pictured Aunt Drusilla alone in the study, checking through the filing drawer for any letter which might give her away. And removing it, without realizing that Frank had stored a copy of his letter to the enquiry agent on the word processor.

Now Aunt Drusilla had had no idea that Frank had discovered her little secret – if that is what it was – until after his death, because she had failed to visit him in hospital. So if any removing had been done, it would have been done by Aunt Drusilla after she had discovered that 'her' house had been left to Ellie – or by Diana?

Ellie looked for the agency in the local phone book, and rang them. She explained that she was Frank Quicke's widow, needing a copy of the report they had recently sent him … no, she understood they couldn't give her any details over the phone, but if they could send her a copy …? Thank you.

She carefully followed the manual to exit from the letter. The screen now reverted to its blank state. Ellie considered giving up for the day.

Then she had another mental picture. Of Stewart removing Frank's pen and cufflinks from the bureau. Or had it been Diana?

She went back through File, through 'Home' to 'Quicke Di'. She opened it, to find a bland newsy letter, dated some months previously. Nothing about the loan for the house, or about Diana's request for more money. Of course, Frank had confined himself to e-mail for his weekly communications to her when he went 'on line', if that was the right term.

She explored the cabinet of office files in the drawer below. Nothing for Diana, not even the birth certificates, and certificates for swimming and GCSEs, which Ellie knew had always been kept there. Which meant that Diana had removed them since her father's death. You didn't need to read anything sinister in that, did you? But what about all those important and very private phone calls she'd been making that morning?

Ellie stared at the computer screen which obligingly switched to a pleasant picture of clouds and biplanes. She picked up the mouse and found to her astonishment that the clouds vanished and she was back to Frank's last letter to Diana again. Close it. It was of no use to her. She would make one more try. Back through Open File to 'Home' and scan through the other names. One caught her eye. Bill.

Bill as in account? Or Bill as in solicitor Weatherspoon? Open Sesame.

Bill as in Weatherspoon. The date was in that short period before Frank finally had to return to hospital for good, asking Bill to call to see him on a Thursday morning when Ellie would be out. Explaining that he wanted to make his will and hadn't much time. Details attached.

Using the down arrow, Ellie arrived at the details. In substance the instructions were as she had seen in the will. But Frank had added a comment which helped to clarify his decision to leave nothing to Aunt Drusilla.

'Nothing to Miss Drusilla Quicke, my aunt, as she has already provided well for herself.'

With regard to Diana, he had written '… she already knows why I'm not prepared to let her and Stewart have any more money at this time. Give her £5000 for a new car, my share of this house to go to Ellie for life, and Diana after Ellie's death.'

Ellie sighed. That whole affair had been very upsetting. Frank had felt as if his beloved daughter had cheated him. She seemed to think he'd been made of money. Perhaps in her terms he had been made of money, but he'd also believed that young people should pay their way and not rely on handouts from the previous generation.

Ellie flicked tears from her eyes. How sad that Frank should have been disillusioned about Diana in the last month of his life. Ellie had always feared that Diana would not be a great earth mother type, but she had hoped that once the baby was born Diana would stay at home most, if not all of the time.

But Diana had gone straight back to work, claiming the need to earn a good salary since her father had refused to increase his gift to them. Although she had assured Ellie that the crèche was first class, still it was not the same thing for the little boy as having his mother on tap, so to speak. Ellie was sure that baby Frank was backward through lack of stimulation. The only thing that could possibly get Ellie to move north would be the idea of looking after little Frank. But then, Diana hated what she called 'interference' in her handling of the baby, and on her parents' visits after the baby was born, had managed to make Ellie feel totally out of date whenever she had tried to do anything for the baby.

And now, Ellie thought, Diana must be fuming about her father's will.

Oh dear.

Ellie switched everything off as the Tesco van made a delivery. Packing all the food away was an effort, but at least she would not need to go out again that weekend. She ate some pot noodles – she'd never had them before and had always wanted to try them. Quite good. Not very sustaining. Chocolate filled the corners.

Sipping a cup of coffee, she went to stand at the back window, looking down over the garden and up towards the church. Usually she felt soothed, looking out on the familiar scene, but today she felt … uneasy. It was the weather, of course. The wind was getting up. Frank's barometer was falling. It looked as if it might snow. She peered through the trees to see if she could see any sign of habitation in the derelict house, but there was none.

She shifted her shoulders under her sweater and shivered.

Then she went up to have a nap. And slept through the phone and doorbell ringing.

The fat man phoned in. 'No movement, nothing. She must have gone north.' The errand boy reported. 'The woman who stayed last night, she went off in a taxi at midday, alone. A local woman came, but didn't stay long. Then Policeman Plod. Only there for a quickie. Then Tesco's came, unloaded five bags of goodies. Looks like she intends to stay for a while. I went and rang the doorbell, see if I could do the old gas trick, but she didn't answer. I could hear the phone ringing. She didn't answer that, either. Perhaps she's gone north already ... well, I could have missed her when I went for some more fags ... bleeding cold out here and I can't keep the engine running all the time, can I?

'No, I suppose she's not intending to go north, not if she's got all that stuff in from Tesco's. Ha, another visitor. A woman, fiftyish, not seen her before. Ringing and knocking ... persistent, I'll give her that ... Ha. She's going in. So the one we want's still there ...'

Ellie stumbled downstairs, hearing someone at the door. And the phone ringing. She ignored the phone to open the front door.

Liz Adams, the vicar's wife, who'd been such a comfort to her last Sunday ... was it only last Sunday? So much had happened since then.

Liz was the sort who believed a good hug did more good than a dozen platitudes. She hugged Ellie tightly, rocking to and fro.

'Oh, Liz!' Ellie sniffed and sought for a handkerchief. For once, she found one in her skirt pocket.

'We've been so worried about you. We took turns ringing you …'

'I had to take the phone off the hook last night. Reporters, you know. And then Diana was using the phone all this morning.'

'Yes, Mrs Dawes told me.' She cocked her head, listening for another presence in the house.

'Diana's gone back home. She wants me to go up for a visit or move to a small flat up there or something, but Liz! I don't want to go.'

Liz hugged her again. 'Come on, my dear. I'm taking you home with me for the weekend. Gilbert has got some kind of function he has to attend tonight, the children will be out and I've got a casserole in the oven. You and I can sit by the fire, eat chocolate and drink wine. You won't need to worry about cooking for yourself, or the phone or answering the door because no one will know where you are.'

'I have to ring Diana. I told her I would. Liz, I have a horrible feeling that Diana is plotting something and as you know, she can be so *forceful*.'

'All the more reason for coming to stay with us this weekend. Ring her now, while I'm here to back you up.'

Ellie took a deep breath and squared up to the phone. A blinking light on the answerphone indicated that various messages were waiting for her to listen to. She pressed 'Play'. Two newspapers, one after the other.

Aunt Drusilla, very angry. 'Pick up the phone, Ellie. I know you're there. Unless, of course, you've gone back with Diana … I didn't think of that. Yes, probably that's what's happened—' The phone was put down abruptly.

Someone calling from a public phone box. A woman's voice, speaking low. 'Ellie, it's me, Kate. I'm all right. Quite safe. I hope you're OK, too. I'm taking a few days off in the depths of the country. Horrible weather, but it gives me time to think … I'll ring you again in a couple of days' time …'

The boy Tod. 'Hi, Mrs Quicke! It's me, Tod! I've borrowed me mum's mobile phone, so I can't be long. Are you all right? Shall I come over? Me mum says I mustn't bother you, but … I've got a lot of homework, it's true. Hey, it looks like snow! Wow! It really is snowing hard! Ring Mum if you want me to come over … Bye!'

John, from the charity shop. 'Ellie, are you all right? We're all desperately worried about you … well, except for Madam, of course. She's being most mysterious about your not coming into the shop this week. Ring me if you want any shopping done, and I'll be right round … I'll ring again later.'

The answerphone clicked off.

Liz remarked, 'Kate …? Kate from next door?'

'Yes. I'll tell you all about it this evening. Liz, so much has been happening … I'm so worried about everything. It would be a great relief to talk to you, if you've got the time.'

'Ring Diana, and let's get out of here.'

Ellie pressed the memory button for Diana's phone number, and waited. And waited. The answerphone clicked on at the other end. It was a relief in a way, not to have to speak to Diana direct.

'Diana, it's mother here. I'm quite well, and going to spend the weekend with an old friend. I probably won't be coming up to stay with you next week. There's too much to do here. I'll ring you again next Thursday, as usual.'

The phone rang again as Ellie put the receiver down. Ellie let it ring as she climbed the stairs to her bedroom, but she could hear the voice recording a message. It was Archie Benjamin, enquiring if he might 'take the little lady out to supper …'

Ellie threw a few things into an overnight bag, remembered to switch off the immersion heater, bolt the back door, draw curtains up and down, leave the lamp in the sitting-room switched on as a security light and turn the central heating down a fraction. There was nothing worse than coming back to a freezing cold house and frozen water pipes.

'Bring your umby. It's snowing really hard now.'

Liz took the bag from her, and they walked slowly up the road and across to the vicarage.

The errand boy reported. 'Looks like she's going away for a bit. Drawn the curtains, double-locked the front door, left a security light. Got a small suitcase with her. Probably going to catch the bus from the corner and take it to the station. That looks like it for the moment. Shall I knock off now? I'm bloody well freezing here …'

The fat man reported. 'Yes, she went across the churchyard, and crossed the road … going to the bus stop, I suppose. The other woman was carrying the bag for her. Must be going up north. It's snowing so hard, I can't see her any more. That looks like it. She's gone, and we can forget about her …'

12

The two women experienced a white-out when a flurry of snow hit them crossing the Green. Only the orange of the beacon on the pedestrian crossing told them where the main road was. The wind was still rising.

Ellie gasped for breath as they pulled themselves inside the vicarage porch. The office was closed for the night, but as Liz opened the front door the usual familiar mix of smells wafted around them. Ellie sniffed traces of polish from the floor tiles, dust from cardboard boxes stacked in a heap at the bottom of the stairs, and the smell of pine from the giant Christmas tree which Gilbert was cack-handedly trying to wedge into a bucket.

'Hi, there!' He had the phone clamped to one ear while he tried to hammer a wedge into position at the base of the tree. 'No, I didn't mean you, Nora ... Liz has just come back from collecting waifs and strays ... no, I didn't mean that literally, of course ...'

Liz and Ellie laughed, shedding coats, shaking their heads at him, going through to the big drawing-room at the back of the house. From upstairs came the chumpety-chump of a CD being played by the teenage daughter, a screeching sound from the slightly younger son playing a computer game, and from further off the scratchy noise of a not-soheavenly choir belting out a chorus from the curate's flat. In the drawing-room, a CD was playing something soothing by an old-fashioned crooner.

This room was, as usual, on the chilly side, since the antiquated central heating failed to heat the vicarage properly. However, a gas log-effect fire was doing its best, the third-hand velvet curtains almost managed to meet over the gigantic windows, and there were plenty of odd cushions and throws on the bumpy settees around the fireplace.

Ellie relaxed at once. Gilbert came in, his specs gleaming as brightly as his smile. 'Guess what! I've got the evening off. The meeting's cancelled because of the snow, and I've got a … whole … evening … to myself!'

He whirled Ellie round and gave her a smacking great kiss.

'Oh leave off!' said Ellie, laughing as she pulled down her sweater again.

'Don't take any notice of him!' advised Liz, uncorking wine with expert haste. 'I'll shove some more potatoes through the microwave if he's going to join us for supper, and we'll eat straight away.'

Gilbert danced around, a schoolboy given an extra holiday. 'I've turned the answerphone on and told Nora she is not to ring me back this evening about anything short of the church steeple falling down. The best of it is, everyone knows I should be out at this meeting, so they won't think to ring here!'

They ate in the big kitchen with the teenage daughter and son, both wanting to know what it felt like to be blown up by a car bomb, what Kate was really like, and what the police had said … until Liz said that that was Quite Enough! When the younger ones disappeared about their

Saturday night business, Gilbert and Liz sat Ellie down before the fire in the drawing-room and said, 'Now tell us all about everything.'

'Well, to start at the end,' said Ellie, 'Madam from the charity shop came round to see me, and before you say "about time, too!", I must tell you that she's given me the sack!'

'What!' Gilbert lost his glasses in his astonishment. 'Has that woman gone raving mad?'

'Possibly,' said Liz dryly. 'But let the girl speak. And this time, Ellie, start from the beginning.'

'It would be good to talk about it, get things into perspective. After Frank died, the doctor insisted on giving me these pills. I felt totally withdrawn. I was having nightmares, too … chasing Frank along long corridors – the hospital, I suppose – and through different doors … and I still wasn't sleeping properly, so half the time I was in bed trying to sleep, I was more or less awake. And half the time I was supposedly awake, I think I was … away with the fairies!

'The first thing I can remember clearly is watching Kate run down from the church … I suppose it was just before Ferdy was killed, but I really don't have the slightest idea what time it was. Next day Mrs Dawes came to say she'd found the body, and that night I saw Mrs Hanna and …'

With many a false start and recap, Ellie poured the whole story out. She had meant at first only to talk about the murder and why she didn't think Kate had done it, but as she went rambling on, she found she was including details of Armand's interview with the police, and going to order a new bed – due to be delivered Monday afternoon – when that poor man fell on the bridge, and the flowers Tod had left on her doorstep … because she was worried about Tod, he was left alone too much … and then it was on to Aunt Drusilla and the mystery of her source of income, and Diana wanting her to go up north and such odd things had been happening to her, like – oh, she didn't know what, exactly, but there it was. Life was quite different, now, what with trying to make sense of the computer, and phoning Tesco's for food, and eating pot noodles and getting quite tiddly not just once but several times and going out in Kate's car. Everything. And perhaps that was a good thing, helping her to move forward, get over Frank's death.

'Only,' she said, 'I wish I understood what was going on … so many loose ends. I don't like loose ends.'

She stopped, feeling a lot better. I'm emptied out, she thought.

Gilbert was humming to himself. Leaping to his feet, he began striding around the room. 'You do realize you're ducking the main issue, don't you? Of course you've got lots of little problems to deal with, but the important thing as I see it, is that you're refusing to face the facts about the murder because you're fond of Kate.'

Ellie would have protested, but he held up his hand to stop her. 'Come off it, Ellie. If Kate didn't kill him, then who did? Did anybody else – anybody at all – have a reason for killing him?'

Ellie shrugged. She simply did not know.

'The jealous husband?' suggested Liz.

Gilbert hummed to himself. 'Mm … possible, but unlikely. He's violent, possessive, jealous. He had a possible motive and he can't prove where he was at the time. But why would he have gone on to kill Mrs Hanna?'

'We don't know that she's dead,' argued Ellie. 'In fact—'

'He had no reason to do so. The only possible reason why anyone would have wanted to kill Mrs Hanna is that she was a threat to them. But Mrs Hanna didn't know anything about the murder, did she? Because she asked Ellie to investigate it for her. I think her disappearance is a separate issue.'

Both women protested. How could it be a separate issue? It was asking too much to expect them to believe it was a coincidence.

Gilbert continued, 'All right. Let's consider the case against Kate for murdering Mrs Hanna. Kate had opportunity, I think. We don't know what she was doing the evening Mrs Hanna disappeared, do we? Could Mrs Hanna have found out something linking Kate to Ferdy's murder? That would have done it, wouldn't it?'

Ellie broke in. 'I'm not at all sure that Mrs Hanna has been killed. I admit I was worried when they found that body in the park, but the police said that was a psychiatric patient from the hospital. I saw inside Mrs Hanna's fridge, you see. The kitchen looked a mess with furniture pulled over and shoved around, but there was a tea towel hanging over the door of the fridge, and the door was wide open. There was nothing but a couple of jars of jam inside.'

'Yes? So?' said Gilbert impatiently.

Liz uncurled her legs and recurled them another way. 'Really, Ellie? Are you sure?'

'Well, not a hundred per cent sure. I wanted to take a closer look, only the policeman threw me out. But if the fridge hadn't any butter or milk or cheese or bacon or anything like that in it …'

'… and if the door had been left open, so the fridge would defrost … was the electricity turned off?'

'I couldn't see. I tried to discuss it with the policeman who came to see me today, but he didn't want to know. I suppose only a woman would see the significance of it.'

Liz nodded. 'You're right. Oh, stop gawping, Gilbert. If Mrs Hanna had been taken unawares and killed, her fridge would still have contained perishable foods. But if she'd planned her departure, she would have disposed of every-thing that might go off, unplugged the fridge or switched the current off at the wall, and put a tea towel over the door to stop it closing, so that the air could get in and stop the fridge going mouldy inside.'

Gilbert looked bewildered. 'But you said the place was in chaos, that there was every evidence of a fight.'

'In the kitchen, yes,' said Ellie, 'but the rest of the flat was in pretty good order, even though someone had gone through the drawers in the bedroom. You could say that a burglar had been at work … or you could say that Mrs Hanna had been packing for a getaway. There's something at the back of my mind about her flat … I want to go back and have another look if I can. If the police will let me.'

Gilbert recommenced his striding around the room, waving his arms like a scarecrow. 'The fact remains that Kate is the only real suspect. I don't see how you can deny it.'

'I don't deny it. I just don't believe it. Did you know Ferdy well?'

'I suppose – in a limited sort of way. He was brilliant at keeping our old banger on the road, and you could always find him outside the church if you needed him. Of course, some people objected to his using the road outside the church grounds as a garage and workshop. I tried to get the PCC to agree to his renting the yard behind the church hall to use as garage space, but they wouldn't agree. They said if we ever got the money through to rebuild, we'd need that space, and of course they were right. But still, if it were only for a few months …'

He sighed. 'I wish I hadn't got so angry with him that day, but he had no less than three vehicles out there the evening he was killed. His van, and two others that he was working on. The van was blocking the entrance to the church hall, which was why I sounded off at him. He promised to remove it and I suppose he did, because it's not there now.

'The other two cars were both there for a couple of days. The Bentley was taken away a couple of days ago, I suppose by the police. The Mondeo is still there. I was going to talk to Mrs Hanna about getting the cars removed because I suppose they belong to her now, but then she disappeared. I don't know what to do about it.'

Liz sighed. 'Ellie, I know you like Kate but everything points to her. You say you've been asking around. The police have, too. Have you turned up anything – anything at all, which points to someone else?'

'I haven't,' said Ellie, unhappily. 'If only he'd been dealing in drugs then we could all have shrugged it off as some sort of gang warfare. But everyone seems to agree he was clean in that respect. I did once think I might talk to Joyce McNally since she used to be Kate's best friend …'

Gilbert pointed a bony finger. 'Joyce sings in the choir. You could speak to her after church tomorrow. If she turns up in this bad weather.'

Ellie yawned. 'I'll try to, though I can't see that it will help.' She yawned again.

'Time for bed,' said Liz. 'You look worn out, Ellie. Have a good lie-in tomorrow, and don't bother to turn out for church if you don't feel like it.'

'Of course I will,' said Ellie, sleepily.

Liz kissed Ellie. Gilbert kissed Ellie. They were a very touchy-feely family.

Liz took Ellie up the chilly staircase and put the electric radiator on in the guest room to supplement the barely functioning central heating.

Liz tried to yank the inadequate curtains closer. 'My dream is that one day we'll have a parish with a modern house, with a proper built-in kitchen and good central heating. Goodnight, Ellie.'

'Goodnight, Liz. Smashing evening. Thanks.'

In the morning the scene was like a Christmas card, with the church and spire, the bare-branched trees and the Green all covered with snow.

At breakfast in the huge inconvenient kitchen, Gilbert slurped tea, sharp-set after returning from an eight o'clock service at the church.

'Long live the snow,' he said. 'It's given me a brilliant idea for a sermon.'

Liz laughed. 'Does that alarm or delight me? Well, I don't suppose many people will get to church today.'

'Oh, some will,' said Gilbert. 'They'll struggle in even if their cars won't start, all bright-eyed and cheery, having overcome all the temptations that Satan has put in their way to get there.'

Ellie went with them and sat at the back as usual. Liz whispered to her, 'Hardly anyone's turned up for the choir, though Joyce has, you'll be glad to hear. Nora is in her usual muddle, Mrs Dawes is looking down her nose at the flower arrangement one of her assistants did, and I've got to read one of the lessons for someone who's phoned in sick.'

Ellie noticed Mrs Dawes' granddaughter Chloe moving into a back pew with a stolid-looking young man at her side. He wasn't black, exactly. Possibly of mixed race? Ellie frowned. Hadn't she seen that young man somewhere before?

Mrs Dawes swanned down the aisle to where Ellie was sitting and grasped her by the arm. 'I know you haven't formally joined the choir yet but you can help out today, can't you, now you're here and we're short of sopranos? Did you see my granddaughter with her new young man? Wonders will never cease!'

Ellie was terrified at the thought of being put into the choir, just like that! But she could see that even her small voice might be of use, and she wasn't the type who would refuse to help. In the vestry she submitted to being inserted into a long red gown and given some hymn books to carry. She went back into church in Mrs Dawes' wake, hoping she wouldn't trip up, lose her place in the hymns, or otherwise disgrace herself. She wondered fleetingly what Frank would have said if he could have seen her.

It wasn't so bad, really. She stood up and sat down when the others did. Mrs Dawes whispered – piercingly – what to do and when. Ellie found she knew all the hymns they were planning to sing, and she sat out while the choir attempted – somewhat disastrously – an anthem.

Gilbert's sermon was brief, amusing, and left them thinking.

'Well, so you all made it through the snow. Congratulations. Adversity brings out the best in the British, doesn't it? Of course this amount of snow is just a minor inconvenience. We're not going to be cut off for days or weeks. Our electricity supply, our gas and telephones are still working. Our Christmas shopping will not be affected.

'Some years ago in a small town in Austria, it was a very different matter. They were thoroughly cut off from the world. Well-laid plans for a Christmas Eve spectacular at the church had to be cancelled. Only a few people could be expected to turn up, that didn't include the movers and shakers. Sadly the local organist put away the music which it had been planned to perform on Christmas Eve.

'What was a celebration of Christ's coming into the world, without some joy, some music? Sorrowfully, he asked God to understand the situation, and to show him some way that they might still celebrate God's coming.

'He began to hear a tune in his head. He remembered a poem the local pastor had shown him. The poem and the music went together perfectly. He played the music through on his guitar, and it moved him almost to tears. He paced around, singing the words. Yes, it was good. Unlike anything they'd planned. It wasn't grand. It didn't have a big chorus, or complicated harmonies. It didn't even need the organ.

'But it told the story of Christmas perhaps better than any of the well-known pieces the choir had been practising. That piece of music is now known as "Silent Night". It was born out of adversity, and is perhaps the best carol ever written.

'The snow here is only a minor inconvenience to us today, but this past week we have suffered other blows from outside forces. A young man we knew well has been murdered. His mother has disappeared. A car has been blown up. A young woman has gone missing. The body of a poor distraught woman has been found in the park. We have been besieged by reporters, gossip is rife, and not everyone has been kind to those people most affected by these events.

'The man who wrote "Silent Night" put his problem in the hands of the Lord, and asked for help to solve it. The result was a carol to touch the heart. Let us now in silence ask the Lord to take us, too, under his special care at this difficult time. Let us ask him to have a special care of all those who have been touched by what has been happening. Let us ask him to be with the police, working to solve the case and bring those responsible to justice. Let us ask him to comfort the bereaved mother, and all Ferdy's friends. Where there has been evil, let us ask him to cleanse our hearts and minds … so that we too may bring forth a new spirit at Christmastime …'

Later, they did sing 'Silent Night'.

'I'm Joyce. Mrs Adams said you wanted to speak to me.' Joyce McNally was a well-brushed, tidy girl with hostile dark eyes. The very picture of a teller behind a bank counter. Ellie wondered if the girl were always hostile, or just feeling anti today.

'Thanks, yes. It's about Ferdy Hanna, of course.'

The girl pinched in her lips, and then expelled air. 'Puh! I knew him once, a long time ago, but I don't know anything about what he's been up to recently. Sorry, I can't help.' She turned away, disassociating herself from Ellie.

Ellie persevered. 'Just one question. Was Ferdy doing well with the cars?'

'I suppose.' Was the girl being deliberately vague? 'He didn't rip people off too much, so they used to go back to him for their next car, and for repairs. Yes, I suppose he did all right. He used to boast he'd make a million before he was thirty. Don't suppose he would have done. Though he did say …' She frowned and stopped.

'Yes?'

'He did say …'

This was like drawing teeth out of a toffee apple.

'… well, I expect it was a joke, but he did say something about an offer being made to him for the business. It must have been a joke. I mean, who would want to work that hard, in the open, no proper site or garage or anything? I must go.'

Joyce smiled invitingly at a bony young man who was holding up her coat for her. No doubt this was the acceptable suitor, the scout leader. Joyce slid into the coat and departed.

Well, that was a waste of time, thought Ellie.

Lunch at the vicarage on Sundays was a feast that expanded to include whoever Gilbert and Liz felt needed feeding either in body or spirit. So Nora was invited, and two elderly women. Archie Benjamin angled for an invitation but to Ellie's relief was not asked. The curate and his wife came, plus their five-year-old boy. The lad was badly behaved but his parents' pride and joy, so no one said anything when he spread his food all over the table.

Ellie noticed that Liz got a little tetchy when Nora burst into tears in the middle of lunch and fled from the room, followed by a worried-looking Gilbert. They were absent for a good ten minutes, by which time everyone else had finished their pudding, and Ellie was helping Liz to clear away and stack dirty plates in the dishwasher.

Ellie whispered to Liz, 'What's up with Nora?'

Liz said, 'I'll tell you as soon as we've got the place to ourselves again.'

The elderly visitors drifted away for their Sunday naps,

but the curate and his family, plus Nora and Ellie, helped the vicar secure the Christmas tree in the chilly hall, resurrect dusty decorations from their boxes and hang them on the branches.

After tea Nora went home, and the curate withdrew with his wife into their flat at the back of the house, taking their fractious son with them.

It had begun to thaw outside, and to rain in a spiteful, hard-hitting way. With their other guests gone and the teenagers out, Liz switched on the fire in the drawing-room while Gilbert drew the curtains.

'Gilbert,' said Liz, 'I think Ellie might find it helpful to know why Nora is in such a state these days. It wouldn't be breaking a confidence, because Nora will talk about it to anyone who'll listen.'

13

'Yes, I've been thinking that myself,' said Gilbert. He sat on the arm of Ellie's settee and took her hand in his, patting it. 'You know that Nora used to live with her father in one of the nice flats overlooking the river? He'd been a headmaster somewhere, had a good pension. Horrible old tyrant, though I say it as shouldn't. Never wanted Nora to do anything but dance attendance on him, but let her play the organ because it was "a nice hobby for a woman". Well, when he died, she discovered that not only did his pension die with him, but he'd only got a short lease on the flat, and didn't own it.

'She has no proper job, is completely untrained for anything. She does go into the primary school here to help children to read, but that's not going to get her a mortgage to buy a flat, is it? Especially not a spacious luxury flat over-looking the Thames. She simply didn't know what to do.'

'Came round here, crying, all hours of the day and night,' said Liz, crossing and recrossing long legs.

Gilbert continued to pat Ellie's hand. 'She was distraught. Had no friends who would put themselves out for her. So I went with her to her father's solicitors – very old-fashioned firm, miles away, and made them take her case up, try to get an extension of the lease. We thought that if she could get the lease extended, she could continue to live there, perhaps take in lodgers to make ends meet. The solicitor found out that the building was managed by Jolleys, the estate agents at the bottom of the Avenue here. They refused to extend. They said she could negotiate a new lease if she liked, but the price asked was wildly beyond her means.

'So I went down to Jolleys and had words with them. The interview became somewhat – ah – heated, I'm afraid. I demanded the name of the owner of the flat so that I could contact him direct. They refused to give it to me, but as I was leaving I bumped into old Miss Quicke coming in. I said something rather sharp about hoping she wasn't planning to do business with Jolleys because they were a load of sharks and she pulled herself up and said she had done business with them for many, many years and that as far as she was concerned, they were the best in the business …

'I jumped in with both feet and asked if she was responsible for turning poor little Nora out into the cold, and she said that if someone wanted to live in one of her flats, then they must pay the market price!'

Ellie savoured the words. 'One of her flats? You mean, she owns more than one of the flats in that block?'

'That's what it sounded like. So I asked Frank if he had any influence with his aunt in the matter. He said I must have got the wrong end of the stick. He said his aunt had nothing in the world but her old age pension. I told him I was absolutely sure she owned some property in that block, and eventually he promised me to look into it.'

'And that's when he wrote to the enquiry agents,' said Ellie. 'He paid for their report, but the actual paperwork is missing. I thought Diana must have taken it, because she's hand in glove with Aunt Drusilla at the moment. I rang the enquiry agents and asked them to send me a copy of their report. I wonder …'

Liz uncurled her legs. 'Nora's still hoping Gilbert will be able to swing something for her, though he's told her again and again there's nothing that can be done. She says he's the only one who cares tuppence about her. And maybe …' she shrugged, '… maybe that's true.'

Gilbert said, 'Come on, Liz. You know you've been marvellous, listening to her, mopping her up, all hours.'

'Mm, but it's really your shoulder she wants to cry on.'

Ellie frowned. 'What's going to happen to her?'

Gilbert shook his head. 'I don't know. She's lived in that flat all her life. It's true she can't afford to purchase a new lease at the price Miss Quicke is demanding. I told her to put her name down at the council …'

'Oh, she wouldn't do that!' said Liz, half ironical and half sympathetic.

Ellie sat up straight. 'I always thought tenants had rights in these matters as well as landlords. Is her solicitor any good? Can't he see what can be done under the law? Do you think it would be a good idea for her to go to Bill Weatherspoon instead?'

'She can't afford solicitor's fees.'

'Well!' said Ellie, breathing a little faster. 'I think that's a pretty poor show. I'll ask Bill to take her case on, and see what can be done. If the worst comes to the worst, I'll pay his fee myself!'

'Bravo, Ellie!'

'I hope that by tomorrow morning I'll have a copy of that report. Hopefully that'll give me some ammunition to deal with Aunt Drusilla.'

'Double bravo!'

'And I suppose …' with a sigh, 'I ought to tell the police what I think about Mrs Hanna's disappearance … that fridge, you know.'

'To be fair,' said Liz, 'she could have planned to disappear, and been abducted after she'd gone to all the trouble of clearing out the fridge.'

'Would her abductors carefully take away with them the perishables she had removed from the fridge earlier? I don't see that. But I'll look into it tomorrow.' She put her hands to her head in mock despair. 'So many things to do. Do you think I'll ever get myself sorted?'

Gilbert leapt to his feet and fled the room saying, 'I think I've got the answer!' He returned dragging a metal stand with a flip chart on it.

'Oh no!' said Liz, laughing. 'That's what we use for parish meetings!'

Gilbert tore off used sheets and produced a large pen. 'It concentrates the mind to write down your aims in life. Ellie, tell us what you have planned.'

'Find out where Mrs Hanna's gone … take delivery of my new bed … see Bill Weatherspoon about Nora's lease …'

Gilbert, writing rapidly in enormous letters, added, 'See the police about Kate …'

Liz put in, 'Have a showdown with that awful woman at the shop …'

'No!' said Ellie. 'I was shocked – humiliated even – when she gave me the sack, but even if she begged me to, I wouldn't go back.'

'Oh yes, you would!' said Liz. 'You've been the backbone of that place for ever.'

'Not really. Oh, perhaps. I was devastated at first. At first I couldn't imagine my days without the framework of

helping in the shop. It's been my life for so long. But now –
it's hard to explain, and you'll think I'm being very selfish –
but when I think about working in the shop I keep remembering how I always have to be so kind and patient to
everyone there—'

'But you are naturally kind and patient!' argued Liz.

'You won't believe what dark feelings I've been having
lately. About my nearest and dearest, too!'

Gilbert ran a thick black line through 'Charity shop'.
'Scrub that, then. Shall I put "make peace with Diana"?'

Ellie didn't object, but she didn't say she agreed, either.
She still had a nasty hard place inside her when she thought
of Diana. Maybe in the morning she'd feel better.

She said, 'There's so many things I have to do. Finish
writing ta notes for everyone's sympathy letters. Book
myself in for driving lessons … yes, I mean to do it, I really
do. I don't care what you say about Kate, she's been marvellous to me. Then I've got to find the PCC notes on Frank's
computer. Gilbert, you've been an angel, not asking me
about them. They're there somewhere, of course. Only he's
put them in a file or a folder or whatever you call the
wretched things, and I can't find out where.'

Gilbert wrote down 'Sympathy letters. Driving lessons.
PCC notes.' He said, 'Don't worry too much about the
minutes. If the worst comes to the worst, we can recon-
struct them from what everyone remembers at the next
meeting.'

'Yes, but it irritates me, not being able to find them,' said
Ellie, crossly. 'Gilbert, what would you file them under, if
you'd done them?'

'Frank might have filed them under the name of the
property committee, because that was the committee he sat

on. Or under church hall? Because he was so involved with getting the grant to rebuild it? Or perhaps the initials or name of the church, St Saviour's?'

'I'll look tomorrow.' Ellie sighed. 'You've been so good to me, you two. I don't know what I'd have done without this weekend away from it all.'

Gilbert solemnly tore off the sheet of suggestions, folded it, refolded it, and folded it again to form a neat package which he handed to Ellie with a bow. 'My dear … any time.'

'Bed,' said Liz. She turned out the fire. There were kisses all round, and Ellie went upstairs thinking that she would be glad to get back to her own bed tomorrow …

'… and SNAP!' The errand boy slapped down his last card and scooped the pile. They'd been playing for hours. First they'd played for who was paying for their supper. The fat man lost that one. Two more cartons of pizza had been added to the pile on the floor, plus another six-pack of beer.

Then they'd upped the stakes and played for the fat man's car, which he won back after a hard-fought contest. The errand boy gave in with apparently poor grace, keeping to himself the fact that he was going to have to get rid of it sooner rather than later, since it had the turning circle of a tortoise. Definitely something wrong, there. He said he'd get hold of something else to use tomorrow, and leave the Saab outside Ellie's house, dropping the keys back to the fat man the following evening.

The fat man said, 'About time, too.' He'd been taking minicabs to get to and from the council flat he called home. He didn't bother to say it, but with his leg in plaster he couldn't have driven anyway.

Now they were so bored, they'd been driven to playing Snap, using matches for stake money.

They were gradually making the upper room more comfortable with a deckchair, a fan heater and some sacking tacked over the windows. The errand boy had managed to turn the electricity supply and the water back on that day. The fat man had brought in a sleeping bag, so that he could spend the night there in the chair. The stairs were difficult for him to manage.

For the umpteenth time, the errand boy lifted the sacking at the window, and looked out.

'No change. I reckon she's gone north, all right. Can't think why we have to keep watching.'

'She says she has to be certain. You-know-who can't risk being seen until we're dead sure the old lady's hopped it.'

'Reckon she has.'

'Try telling her ladyship that!'

Neither had forgotten – or forgiven – their past rivalry, nor the matter of the fat man's 'borrowed' car. But for the moment, they were as one.

'If she does come back,' said the fat man, eyeing his companion over the rim of his can. 'If she does, then I reckon the best way is a quick hit and run with the motor. Not mine, of course.'

The errand boy gave no sign that he approved this suggestion, although he had in fact thought of it himself already. 'Nah, if she does come back, I'll get in and fix the gas.'

Slap, slap went the cards. 'You said she got a gadget which goes off if there's a gas leak.'

'I can turn that off, easy. Five minutes, that's all.'

Slap, slap.

'She won't let you in.'

'Do it when she's out.'

Slap, slap … 'Bingo!' said the errand boy and lifted both the pile and the stakes.

'I need some more painkillers,' sighed the fat man. 'Bring some in for me in the morning, will you?'

'Sure … if she's not back.'

A cold, wet and thoroughly wretched Monday morning. Liz had gone off to her counselling job and Gilbert had a long list of sick to visit. Ellie took her time sponging around her grazes, stripping her bed after breakfast, hoping the rain would stop before she had to cross the church grounds to get back home. The rain didn't stop.

She was trying to remember exactly what food she had in the fridge and freezer as she turned into her driveway. A pity she couldn't have gone up through her garden to the back door, but she'd bolted the kitchen door on her way out.

A cruel gust of wind and sleet caught her as she reached the porch and felt in her handbag for her key. Shaking down her umbrella, she tried to hold on to the door as the wind took it from her. It flew into the house with a bang. She dropped her umbrella and overnight bag and, using both hands, eased it shut.

She stopped. Opened the door wide. And stared.

On the gatepost at the top of the drive was a For Sale sign. Jolleys. By appointment only.

Ellie blinked. It was still there. Advertising her house for sale.

Wind and rain blew into her face. With shaky hands she closed the door. The red light was blinking on the answerphone. She was standing on the daily newspaper, and she'd left a fresh pint of milk on the doorstep.

Diana. It must be.

Diana had put her house on the market, without telling her.

Of course Diana had planned that Ellie would go back up north with her, and so would not see the sign. Once up north, Diana had no doubt intended to present Ellie with a fait accompli. 'You can't go back. The house has been sold. Now you can buy something close to me.'

It might have worked. Yes, it might very well have worked.

There was something at the back of Ellie's mind, something Bill Weatherspoon had said. Ellie already owned half the house. Frank had left the other half to her for her lifetime. After her death, his half would go to Diana. But if this house were sold, then what happened?

Ellie felt sick. It was one thing to know with your head that your daughter was a bit of a bully, but to be bullied like this was … devastating.

Ellie pushed herself off the wall, hung up her wet coat and, turning the central heating indicator up to normal, went into the kitchen to make herself a cup of tea and to think. She could of course ring up Diana and scream at her. No, no good. Diana would be out at work. And Diana could shout louder than Ellie.

She could get Bill Weatherspoon to write to Diana. Yes, of course. But wasn't it a little weak to rely on someone else to fight her battles for her?

She would deal with this herself. She opened curtains, switched on the immersion heater, rescued the milk from the doorstep, picked up the post – nothing from the enquiry agents yet – threw dirty washing into the machine, switched it on and listened to the messages on the answerphone. Nothing much there, except another message from Kate saying that she was just fine and would be in touch again soon. Oh, and a blustering threat from Armand, to the effect that if Ellie didn't tell him where Kate was hiding, he'd come round and make her.

'Let him try!' thought Ellie.

She phoned Jolleys, who billed themselves as THE Neighbourhood Estate Agents, and asked for an appointment with Mr Jolley. She was told he was busy with clients all morning. Check. She phoned Bill Weatherspoon, only to be told ditto.

Right! Up to me, she thought. She put on her heaviest winter coat and fished out Frank's extra-size umbrella. She remembered that Diana had not used her own house keys when last she returned to the house. If the For Sale sign said 'By appointment only', it meant that the house agents had a key to get in with. Had Diana given them her key?

What a horrible thought!

Ellie did not, definitely did not wish to have would-be buyers looking over her house while she went up to the Avenue. Also there was that very dodgy gas man hanging around … she ought to have rung the gas board when he presented himself with a half-smoked cigarette butt behind his ear. Suppose he tried to get back in, while the house agent was showing someone around?

Yet to get this matter sorted, she must leave the house. Who could she trust to house-sit for her?

She rang John at the charity shop, hoping he might have gone in to get some books sorted. Thankfully, he was there and willing to house-sit for a while.

He wanted to discuss the matter of her returning to work at the shop but she couldn't be bothered with that just at the moment. By the time he arrived, she had the house warm and some coffee and biscuits ready for him.

He goggled at the For Sale sign just as she had done. She really didn't like having to expose Diana's little plans to strangers, but in this case it had to be done. John exclaimed with horror, with sympathy, and settled down with the papers to guard the house.

'Bolt the front door behind me and if anyone comes from Jolleys, tell them I'm at the shop, sorting it out … and don't let any fake water, gas or electricity men in while I'm gone, will you? I think there's one hanging around this area.'

'Trust me!' said John. He drove the front door bolt to behind her as she stepped out into the rain.

Jolleys, THE Neighbourhood Estate Agents, was across the road from the charity shop, near Sunflowers café. The café looked bright and welcoming on this murky November day. Ellie could see Chloe flitting about inside. Was that her new boyfriend sitting at a table in the window? Mrs Dawes had seemed surprised that Chloe had taken him to church. Fleetingly, Ellie wondered why.

She had something more important to deal with now. Jolleys looked prosperous. There were three desks inside. Solid, impressive-looking desks, staffed by two middle-aged women, and a balding, smiling, rubicund man who Ellie supposed must be Mr Jolley himself.

There was a client with him. A nervous-looking young man probably trying to find something within his means to rent.

'May I help you?' One of the middle-aged women.

'Thank you. I'm here to see Mr Jolley himself.'

'Do you have an appointment? I'm afraid he's busy all morning. Perhaps I—'

'My name is Mrs Quicke, and I think,' said Ellie rather more loudly than was usual with her, 'that Mr Jolley would prefer to deal with this rather delicate matter himself. Now. At once.'

Mr Jolley looked up, recognizing trouble when he saw it. He frowned, looked impatient. Then slightly bewildered. Lastly, cautious. He waved the man he'd been interviewing to an assistant's desk.

Ellie seated herself in front of him and said, 'Mr Jolley, you've put a For Sale sign up outside my house.'

He treated her to a fat smile. 'Ah, Mrs Quicke. Sorry to hear you're leaving us, but you'll be delighted to hear that there's a lot of interest. In fact, one of my assistants will be showing two couples around this morning.'

'On whose authority? I have not asked you to put the house on the market. I was astounded to see the For Sale sign up this morning.'

Mr Jolley began to perspire. 'We were instructed by your daughter. It is all perfectly in order—'

'No, it isn't. The house is mine, not hers. And I have no intention of moving.'

'But we understood—'

'You were … misled. I must ask you to have that sign taken down immediately. Today. And I believe you have a set of keys belonging to me? I want them back.'

'But … we understood that you needed a quick sale, that you are negotiating for a small flat near your daughter …'

'… and you didn't check with me first?'

'We understood that your daughter already has title to half the house, and that you were not well … unable to look after yourself …'

Ellie thought she had been keeping her anger under control, but now she let it slip. 'You were misinformed. Check with Bill Weatherspoon if you wish. Do I look as if I were senile and ready for a nursing home?'

'Er, no.' He scrabbled unhappily in a file at his elbow. 'Our instructions were signed, all in proper form … the photographer has been asked to take the usual … we have even booked a quarter-page advertisement in—'

'Then you'll have to unbook it, won't you?'

His colour, which had been unhealthily high, began to fade. He thrust a form at her, on which Diana's signature was prominent. 'We acted perfectly legally. Your daughter was very clear that she owns half the house. I will of course check with Mr Weatherspoon, but … you must understand that we acted throughout in good faith … we have incurred various expenditures …'

'Send the account to my daughter. I am certainly not responsible for it!'

She stood up. 'My keys, please.'

'I'm afraid that they are with my assistant, who is even now taking someone round …'

'I expect he has a mobile phone. Ring him. Get him back here. Return my keys, and we'll say no more about it.'

'He may already be showing someone round the house. It's a prime property. Selling this would give you a nice bit of capital. You could afford to buy something really exclusive with the money …'

'You underestimate me, Mr Jolley. A neighbour is house-sitting for me at the moment and he will not be letting anyone in during my absence. Please ring your man and get my keys back.'

He caved in, as bullies always do. 'Of course. Please take a seat.'

He's a smarmy git, if ever there was one, thought Ellie. She was surprised at herself for even thinking such a thing. Her anger was cooling to a leaden dullness. She hated this. That her own daughter could do this to her ...!

Then she thought of something really sneaky, but potentially helpful.

14

Mr Jolley was fast recovering his usual smiling demeanour. 'My assistant will be a few minutes, Mrs Quicke. Would you care for a cup of coffee while you wait?'

The pale young man had left. Another client had arrived. Bent on smoothing Ellie down, Mr Jolley signalled that one of his assistants should deal with him. Ellie was prepared to be smoothed.

She said conversationally, 'It might be just as well if you did check with Mr Weatherspoon about the ownership of certain properties. The house presently occupied by my late husband's aunt, for instance …'

His eyes began to bulge. 'Miss Quicke?'

'It is possible that I may be putting that house on the market. What do you think it would fetch?'

He gobbled, perspired and mopped. His voice came out as a squeak. 'You … you own that house? But …'

'Yes,' said Ellie with a stony smile. 'I own that house, too. I haven't really thought about what I shall do with it, yet. It would cut up into several nice flats, wouldn't it? Or perhaps a developer would be interested, because there is almost an acre of garden attached. How many town houses do you think we could get on that piece of land?'

Mr Jolley appeared to have lost his voice completely.

The coffee came. Ellie sugared it, and sipped. Really good coffee. A man who knew what his customers liked, Mr Jolley. Now did he care more about managing the flats for Aunt Drusilla, or about handling the sale of the big house? Which would bring him more money and kudos? Ellie rather hoped he'd be loyal to Aunt Drusilla, having worked for her, presumably, for a good many years. The degree of his loyalty might rather depend, Ellie thought, on how many flats she owned and he managed.

He smiled, revealing teeth far too even and white to be natural. 'Well, well. You have come to the right person, haven't you? Now that our little misunderstanding is out of the way, we can look forward to a splendidly rewarding relationship …'

Two flats only, thought Ellie.

'… and if you would just like to give me time to check … perhaps by tomorrow … and then, I can save you waiting here, bring your keys round to you myself, just to show there's no hard feelings, ha ha!'

I underestimated him, thought Ellie. The man is going to back-pedal, check with Aunt Drusilla, who when all is said and done must have brought a lot of work to him over the years … and maybe it's four or five flats … and then try to smarm me into forgetting his sharp practice. Because he was just that little bit too eager to fall in with Diana's wishes on this one, wasn't he? Just a little too quick off the mark with his For Sale board and camera and adverts.

She adhered to her seat, although he had risen to his feet obviously trying to get rid of her. 'I'm in no hurry,' she said. 'I only have to call in at the police station after this …'

He sat down, abruptly, his colour fading again. 'You're going to involve the police in this … this stupid little misunderstanding?'

Ellie gave him a limpid smile. 'Why should you think that? If you will give me the original of the form with Diana's signature on it – keeping a photocopy for yourself, of course – then I shall certainly not be mentioning the matter to the police. For the moment.'

'Of course, of course.' He was perspiring again. It had been only a guess on Ellie's part that he had known the truth about the ownership of her house before he took it on. Or maybe he had had his suspicions but stifled them. Either way, he was going to give her the weapon she needed to checkmate Diana.

Oh dear. How horridly businesslike she was being today. And tough! She hadn't thought she could ever outface a man like this.

A young man burst into the office, looking thunderous. He was carrying a clipboard and flourishing a set of keys. Ellie recognized Diana's owl keyring.

'What's going on? I couldn't get into the house. The front door was bolted and the back door, too. Did you send me to the wrong house? The client's furious. Loved the area, loved the house, was prepared to go the asking price, subject to a survey, of course.'

Mr Jolley had been making shushing noises, but the young man was too angry to care.

Ellie said with saccharine sweetness, 'Oh, you poor thing. Mr Jolley sent you on a fool's errand, I'm afraid. Are those my keys? Thank you. And the form – yes, yes, with my daughter's signature on it. Splendid. And Mr Jolley, I shall think over what you said about the big house. Quite a large development, I agree. A real goldmine. Good day …'

Ellie swept out into the street, got herself round to the Sunflowers café, and sat down to have a good laugh. A laugh which was also nearly a cry.

How could Diana have done that to her? She ordered coffee, used the café's public phone to tell John that the crisis was over, and that he had been perfectly splendid, repelling boarders for her.

She was surprised to hear that the fake gasman had been back again. John had carefully watched where he went after trying to get into her house, and the man had gone off to sit in a green Saab, registration number unknown. Definitely not a gas board van. Had John rung the gas board? And the police? He had? Good. You couldn't be too careful nowadays, could you?

She owed him a meal, if he cared to join her at the café for lunch.

Fancy that! she thought. Frank not dead three weeks, and I'm inviting another man to have lunch with me!

The errand boy was reporting on his mobile. 'Yeah, she's back all right. The For Sale sign is still up, so she's probably not going to be around much longer … yeah, yeah. Even one day's too long, and yeah, I understand we can't afford to take any chances. Well, she's up at the shops now … Yeah, I did try the gas trick but she'd got a minder in the house and he wouldn't let me in. Some retired colonel type. Threatened to ring the police. Don't know if he will, but he looks the sort that might. So we'll forget the gas. I've got the Saab with me today. She's in the caff. Broad pavements, double yellow lines. I can knock her over easy peasy, especially in this weather when they're all keeping their heads down …'

Chloe brought Ellie a coffee which she didn't really want after all the coffee she'd been drinking that day. She tried to lift the cup to her lips and found her hand was shaking so much that she had to put it down again. She clenched her teeth, trying to still the shivers.

She'd been through too much lately, that was the trouble. Any little thing set her weeping like a baby. Not that she was going to weep now. No. She sniffed, found a hankie and blew her nose. No. The woman who had outfaced Mr Jolley and retrieved Diana's set of keys, was not one to be overthrown by the shakes.

Definitely not.

She would just sit there till she felt better. When John came they would have lunch together, and then she would think about what she ought to do next.

She wouldn't be able to ring Diana till the evening. She had a horrid feeling that Diana and Stewart might have got themselves into debt by moving into that big house. Especially since Diana had only been able to get a part-time job. Perhaps she ought to help them out. Perhaps it had been mean of her not to pay the estate agent's expense bill.

But no. Diana ought not to have done it. Not any of it. She ought not to have chosen such a big house when her father had only given her enough for them to afford the mortgage on a smaller one. Diana ought not to have been greedy.

Well … she had always been a greedy child, wanting more than her fair share of whatever was going. Perhaps it was time for her to face up to the realities of life. Buying what you can't pay for equals misery. See Mr Micawber.

But she could afford to bail them out.

Would that be a good idea? Considering how Diana had just tried to bully her into a move she didn't want? Ellie supposed Diana's idea was that selling the house and having her mother move into a rented flat would release a lump of capital, which Ellie could easily be persuaded to pass over to her daughter. Or half of it, at any rate.

Ellie sighed. No, it wouldn't be a good idea to bail Diana out. It was never a good idea to give in to bullying. Or emotional blackmail. Diana would just go on and on and …

Well, what would Frank have done?

Frank had been furious with Diana buying that big house. He had made it clear in his will that he didn't want her to have any more of his money for the time being. He was, of course, old-fashioned in some ways. But very sound.

John swept through the door of the café, shaking out his umbrella. 'I don't know which is worse, the snow or the slush or the rain!'

He kissed Ellie's cheek and, rubbing cold hands together, sat down beside her. He looked, she thought, like a knight of old, having vanquished dragons for the sake of his fair lady.

'Dear John, what will you have? Chloe recommends the beef stew. She says, "It's called some foreign name on the menu, but that is what it is." Complete with dumplings. I can't remember when I last had dumplings, but it's certainly the weather for it.'

'Two beef stews it is, then,' said John. He drew his chair up closer to Ellie. 'I rang the gas board and they said they hadn't had any leak reported in our area. What's more, they don't employ a man answering to his description. They said we should phone the police, so I did. The police said they'd want to speak to you about it, too, because you saw the man yesterday and someone less clued up might easily let the man in. I dread to think what might happen next. At the least, some old age pensioner might lose their savings.'

'I have to call in at the incident room, anyway,' said Ellie, leaning back for Chloe to lay the table.

Chloe was wearing a bright green streak in her hair today, with matching emerald T-shirt under a black blouse. Jeans, of course. Colourful.

Chloe said, 'Excuse me, but did you say you wanted to talk to the police? If you wait a bit, my boyfriend will be in about two and he could maybe fix it for you, whatever it is.'

Ellie's mind swivelled back to the face of the man she'd seen beside Chloe at church the day before. 'He's a policeman at the local station?'

'Just joined recently,' said Chloe complacently. 'He's not as thick as he looks, but he's got a long way to go yet, so if you've got something that he can deal with … it'll give him some brownie points and save you a trip to the nick. Anything to drink today?'

'Tea please, later.'

Chloe removed herself.

'She's got something there,' said Ellie to John. 'The incident room gives me the horrors. I suppose it's the contrast between knowing what usually goes on in the church hall, and what's there now.'

'Pictures of Enid Blyton's Noddy on the wall, looking down on real-life policemen?'

'I'd forgotten how terribly shabby it is in there. No wonder the vicar wants to rebuild. As for the police, they all treat me as if I'm just a silly woman reporting a missing cat.'

'I didn't know you had a cat.'

'I might get one just to be able to report it missing, and cause them maximum aggro.'

John laughed. 'Bravo, Ellie. Don't let them grind you down.'

'No way!' said Ellie, smiling. 'John, I really appreciate what you did this morning. I made Mr Jolley eat his words and I got my keys back. Now I suppose I have to face Diana with what she's done.' And wasn't that a depressing thought!

Chloe brought two steaming platefuls of rich, spicy stew with dumplings, carrots and mashed potatoes. John almost crowed with delight. 'Wait till I tell my wife about this. Although she'll probably say it's bad for my cholesterol.'

'I have come to the conclusion,' said Ellie, speaking through a mouthful of dumpling soaked in gravy, 'that every now and then we ought deliberately to try something new and possibly risky. Just to keep our minds bright.'

'As if you needed it!'

'Oh, I do. Or rather, I did. You've no idea what a scared little mouse I am, really.'

'It doesn't show.'

'John, you are sweet. Of course it showed. Why else did I let other people dictate the course of my life for me?'

'You did?'

'Yes. I did.' She thought, John is a sweet old so-and-so, but he hasn't a clue what I'm on about. She also thought, I'm eating this too quickly. I'll get indigestion. But I don't care.

John put his knife and fork together on his empty plate. Really, he'd eaten that even faster than her! Just like a Hoover.

'Ellie, we do need to talk. Last Friday, when we heard that there'd been a fire in your road and that you'd been taken off to hospital, Madam said she was going round to see you when you came out. Rose and I suggested getting some flowers for you. Madam said we could do what we liked, but she didn't think it appropriate seeing how little you'd been contributing to the running of the shop these last few weeks.

'So there was a bit of a bust-up. Donna and Anita for once were in agreement with one another. Rose cried. We had to shut the shop up at lunchtime, there was such an uproar. On a Friday, too. People were banging on the door, wanting to come in. But once you start winding up people like Madam, well … things were said. Anita, in particular. You know how rude she can be when she tries. She told Madam that the only person who didn't pull her weight was Madam herself. She said everyone wanted Madam out and …'

Ellie put her hand over John's. 'I get the picture. Madam couldn't face the idea that I might be more popular than her in the shop, and so she took the opportunity to get rid of me. Well, I admit I was upset at the time, but now—'

'Hear me out. When she told us on Saturday that you weren't coming back, Anita left, and so did Rose. Madam was livid. Apparently she'd lined up some old friend of hers to take your place, but she hadn't counted on two others leaving. I told her straight, "Get Ellie back, or you'll have no one left to staff the shop." And that included me!'

'Dear John, that's awful. You can't go. As for me, I've been thinking hard about the shop all weekend and I honestly do feel that Madam is right. I haven't been pulling my weight recently and at the moment I haven't the slightest desire to come back. Oh, I know what you'll say. That I'm suffering from false pride and yes, the way she sacked me did hurt, but in a way it's a relief. One less thing to think about. There's so much going on, I have so many adjustments to make … heavens above! I forgot! My new bed is being delivered this afternoon and I must be there to let the men in! Oh dear, and I was going to indulge myself with a dessert, too! Never mind. Another day. Chloe dear, can I have the bill? And if your young man could see his way to calling on me, I'd be grateful. What's his name, by the way?'

'Bob,' said Chloe, busily writing out the bill and taking money. 'I've known him on and off all my life. Didn't think of him that way at first, he's older, you see, been around a bit. But he fixed on me and kept coming back and back at me, asking me out. So I said I would if he got himself a decent job and now he's really keen on it, wants to do all these courses and that. I'm not so happy about his being with the police, myself. There's a lot of violence out there, isn't there? But I can't go back on my word, can I? And I quite like him, you know, that way …'

Ellie and John exchanged fleeting glances, trying not to laugh. Then Ellie did a double-take. 'Chloe, he's not Ferdy's schoolfriend Bob, is he? The one that used to go out with Joyce McNally?'

'S'right. And others. Chasing butterflies, he called it. He can be quite poetic when he likes. Surprised me that, him being so soft inside. Mind you, it's easier for a woman if the man is a bit soft inside … so long as nobody else knows about it.'

Ellie tried to unravel this. 'Now you two were in church yesterday because he wants to put up the banns, or because he wanted to see where his friend had been killed?'

Chloe looked horrified. 'Banns? Over my dead body. All that sort of thing went out with my mother's generation.

No, he had some idea about soaking up the atmosphere. Been reading too much detective fiction, if you ask me. Said the murderer might be in church and show some guilty feeling.'

She shrugged. 'Load of baloney, I thought. What he really meant was that he was really upset over Ferdy, couldn't get it out of his mind. Well, it's been on my mind too. A lot. So he said we both needed to go. Make our peace, sort of. He said he'd seen photos and all, but he wanted to see it properly. Ferdy was part of our lives for so long. I understood.'

'Wait a minute. Have I got this right? Did you go out with Ferdy too, at one time?'

'Sure. Who didn't? But not serious like, just in passing, doing my butterfly bit, you could say. Then Ferdy introduced me to Bob one night in the pub and as I said, he got a fix on me, and didn't let me alone till I said I'd go out with him.'

John was curious. 'You see him as husband material?'

Chloe laughed. 'I'm not thinking along those lines for quite a few years. Mrs Quicke, if you've got to go I'll tell him to call round, but it might be after he comes off shift. They're going mad, trying to find that Kate that ran off after the murder. They've got people watching the airports and the stations and Eurostar and everything, but there's been no sign of her yet. Of course, it's only a matter of time till the money runs out and they'll get her in the end.'

'Oh dear,' said Ellie, gathering her things together. 'I'm getting into deep waters. I'm going to have to confess all, I can see it. Don't look so shocked, John. I don't mean that I'm involved, but … well, I'll explain later.'

Putting up her umbrella against the rain which was still pelting down, she hovered on the kerb, wondering if she had time to pop over to the bakery to get some fresh bread, or whether she really ought to get straight back home … and was just going to cross when someone hailed her from under an umbrella which had certainly seen better days.

'Ellie! Oh, look out!'

Ellie stepped back just as a big dark-green car came slashing through the traffic and drove across the pavement exactly where she had been standing … spraying Ellie with surface water … and then roared off down the Avenue.

Ellie screamed. It wasn't a very big scream, but she had been badly frightened.

'What did he think he was doing!' demanded Rose McNally, looking out from under her umbrella exactly like the dormouse from under the teapot lid. 'You could have been killed!'

Ellie told herself to calm down. 'He was probably on his mobile phone, and didn't see how close to the kerb he was. Thanks for warning me, Rose. I was just about to step off into the road. He came from nowhere! Did you get his number? We ought to report him.'

'I'd know that car anywhere, because my Joyce's boss has one just like it. It's one of them German makes. A Saab, that's it. But the licence plate was all muddy, so that's no help. Are you really all right, Ellie?'

'Wet through. I'll have to change everything when I get back home.'

'Oh, I was hoping … but I won't keep you, then.' Rose was obviously dying to talk.

'Look, Rose, I've got something being delivered this afternoon. Are you free? Would you like to drop round later? The only thing is, I've no fresh bread, and I'm late already. You couldn't possibly get me a loaf of bread, a bloomer, not sliced white, and some cakes? Bring them round to my place and we can have a good long chat together?'

Rose lit up with relief. 'Love to. My treat.'

'No, mine.' Ellie thrust some coins into Rose's hand and, cursing the wet coat which clung around her legs, made her way home as fast as she could. Hoping that the delivery men had not yet called … and that Mr Jolley had removed his For Sale sign.

Only to find a taxi parked outside her gate, with the meter ticking over. Aunt Drusilla, as large as life, and twice as threatening.

'Oh, there you are, Ellie. I've been waiting for you for ages. Will you pay the man, please? I can't possibly afford the extortionate amount he wishes to charge.'

The errand boy was on the phone, shaking with fury. 'Yeah, some old bint just pulled her out of the way just as I was driving straight at her. As close as that! Nah, she didn't see nothing, what with the rain, and anyways, the number plate's been properly muddied. She's back home now. Another visitor, arrived in a taxi. Looks like the same old cow who came the other night. What would you like me to do now?'

15

Out of habit Ellie reached for her purse to pay Aunt Drusilla's taxi fare and realized that she had only a few coins left. She hadn't been to the bank for ages. She'd shopped almost daily, paid for her lunch and John's, and given her last few pound coins to Rose.

Aunt Drusilla was getting out of the taxi in anticipation that the slave would do as she was told, as usual. Upright, bony, Weatheralled, unfurling a closely wrapped man's black umbrella, and supporting herself with a silver-knobbed cane which could occasionally be used to rap knuckles with. An outsize and ancient handbag of crocodile skin which from experience Ellie knew contained everything bar the kitchen sink – and cash.

'I'm so sorry, Aunt Drusilla,' said Ellie, trying to look sorry while concealing a desire to giggle. 'I don't seem to have any money on me.'

Aunt Drusilla didn't like being kept waiting in the rain. She was also astounded to hear Ellie declare she had no money. 'Then how do you expect the man to be paid?'

'Perhaps you'd better ask him to drive you round to the bank, so that you can draw some money out to pay him?'

'Now look 'ere!' The burly driver was not amused.

Neither was Aunt Drusilla. 'Ellie, I cannot believe that you have no money. Hurry up, I'm getting wet!'

Ellie pulled out her purse and wallet and showed their state of play. Aunt Drusilla was affronted. She started down the path to the house, ignoring the taxi. 'Then fetch some from indoors.'

'We don't keep cash in the house.'

'Yes, you do. In the bureau.'

Ellie smiled, grimly. 'We used to when Frank was alive, but there's none there now. I'm afraid you will just have to find some cash yourself.'

Aunt Drusilla reached the porch and shook out her umbrella. She pushed at the front door, which of course failed to open. With hands shaking from fury, she delved into her bag, extracted some money and gestured to Ellie to take it to the taxi driver.

'Don't give him a tip. He's an exceedingly rude man!'

Ellie and the taxi driver exchanged rueful glances. The amount on the clock was very nearly the whole of the ten-pound note. 'Sorry,' said Ellie. 'I really haven't any money today.'

Resignedly, he drove off as the furniture van drove up with Ellie's new bed in it. Letting Aunt Drusilla into the house, Ellie supervised the delivery of her new bed and bedding, and the removal of the old one. Her bedroom looked surprisingly spacious now but the carpet was a much stronger colour where the old bed had covered it. Perhaps she should be daring and get a new carpet, too. And new curtains while she was at it? What luxury!

She saw the delivery men off and found Aunt Drusilla sitting upright on a chair in the hall.

'Well, help me off with my coat!' Ellie did so, realizing

her own clothes were clinging to her in a most unpleasant manner.

Ellie ushered Aunt Drusilla into the living-room saying, 'Excuse me a moment. I'm wet through. Make yourself a cup of tea if you like.'

She stripped, rubbed herself dry and got into warm, clean, comfortable clothes. Bliss. And Rose would soon be here with cakes for tea. Ellie hoped they'd be cream cakes, the ultimate extravagance on a wet afternoon. Or perhaps pikelets. Or tea-cakes which they could toast and slather with butter.

In the meantime, she had to face Nemesis. Or Aunt Drusilla. And try to work out some way to help poor Nora get a new lease on her flat. Oh dear. Was there really a tie-up with Diana? If so, had Aunt Drusilla been behind Diana's putting the house on the market?

Looking out of the front window, she saw that the For Sale sign had been removed. Well, that was something. Now to face the music.

'About time, too!' Aunt Drusilla believed in attack. 'Forcing me to come out in this terrible weather, at my age … and then refusing to pay the taxi fare. What would poor dear Frank have said?'

The phone rang. Ellie ducked back into the hall to answer it.

Kate, speaking low. 'Ellie …? Is that you?'

Ellie tried to push the door into the living-room shut with her foot, but it was just too far to reach, and Aunt Drusilla had ears like a bat.

'Yes, it's me. Were you trying to ring before? I've been out so much, and now I'm inundated with visitors …'

'You can't talk freely? You're not alone?'

'That's right. How are you?'

'I'm fine. Bored with doing nothing, eating three meals a day, looking at telly. Missing work. And Armand. How is he?'

'Missing you, too. Asking for news. Naturally.'

'Is he very angry? I miss him terribly. Is there any news about who killed Ferdy? I keep going over and over it in my mind, but you know I really didn't see anything that night, either before or after I spoke to him. The police don't seem to believe me, but ... shall I come back?'

'*No!* I mean, not yet. The police are watching all the ports, Eurostar, everywhere. They're very one-track, aren't they? Do you remember Chloe at the café? She's got a new boyfriend and guess who, it's your old friend Bob. Would you believe, he's a policeman now! He's supposed to be coming round to see me later today. We've had a conman going round, pretending to be from the gas board, and I have to register a complaint.'

Aunt Drusilla had come to stand at Ellie's elbow, pale eyes sparking with annoyance at the way Ellie was ignoring her. Could she perhaps overhear what was being said on the phone?

Ellie said hurriedly, 'Bye, dear. I must go. Got a visitor, as I said. Ring again soon, won't you? I want to hear all about your holiday.'

She put the phone down.

'I really don't know how you can waste time gossiping with friends when you have a guest!' observed Aunt Drusilla. 'Now I should like some tea, please. I could fancy a couple of your chocolate biscuits, too.'

'No biscuits, I'm afraid,' said Ellie, automatically falling into servant mode as she put the kettle on and laid a tray for tea. 'Someone's bringing some cakes in later on, though.'

'Can't you get them to bring them in now?'

'Afraid not.'

'Well!' Aunt Drusilla stalked back to the living-room. Ellie raised her eyes to the ceiling and counted five. Aunt Drusilla never, ever came to tea without making derogatory remarks about something Ellie had done, or not done. She waited for it.

'You haven't dusted today.' Aunt Drusilla held up a dirty finger and wiped it on her handkerchief.

'Sorry,' said Ellie. 'Been busy.' And bit her lip, thinking that she ought not to have apologized.

'Have you indeed!' said Aunt Drusilla, in tones of suspicion. 'I thought you were going back up north with Diana. You're certainly needed up there. Poor Diana was in quite a state the other night when I called to see you. I understand the house is up for sale. Very sensible. But that's not what I came to talk to you about.'

Aunt Drusilla smiled. Smiling was difficult for her, and often terrified the beholder. Ellie quailed.

Aunt Drusilla tapped her handbag. 'I do realize, Ellie, that you had nothing to do with that most extraordinary will of Frank's. I admit that at first I thought you might have done, but Mr Weatherspoon assures me that this was not the case. There is only one conclusion that I can come to and that is that Frank's illness affected his mind. He simply could not have made that will if he had been in his right mind. It has always been understood that the house which has been my home practically all my life, the house in which I was born and in which I intend to die, should be mine for life. There is no way that Frank would not have left it to me, if he had been in his right mind.'

'Mr Weatherspoon insists Frank knew what he was doing.' Ellie hated herself for sounding so apologetic, but years of kowtowing to Aunt Drusilla had taken their toll. She said, 'I think it was something to do with the riverside flats you own.'

Aunt Drusilla gave Ellie a sharp look. 'I? Own flats? Nonsense.'

'Not according to the enquiry agents' report.' Ellie was bluffing, but it seemed her guess had been correct.

Silence. Aunt Drusilla stared into space. Ellie poured more tea for herself, but didn't drink it. She wondered where Rose had got to. Come on, Rose! Rescue me!

Aunt Drusilla inched forward on her chair. 'I shall contest the will, of course.'

'Then I shall put the family house on the market.'

A sharp intake of breath. 'Not even you could be so callous!'

'Talking of callous … why don't you allow Nora to renew her lease at a reasonable rent?'

'That remark merely proves how ignorant you are of business affairs.'

'And how accomplished a businesswoman are you? Well, perhaps I didn't know much about these things, but I'm learning fast.' Ellie was amazed how easy it was to stand up to the old terror, once she'd started. 'Frank's will is sound. He left his estate as he did because he felt you – and Diana – had been greedy. If you fight the will, then I will put your house on the market.'

Aunt Drusilla looked incandescent with rage. Ellie was reminded of Armand's similar, but uncontrolled rage. How calm life used to be, she thought. What a whirlwind I'm living in now …

Aunt Drusilla jerked her head back. 'And if I don't contest the will, you leave things as they are?'

Ellie leaned back in her chair and steepled her fingers. She must be careful not to assume that she'd won, but it certainly felt like it. 'I might. I might not. I might ask you to buy the family house from me. Or I might want to live in it myself. I haven't decided yet.'

'You? Live in my house? How dare you!'

Now she's going to turn on me, Ellie thought, berate me for a failure as wife and mother, tell me I am worthless, et cetera, et cetera. Perhaps she's right, Ellie thought, numbly. Perhaps I am being selfish and lacking in respect for the older generation … for her.

The doorbell rang. Rose, thank goodness.

Ellie got to her feet. 'I must ask you to go now. I have another visitor.'

'Get rid of her. We haven't finished this conversation, not by a long chalk.'

'My visitor might be a "he".'

'What? You dare to stand there, with Frank only just in his grave …'

'… cremated …'

'… and tell me that you are entertaining someone of the opposite sex …'

'Either a policeman. Or someone from the charity shop. Or both. Which would you prefer?'

'You are getting above yourself, my girl! I've never been so insulted in all my life! If my poor dear Frank were here …'

'But he isn't!' Ellie spoke more sharply than she had intended. She felt angry and tearful. She ushered Aunt Drusilla out into the hall, and handed her coat to her while opening the front door.

Rose McNally stood on the doorstep, under an umbrella which seemed to have broken a spoke since they last met.

'Come in!' Ellie threw the door wide. 'Miss Quicke is just leaving!'

Flustered though she might be, Aunt Drusilla was not beaten. 'We will continue this conversation later, when you are less overwrought. I can assure you that I shall not give way to your crude blackmailing tactics. There is no way that I can allow you to dispossess me of what is rightly mine. Now, will you please call me a taxi!'

Rose's mouth had fallen open. Aunt Drusilla's ravings would be all round the neighbourhood by nightfall.

Ellie considered letting the old bat walk. It was only the other side of the Avenue, after all. Then she thought that really would be mean of her, so she gestured to Rose to come in and remove her coat while she rang for a taxi. And as she did so, the doorbell went again. This time it was Chloe from the café, with her stolid-looking young policeman friend, Bob. Ellie invited them in, too, took their coats and ushered them into the living-room.

Rose had shed her coat and umbrella but hovered in the hall, still clutching several interesting-looking boxes from the bakery. 'You won't want me to stay, if you have guests.'

'Oh, but I do,' said Ellie, smiling at her. 'Do stay. The others won't be long, and then we can have a really good chat together.'

Aunt Drusilla was furious. 'Do you actually propose to leave me here in your hall like a servant, while you entertain these people?' It was clear she had placed all three of 'these people' in the slave class.

'Of course not,' said Ellie, with a smile. She had had more than enough of Aunt Drusilla. 'Of course you'd prefer to wait for your taxi outside.' She opened the door wide and ushered Aunt Drusilla out on to the porch. She rather hoped that the taxi driver who responded to the call might be the one who was refused a tip by Aunt Drusilla earlier.

'Cup of tea, everyone? In a minute, perhaps?' She smiled at the others' startled faces. 'Rose, let's put the shopping on the kitchen table and your umbrella in the sink. There. Now come and join us, there's a dear.'

Her visitors all looked uncomfortable as Ellie went around putting on side lamps and drawing the curtains. Rose hovered, hardly daring to sit on the edge of the seat of an upright chair. Ellie stifled impatience. Rose was a timid soul who always wanted to fade into the background, but had the irritating knack of becoming more visible in proportion to her wish not to intrude.

Chloe said, 'Oh, Mrs Quicke, I hope you don't mind my coming with Bob, but we're going out for the evening afterwards.' She sounded aggressive. Ellie wondered why. Did policemen usually take their girls on police business?

'Of course not, dear,' said Ellie.

Chloe threw herself back on to the settee, watching her boyfriend the while. Ellie identified tension between them, and was put on her guard.

Bob seemed very sure of himself, sitting with knees apart and beefy features set in stone, the very picture of a small-minded policeman about to book an old lady for inadvertently parking with one wheel on the pavement. Ellie was not sure she liked him.

But she did like Chloe, so she said, 'Well, this is a nice surprise. Are you sure no one would like a cup of tea?'

Bob produced a notebook and pen and squared his elbows. His attitude proclaimed that he was still very much on duty.

Chloe said, almost sulkily, 'Mrs Quicke, when I told Bob you had some business at the station, all I was thinking was that he could save you a journey. But now he's started to go on about people withholding information—'

'Let me do the talking, if you please,' said Bob. Ellie wondered if he were just showing off in front of Chloe by playing the heavy policeman, or if he were naturally heavy. 'Mrs Quicke, may I have a word in private?'

'Well, no,' said Ellie. 'I really don't see the need. What I have to tell you is not private in any way.'

'Are you sure about that?'

'Yes, perfectly,' said Ellie, perplexed. 'In fact, the more people who know about it, the better.'

'You want the matter cleared up as soon as possible, then? You're prepared to co-operate now?'

'But of course. I don't understand. It's really quite trivial. No harm was done.'

'You regard murder as trivial?'

'Murder? No, of course not. But I assure you, the man did not gain entry to my house, and nothing has been stolen.'

Rose and Chloe were turning their heads first this way and then that, as if they were watching a tennis match.

Bob pushed himself further forward in his chair. Frank's chair. He was a large man, and more than filled it. He said, 'Who mentioned theft?'

Ellie was bewildered. 'I did. Wasn't that what the man was after?'

'I don't know what you are talking about, Mrs Quicke. I'm referring to the knowledge you've been withholding about the murder of Ferdy Hanna.'

'What?' Ellie changed colour. She glanced at Chloe, who was looking up at the ceiling, divorcing herself from the conversation. Rose gave a little whimper of excitement. Ellie drew back in her seat, and folded her hands before her.

'I'm so sorry. We seem to have been talking at cross purposes. I intended going to the station to report an attempted crime. A man presented himself twice at my door and tried to gain entry to the house, saying that he had to investigate a reported gas leak. He had a half-smoked cigarette butt behind his ear and I thought his manner suspicious. The second time he came, a neighbour was here and challenged the man's credentials. This neighbour subsequently rang the gas board and discovered that they had no such man working in this area, and no gas leak had been reported. We are always being warned to check on IDs and to report anything suspicious. So he reported it, and now I am reporting it, too, formally.

'You'll need a description of the man. He was taller than me, about five ten, bony rather than thin, about forty years old, sandy-ish hair, wearing blue overalls under a denim jacket, carrying a black holdall. He had some kind of photo ID dangling from his overall bib, but I couldn't see that properly. I think that's all I can tell you.'

Bob hadn't taken down a word of this, but sat with pen suspended over his notebook, stolidly waiting until she had finished.

'So let's talk about the murder.'

Ellie gestured helplessly. 'I don't know anything about the murder.'

'Yet you say you were standing at the window, looking out over the churchyard, when it happened.'

'I believe I may have been. But as I explained to Inspector Clay …'

'Explain it to me … if you can.' His tone was menacing.

Ellie opened her eyes wider. 'Why should I have to go on repeating myself all the time? I explained to Inspector Clay that I was on medication at the time. I cried a lot. I wasn't really aware of anything that went on around me. Yes, I probably was standing at the window looking out at the time, but I don't remember seeing anything odd until Kate came rushing down from the church and dashed along the alley.'

'Ah. Yes. Now we come to it. We have your statement to that effect. Do you wish to alter it in any way now?'

'No. Why should I?'

'Perhaps because you really saw a little more than you said you did …'

Ellie understood that she was meant to be flustered by Bob's methods. Instead, she felt amused. Almost. If she hadn't been through so much that day already, she might well have been alarmed. Instead, she just felt annoyed, and rather tired.

She turned off the main light and one of the side lamps, drew back the curtains overlooking the garden and the church and beckoned Bob to join her at the window. The lights were on around the church and in the alley. The side lamp in the living-room was reflected in the window, but Ellie could clearly see what was happening around the church. 'It was about this time of day. Now you can see what I saw,' she said. 'No more, and no less. Satisfied?'

For the first time she felt … exposed, standing there and looking out over the garden. She drew the curtains to, with a shiver. It was cold out there. She hastened to put the main light on again. Should she turn the central heating up a notch?

'No, I am not satisfied,' said Bob. A stubborn man.

Chloe made a sudden movement. She dropped her eyes from the ceiling to meet Ellie's glance and shrugged, conveying that she wanted no part of what was going on. Of course Chloe had known Ellie for many years. She knew Ellie wouldn't lie. Possibly she had already given Bob the benefit of her opinion on the subject, and he had rejected it.

Rose was crouched down in her chair, frightened eyes darting from Bob to Ellie and back again. More grist to the gossip mill …

Ellie looked straight at Bob. 'You're a bit of a bully, aren't you? If I saw anything else, it didn't register. Believe me, if I could help, I would. I liked Mrs Hanna, and was sorry for her.'

'So you say. But you helped the murderess to escape, didn't you?'

Ellie felt short of breath. He was threatening her! And she did feel threatened. She thought of calling for help. She could terminate this interview by ringing Bill Weatherspoon for guidance. Or she could face the music herself.

'If you are referring to Kate,' she said, slowly, 'then no, I did not help her to escape, as you put it. And before you ask, I do not know where she is, and I do not know how to contact her. Let me also go on record as saying that I do not believe she killed Ferdy.'

Bob barked out a laugh. 'How can you be so blinkered? If she didn't kill him then why did she run away? Why has she cleared out her current account and gone into hiding when any innocent person would have stayed around to help with enquiries?'

Ellie thought, I must not let him rile me, because that's what he wants. I must be calm and reasonable, even if I feel like having hysterics. She said, 'Kate ran away because someone tried to kill her by blowing up her car.'

'She staged that "accident", to give herself an alibi.'

'Nonsense! She was as shocked as I was!'

He sneered. 'Face it. She conned you. We have reason to believe that you sheltered her after the explosion and helped her escape. Also, that you are still in touch with her.'

'It sounds to me as if Armand has been making wild accusations again. He's a jealous, perhaps unbalanced man.'

Bob shifted his legs further apart, leaning forward even more. 'All right. Let's look at it another way. We think she killed Ferdy and one of his friends then tried to get even by blowing up her car …'

A slight hiss escaped Chloe. Ellie wanted to say, 'Well, you were one of his oldest associates. Did you blow him up?' She refrained with an effort. She said, 'I suppose that is possible. Have you investigated his circle of friends yourselves?'

'Yes.' Stolidly. 'It led nowhere. So why do you think her car was blown up?'

'It couldn't have been an accident?'

'No, it couldn't. So who did it, Ellie?'

She did not care for his use of her first name. She supposed he did it to throw her off balance. Maybe he would make an effective policeman, some day. She said, 'I really don't know. At first I thought Ferdy must have got mixed up with some drug people …'

'No way. I can vouch for that.'

'… then I thought it might be Armand …'

'The husband? Don't make me laugh.'

'… but I think now it must be something to do with his car sales. A dissatisfied customer, a sudden quarrel that blew up out of all proportion? A blow struck in haste that wasn't meant to kill, but did? I wondered about his cars …'

'His van was found in a lane twenty miles away. Burned out. No fingerprints possible.'

'Ah. Well, what about the other cars he was working on by the church? They've been disappearing at intervals, haven't they?'

This was clearly news to Bob. 'What makes you say that?'

'The vicar told me they'd been disappearing. Somebody's pinching them, don't you think? Maybe he had a quarrel with one of his latest ex-girlfriend's new boyfriends …'

She gave Bob an innocent-seeming look. Chloe smiled slightly.

Bob reddened. 'If you continue to refuse to co-operate, then I must ask you to accompany me down to the station.'

Ellie felt her heartbeat quicken. 'Have you a warrant? No? Then I fear I must refuse. I've told you all I know. Go away and do something useful for a change.'

Is this really me, she thought, telling this man off?

Bob's face went lopsided and ugly. His high colour did not fade. He put his notebook and pen away and thrust himself off the chair. 'Come on, Chloe!'

Chloe looked away. 'You go. Mrs Quicke was so kind as to offer us a cup of tea earlier. I sure could do with one now.' She sounded as if she were suppressing tears. It looked as if his bullying tactics had put an end to their romance.

Bob was appalled. He obviously had no idea how he'd alienated his beloved. He said, 'But …!' He looked furious. 'Well, I'll pick you up later at your place, right?'

'No, thank you,' said Chloe, in a muffled tone.

Ellie pushed herself upright. 'I'll show you out, then.' She ushered him out into the rain, and carefully didn't quite bang the door after him.

'Wow,' she said. 'Next, let's have some tea, and see what goodies Rose has brought us to eat.'

Chloe and Rose followed her into the kitchen.

'What can we do to help?' said Chloe, blowing her nose on a piece of kitchen towel.

'Wouldn't you like me to go now?' said Rose, opening cake boxes to display a tempting array of eclairs, doughnuts and frangipani tarts.

'Bless you both, no,' said Ellie. 'It's been a perfectly horrid day so far, so let's indulge ourselves, shall we?'

Chloe said, somewhat indistinctly, 'I'm sorry I brought him. I'd no idea he was like that. When he said he was going to see you, to question you, he sounded so grim that I got cold feet and thought I'd better come along, too. I wish I'd never said anything to him in the first place. As if you could possibly have sheltered a murderer … What a nerd! I won't be seeing him again, I can tell you!'

Ellie patted her arm. 'He was just doing his duty, I suppose.'

'What dreadful manners …' twittered Rose.

Ellie grinned. 'Yes, if he hadn't been so pushy, I might have shared a couple of thoughts with him. So, ladies, perhaps we three could put our heads together after tea, instead?'

16

The errand boy's eyes crossed with resentment at the telling-off he was getting down the phone. He'd failed again. He was worse than useless. Interspersed with a good many words of Anglo-Saxon origin. And he had to take it in silence. He ground his teeth, took out a cigarette, lit it, puffed, stubbed it out on the dashboard.

He didn't need telling that every day they were letting big money slip through their fingers. You-know-who was ready to move as soon as she gave the word. The territory was wide open, the stock had been moved into the derelict house, and Ferdy's best car was in the garage – a vintage Bentley which would fetch a nice penny. As for the Mondeo, he knew a man at the pub who'd buy it off him, no questions asked.

One frail woman stood between each of them and a fortune.

The errand boy said, 'Look, I'll stage a burglary tonight. Break in. Bash her head in before she knows what's what. Yeah, I know she'll be on her guard, but she's gotta sleep, ain't she? … Yeah, I know she throws the bolts back and front, but her French windows is flimsy. A coupla kicks on the side of the hinges, a quick wrench with the tyre lever and I'll be in, no problem. I do the job, take the telly and video and stuff to make it look like a burglary, and that's it. Just another interrupted burglary gone wrong.'

He switched his mobile off, sweating. This job was getting to him. He'd better find a stocking or a child's mask to wear tonight.

Ellie, Chloe and Rose drew their chairs close to the electric fire. The wind was sweeping hard pellets of rain against the windows and screeching down the chimney. It was no night to be out on the streets. They'd eaten all the cakes and downed two big pots of tea. Chloe was sprawling across her chair, showing an extraordinary amount of denimed leg. Rose was flushed, a little giggly.

Ellie leaned back in her chair and then pulled herself upright. If she wasn't careful, she would drift off to sleep.

She said, 'Well, ladies, shall we hold a council of war? I really do not know who killed Ferdy, though believe me, it wasn't Kate. I think it must have been some business associate of his – something to do with the car business. Joyce said something about Ferdy being made an offer for the business. Maybe it's something to do with that. Or more probably it was a dissatisfied customer. I do feel the police are the best people to solve his murder, but there is another little mystery which I think we may be able to solve between us. The supposed abduction and murder of Mrs Hanna.'

Chloe gaped. 'Supposed? Didn't they find her body in the park?'

Rose said, 'No dear. That was some poor woman from the loony bin. Mrs Hanna's still missing.'

Ellie nodded. As usual Rose's information was accurate. 'I think the three of us ought to be able to work out how she went, and where. Rose, do you remember telling me about Mrs Hanna coming into the shop just after the murder with her little dog under her arm, causing all sorts of upsets to the staff?'

'Do I! Anita and Donna had quite a set-to about it. And then that child broke a teapot and—'

Ellie interrupted. 'I must have seen her with her dog, I suppose, but I can't for the life of me remember what kind it was.'

'One of those nasty little hairy things. Not a Mexican chiwi-something, but not much bigger.'

Chloe said, 'She had a Westie. She was always parading up and down the shops with it under her arm. It used to wriggle, wanting to get down and get in people's way. She used to bring it into the café and feed it titbits on her day off. Ugh! She would have killed it with overfeeding if it weren't for Dagmara taking it out and exercising it every day when she – Mrs Hanna, that is – was working at the bakery.'

'Who's Dagmara?'

'Dagmara Pri-something. I don't know how she spells it. Everyone calls her Dagmara. You know her! Polish. Cleans for us at the café, does a couple of offices down the road and some of the shops, too, after hours. Big woman, dyed blonde hair. Lives in the same block of flats as Mrs Hanna.'

Rose nodded. 'I know her. She comes into the shop, size twenty-two, bright colours. But she never brought a dog into the shop that I remember.'

Ellie said, 'The thing is, Mrs Hanna may have overfed the dog but she loved it, didn't she? She made proper arrangements for it to be looked after when she was working. Now there was no sign of the dog in the flat when the police went in, but I could smell it, and I heard a dog yapping somewhere nearby. Have you seen Mrs Hanna's Westie around since she left?'

Chloe nodded. 'Sure. With Dagmara at the bus stop. She had the Westie on a lead and it was wearing a cute little tartan coat.' Chloe frowned. 'That's odd. How come Dagmara is looking after Mrs Hanna's dog, unless ...?'

'Unless Mrs Hanna asked her to?' said Ellie. 'The question is, when did Dagmara remove the Westie from Mrs Hanna's flat?'

Chloe said, 'Dagmara must have a key to Mrs Hanna's flat because she took the Westie out every day Mrs Hanna was working, including Saturdays.'

Rose twiddled her fingers in the air. 'Mrs Hanna didn't go to work the Saturday after Ferdy was killed. They were ever so cross about it in the bakery, I remember.'

'So let's suppose that on Saturday as usual Dagmara went upstairs to fetch the Westie for its morning walk. I think there was a note on the kitchen table with a bag full of dog food, feeding bowls and so on. I think the note was addressed to Dagmara, asking her to look after the dog for a while.'

Chloe and Rose looked perplexed.

Ellie explained. 'There were no feeding bowls left out for him, clean or dirty. On the draining board was an empty, washed tin of dog food. An untouched tin of dog food had rolled under the table. I thought at first Mrs Hanna had taken the dog with her, but you say that he's been seen around since.'

Chloe shook her head to clear it. 'But ... that means she made proper preparations for going away.'

'What's more, the fridge had been emptied of all perishable stuff and there was no sign of any of that, either. Plus, a tea towel had been thrown over the door of the fridge to keep the door slightly open.'

Both women looked thoughtful. Chloe said, 'That's what my mother does before we go away on holiday. She cleans out the fridge, gives any perishables to a neighbour, and lets her have a key to make sure everything's all right while we're away.'

Rose said, 'But everyone says there were signs of a terrible struggle, furniture overthrown, drawers pulled out and everything. She must have been abducted!'

Chloe was incredulous. 'After cleaning out the fridge and making sure the dog was going to be looked after?'

Ellie nodded. 'I think she packed a large suitcase, something on wheels. She packed in a hurry, leaving drawers half open. Then she dragged the suitcase down the hall, leaving tracks in the pile of the carpet runner. The little dog must have been frantic with excitement, seeing her pack. He would be jumping up and down, creating problems for her. She clipped his lead on, and tied it to the back of the chair in the kitchen while she emptied the fridge, piling everything perishable plus all the dog food into some bags, which she left on the table with a note for Dagmara. She couldn't take the dog with her so when she left the flat with her suitcase, she carefully shut the kitchen door behind her, knowing that Dagmara would be coming by to take him out the following day.

'Left alone, the little dog went berserk. You know how excitable those little Westies are. He ran round and round, dragging the chair with him, upsetting the vegetable rack, jolting the table so that one of the tins of dog food rolled out on to the floor. He pulled down the drying-up cloths hanging by the sink. Finally he was tired out, and went to sleep.

'Next day Dagmara arrives to collect him as usual. She reads the note and takes both the dog and the perishables back to her flat. She doesn't put the kitchen to rights again because she wants to get out of there, fast.'

Chloe bit her finger. 'And why couldn't Mrs Hanna take the dog with her?'

'Because she was going out of the country. I assume someone visited her that evening and frightened her so much that she decided to go back to Poland until things calmed down.'

'And she couldn't take the dog because of quarantine restrictions.'

'But Dagmara must have realized that Mrs Hanna wasn't dead, as we all thought. Why didn't she tell the police?'

Ellie shrugged. 'Polish people all stick together, don't they? If Dagmara believed Mrs Hanna was being threatened, wouldn't she help her cover her tracks? Again, it's possible that whoever frightened Mrs Hanna might be known to Dagmara as well. Every time I try to think who it could be, I can only come up with something nasty in the second-hand car trade.'

Chloe said, automatically, 'Ferdy was clean. He wasn't above bending the truth a bit, perhaps. Say about mileage on a car. But he wouldn't have nothing to do with bent gear.'

'I know. It's a puzzle. But it's the only thing I can think of that makes sense.'

Chloe leaned forward. 'You ought to have told the police, you know. They're still looking for Mrs Hanna, wasting man hours doing it. They could go and see Dagmara, get her to give them the note ... if there is a note.'

'I know,' said Ellie, comfortably. 'But I did try to tell them earlier, and they didn't want to know. Besides, I couldn't be sure my suspicions were correct until you confirmed that the dog was still around, and who it was with. I was thinking maybe I would try to locate the dog that I'd heard in the flats tomorrow, and see if whoever it was who was looking after it, would talk to me. Then perhaps I'd have something more to tell the police.'

Rose twittered, 'Do you think Mrs Hanna managed her getaway all by herself? Getting flight tickets, and all?'

'No. I think she phoned a fellow Pole and got him to help her. It wasn't Dagmara, because otherwise she'd have taken the dog with her there and then, and I believe the dog was left alone in the flat for some time after Mrs Hanna left, because of the mess it made. Mrs Hanna wouldn't have gone by air. Too expensive, and she wouldn't want to be hanging around, waiting for a flight. She would have gone to Victoria and got on that train that takes twenty-four hours to get to Warsaw, but is very cheap. I suspect that if we asked around in the Polish community, someone would be able to tell us how she went ... and possibly even, why.'

Chloe was doubtful. 'The Poles do all hang together. They probably wouldn't talk to us. I suppose they might talk to the police, if there was somebody threatening them. You think it was a sort of Polish Mafia thing?'

'I don't know. Are you going to tell Bob this?'

Chloe roused herself. 'Over my dead body do I give that jerk the time of day, ever again!'

'He was only doing his duty, as he saw it. And I think perhaps he wanted to show off in front of you a little?'

'Hunh!' Chloe took out her compact, and inspected her face. Perhaps she wasn't quite so antagonistic to Bob now.

The phone rang, and Ellie plodded into the hall to answer it. It might be Kate. And what should she tell her?

It was Diana.

'Mother, what's this I hear? I've had Aunt Drusilla on the phone, extremely upset. Whatever have you been saying to her? Are you out of your mind?'

'Diana, dear. Take a deep breath. Count to ten.'

'I do really think all this must have affected you more than you think …!'

'Finding out that Aunt Drusilla owns half a dozen river-side flats must have turned my brain?'

'What? What nonsense!'

'Would you like to see the enquiry agents' report?' Ellie crossed her fingers, hoping it would arrive in the post tomorrow.

'You've actually set a private detective on to Aunt Drusilla? Mother, how could you stoop so low!'

Ellie made an effort to be patient. 'Not I, dear. Your father. Now listen to me, Diana. Listen carefully. I was glad that you came down to look after me the other day, but you must not assume that I am incapable of handling my own affairs. I was extremely surprised, not to say angry, when I discovered that you had put the house on the market without consulting me—'

Diana blustered. 'It was the obvious thing to—'

'No, it wasn't. I have been to see Mr Jolley and taken the house off the market again. I have also retrieved your keys which you so foolishly left with him.'

'What? You had no right … you know perfectly well that half the house is mine—'

'Not until I pass away, dear. Which reminds me that I

must set about making my will. I have decided to leave everything to the nearest cats' home.'

Ellie put the phone down, and bent over with painful laughter. Of course she wouldn't really do it, but somehow or other she had to get it into Diana's head that she must not interfere in her mother's life like this.

The doorbell rang. Ellie opened the front door, and a chilly gust of sleet entered along with the burly figure of Bob.

'Sorry to disturb you again, Mrs Quicke, but I thought you ought to know that when I drove up just now, I noticed a man in a Saab watching this house. It looked like the gas man you mentioned to me, so I went over to have a word, and he took off like a bat out of hell. I tried to get the number, but the plate had been smeared over with mud. Of course, that's a traffic offence in itself. Anyway, I thought you'd like to know that he's gone now.'

He looked beyond Ellie to the living-room doorway, where Chloe was standing, biting her lip as she listened to him.

He looked at Chloe, while still talking to Ellie. 'It's a nasty night out. I knew Chloe hadn't got home yet because I checked with her mum. So I came back, wondering if she was still here and I could give her a lift. It's not fit for a dog out there tonight.'

Ellie peered outside. Indeed, it was not a night to be out. The ground was covered with a greyish slush and the wind was whipping branches around.

Chloe looked undecided.

Bob swallowed. Sounding less confident than his words might appear, he said, 'You're coming home with me, my girl. And no arguments.'

Chloe gave him a brilliant smile. 'Of course, Bob!'

She kissed Ellie on the cheek, pulled on her jacket, and was swept out into the night within Bob's arm.

Rose McNally hovered in the doorway. 'Well! What do you think of that! Do you think she'll tell him what we think happened to Mrs Hanna?'

'I really don't know.' Ellie hoped in some ways that Chloe would do so.

Rose looked at her watch and gave a little scream. 'Look at the time. I'm never out this late at night. I've got my bus pass but are the buses still running, do you think? I couldn't possibly afford a minicab. What am I going to do?'

Ellie thought how much she longed for peace and quiet now. A long, hot bath. Sinking into her brand new soft bed with its daisy-printed covers. Sleep. But she couldn't shuffle off responsibility for Rose.

'I hadn't realized it was so late. Would you like to stay the night? You can't possibly stand around in this weather waiting for buses and I've got a spare room here. Also, we haven't yet talked about what's going to happen at the charity shop if you don't go back …'

'Oh, I'm not going back if you don't.'

'Nonsense, dear. What would they do without you? Now let's see. Diana slept in the back bedroom and those sheets are still on the double bed …'

'Oh, I couldn't possibly put you to so much trouble.'

'I mean it,' said Ellie, trying not to scream.

'Well …' Rose fidgeted, and then burst out with it. 'I don't mean to sound ungrateful but the thing is … do you have a single bed? I haven't been able to sleep in a double bed since my husband died. I kept waking up and feeling the space, if you know what I mean.'

'I do indeed. The small bedroom is full of junk – I do my ironing in there – but yes, I do have a brand new single bed, which I can make up for you.'

Ellie resigned herself to the fact that someone else was going to have first go at the beautiful new bed. Ah well. It was just for one night.

'You are so kind!' said Rose. 'And perhaps a sleeping pill? In a strange bed, you know …'

'And a clean nightie … though I'm not so sure about a new toothbrush.'

Rose blushed. 'Oh, we don't really need to worry about that!' From which Ellie deduced that Rose was wearing dentures.

Upstairs they went to draw curtains and make up the new bed with new bedlinen. 'Very pretty!' said Rose, bouncing on the bed.

'A late night cuppa?' suggested Ellie, finding her guest a clean nightie – a prettily flowered full-length cotton one with long sleeves – and a towel. She showed her into the bathroom and surveyed the back bedroom, deciding she was too tired to change the bedlinen which Diana and Stewart had used. By now Ellie was aching all over and hating her visitor. 'Tea, coffee, hot milk?'

'Thank you, dear. Hot milk would be the very thing.'

Rose followed Ellie downstairs and started poking into corners while Ellie heated up milk, put the chain on the front door, pushed bolts home front and back.

'No poker, dear?' asked Rose. 'I always take the poker to bed with me, just in case a burglar breaks in.'

Ellie forced herself to hold her smile. 'No poker, I'm afraid.'

'Well, a nice heavy frying-pan would do.'

Ellie fished out her heavy frying-pan and handed it over with a sleeping pill. Rose beamed. 'Thank you, dear. Now I feel quite safe.'

Ellie wondered if taking a sleeping pill wouldn't wipe out any benefit that might accrue from taking an offensive weapon to bed, but didn't argue. She was too tired for that.

Rose took a very long time in the bathroom but finally Ellie got in for a quick wash, promising herself that on the morrow she would take the dressings off her grazes and have a really good long bath. Into bed in the back bedroom. The sheets smelled of Diana and Stewart, but she told herself to ignore that.

She hoped to fall asleep at once but was overtired. She lay awake, listening to Rose snoring gently through the party wall. The clock downstairs struck midnight. At one o'clock she half surfaced to hear the clock strike again, and then dropped into a heavy sleep.

The errand boy was on his mobile. 'I'm going in. All's quiet. I've got a Mickey Mouse mask and a tyre lever. Should only take me ten minutes ...'

The battery in the fat man's mobile was dead. He'd been trying and trying to get through and couldn't. He didn't know what to do. He couldn't even call a minicab to get him out of there. The office was too far off for him to walk on crutches. He cursed, shouting into the unresponsive phone, trying to raise the errand boy, to warn him.

'She's sleeping in the back bedroom, not the front ...'

Eventually he seized his crutches and began to make the painful journey down the stairs.

17

Ellie half woke and sleepily wondered why. She concluded that she needed to go to the toilet. She tried to tell herself that she didn't need to, but she knew that she did, really. She felt for the switch of her bedside light and only then realized that she was not in her usual bed, and the bedside light was not where it should be.

With an effort she pushed herself upright, swung her legs over the side of the bed and felt for her slippers. The house was cold. She ought to have left the central heating on, especially – she now remembered – as she had a guest. The room was not completely dark because of the lights in the churchyard outside. She yawned, reached for her dressing-gown and hoped Rose hadn't felt the need to go to the bathroom at exactly the same time as her.

No, Rose was still snoring.

But if Rose were still snoring in bed, then why was a light flickering across the landing? She could see it under her bedroom door.

Suddenly she understood how sensible Rose had been to want to take a poker to bed with her. There wasn't even a phone upstairs. Ellie looked around for a weapon. Anything. But bedrooms don't usually supply an armoury of weapons. The best she could come up with was an elderly but heavy portable radio. The batteries gave it a formidable weight.

The light had gone from under the door. Rose still snored.

Ellie thought, Lord, have mercy!

She tied the dressing-gown tightly around herself, pulled the skirts up to give her more freedom of movement and grasped the radio by its handle. She put her eye to the edge of the door on to the landing and eased it open a fraction.

Nothing. No one. But the door to the front bedroom was ajar, there was a light within, and Rose was still snoring! Even as she watched, her bedroom door swung inwards, as it always did if not firmly closed.

Ellie considered tiptoeing downstairs and calling the police on the phone … by which time Rose would perhaps have been raped or worse. Telling herself to be brave, Ellie inched soundlessly towards her bedroom. Someone was holding a torch beam on to the bed. Behind the silhouette of a man, Ellie could make out the humps of Rose's body under the brand new duvet. Rose was lying propped up in bed, fast asleep, with her cardigan draped over her head.

The silhouetted figure laid his torch down on the bedside table, with the beam pointing towards Rose's feet.

He lifted a heavy bar above his head …

Ellie tried not to let herself think about what she had to do.

She screamed.

Grasping the heavy radio with both hands, she swung it against the man's backside. And screamed again as he fell across Rose's body.

The man grunted with pain. To her horror Ellie saw that he had not let go of his weapon.

A nightmare of a face turned towards her. She had hurt but not disabled the intruder. She despaired. She had not hit him hard enough, and maybe you only ever got one chance to hit such a man. If you didn't disable him with your first blow, you might well not get another chance.

She drew back, panting. 'Get out!'

'Bitch!'

The man pushed himself up on to outstretched arms. He was wearing a thick black sweater over black jeans, which must have absorbed much of the force of the blow. He was still strong, and now he was also very angry.

The masked head turned to look down at the stirring figure of Rose, and then turned back to look at Ellie.

'You …!'

Using his knees to lever himself off the bed, he turned his attention to Ellie, lifting the heavy bar to aim at her head.

Horrified, she jerked backwards as he swung again.

The bar missed her cheek by a fraction.

He cursed. Raised the bar high once more.

Ellie lifted the radio high, hoping it might break the force of the blow.

The man took a half step forward, seemed to trip over his own feet, and crashed to the floor.

Rose, sitting up in bed, had seized one of his legs from behind and brought him down.

The bar dropped from his hand. Ellie had just enough presence of mind to stand on it so that he couldn't retrieve it.

The man shuffled back on his haunches, holding on to his right shoulder.

Rose was flailing around, caught up in the bedclothes. And screaming. She had a painful, ear-splitting scream. Ellie joined her.

Unnerved, the man began to crawl towards the open door. He gained it, pulled himself to his feet by the handle and lunged out on to the landing.

'Quick!' Rose had found what she was looking for … the heavy frying-pan.

Ellie dropped the radio, grabbed the frying-pan and rushed out on to the landing after the intruder. In the dark, the man was feeling for the top step.

The hall was icy cold. The front door was wide open, the hall patched with light from the nearest street light.

Right, my laddo! thought Ellie. You've asked for this!

She'd played a considerable amount of tennis in her youth, when her forehand drive had been much admired. She swung the heavy frying-pan with both hands, connecting with the intruder's backside and sending him into orbit.

The man crashed down the stairs, landing in a heap at the bottom. And didn't move.

Beside the open front door lay Ellie's television and video, together with her silver vase and photograph frame. He must have opened the door before he came up the stairs, to facilitate a quick getaway.

Rose peered under Ellie's arm. 'What can we tie him up with?'

'The cord off Frank's dressing-gown. Behind the door in the bedroom.'

Still carrying the frying-pan in case the man was shamming, Ellie switched on all the lights and made her way down the stairs. The man didn't move. She didn't trust him, though. She held the frying-pan ready while Rose managed to tie the man's hands behind his back. Ellie sacrificed her own dressing-gown cord to tie his feet.

Only then did she put the frying-pan down, close the front door and lift the phone to call the police. After that she put the central heating on again.

Rose sat hunched up on the bottom step of the stairs, staring at the man's masked head. 'I've never been so frightened in all my life!' She looked vividly awake, rather than terrified.

Ellie sat on the chair by the phone and tried not to shake. Thanks, Lord, she thought. She said, 'Rose, I thought you'd taken a sleeping pill. How come you woke up at the right moment?'

'Well, dear, I didn't like to say anything, but the sleeping pill you gave me wasn't very strong. I have some special pills from the doctor to help me sleep. So I wasn't deeply asleep, if you know what I mean.'

'But I heard you snoring.'

'Snoring, dear? Oh, I don't think so. Breathing a little heavily, perhaps. I have to sleep sitting upright. My hiatus hernia, you know.'

Ellie pushed herself to her feet and went to investigate where a strong draught was coming from. She found one half of the French windows was off its hinges. She stared at it, wondering what on earth she was going to do about that.

There was another unearthly, banshee-like shriek from Rose as someone pounded on the front door and rang the bell.

As Ellie returned to the hall, Rose leaped at her, and clung. 'He's awake!'

'Yes, dear, but you see he can't get away. And that's probably the police.'

It was Armand, with a greatcoat slung over his pyjamas. 'What on earth is going on? You're not being raped, are you?' He was as angry and unpleasant as ever.

'Do come in,' said Ellie, pleasantly. 'We've surprised a burglar, and would feel a lot safer with a man around till the police get here.'

'What?' Armand stared at the intruder, whose mask stared back at him. Armand inspected the man's bonds, remarked that women never knew how to tie a knot, and tore off the man's mask. He recoiled.

'Heavens!' said Ellie, feeling rather faint. 'It's that gas board man that wasn't!'

Rose transferred her grasp to Armand's arm. 'We've been burgled! I woke up and there he was standing over me, menacing me with an iron bar! So I tackled him and threw him to the ground, and then he got away and fell down the stairs and knocked himself out. Do you think I could sell my story to the newspapers?'

'Good ... grief!' said Armand, blinking.

The doorbell rang again, and this time it was the police. No faces that Ellie knew. They seemed not too sure that they weren't being called out on a fool's errand till Rose proudly showed them the prostrate burglar, and told her tale all over again.

'This your house then, missus?' one of them asked Rose, producing a notebook while the other spoke into his walkie-talkie.

'No, no!' said Rose, with a smile which was almost coquettish. 'I was just staying the night. I always knew I'd catch a burglar some day, and now I have!'

Ellie let Rose ramble on. She was looking at the winking light on the answerphone, and wondering if Kate had left a message on it, and if so, would the police notice and want to listen to it.

At last Rose began to unwind and dark shadows started

to appear under her eyes. Her vivacity drained away and she looked what she really was, an elderly lady whose sleep had been rudely disturbed, and who was beginning to feel shaky.

The burglar was by this time fully conscious, humiliatingly aware of having been defeated and tied up by two women, and uttering threats about prosecuting them for attacking him. Ellie silently led the way upstairs and pointed out the tyre lever in the bedroom to the policeman.

She said, 'I did hit him, it's true. He was standing over Rose with that bar in his hand, and I realized he was going to kill her. Then he turned on me and I thought I was going to die, but she tackled him, and he fell. I think that's when he hurt his shoulder. Then he got away and I hit him again as he was hesitating at the top of the stairs. He fell down the stairs and knocked himself out. That's when we tied him up and rang for you.'

The policeman's eye wandered over to the frying-pan. He didn't ask what Ellie had hit him with. He just nodded and said, 'You two ladies deserve a medal. You pushed him down the stairs, and he knocked himself out. Quite right, too. You'll be prepared to make a statement about this down at the station?'

Ellie nodded.

Armand was by now trying to assert himself, exclaiming at the pile of swag which the burglar had collected by the front door, and asking what the police proposed to do about the broken French window.

Ellie put the kettle on and made tea for them all. The burglar's arms and legs all appeared to be in working order, so he was removed by a back-up car with the assurance that they would have the police doctor look at him soonest.

Rose drooped, and Ellie coaxed her up to bed. No doubt the despised sleeping pill was kicking in by now.

Armand strode about, complaining of the inefficiency of the police in not providing a carpenter to mend the broken window that very night. One of the policemen went to inspect the damage with him, and promised to send someone along in the morning.

Was that man really trying to kill me, thought Ellie … or was he just an ordinary burglar?

The older policeman said, 'Well, if that's all …' He and his companion were ready to leave, and Ellie realized she was not going to feel safe if they did.

She said, 'Officer, one of your men came round this afternoon because I wanted to report that a conman has twice tried to gain entry to this house, pretending to be from the gas board. It's the same man who came here tonight. Do you think we're safe here?'

The policeman was, perhaps, tired. It was, after all, the dead of night. He said, with barely concealed amusement, '*He'll* not be back tonight, that's for sure.'

She nodded, realizing that he thought her a frail, rather stupid woman. She said, 'I think he's tried before. Someone tampered with the wiring of my electric lawnmower. Then there was that very odd incident with a big, heavy man on the bridge … though that might have been just an accident … I was very upset that day … and of course he ended up in hospital with a broken leg, but looking back, I do wonder if perhaps he wasn't intending to hit me with that piece of scaffolding he was brandishing …'

She looked at the officer and from the amused, rather distant expression on his face, realized that he thought she was rambling.

She added, 'Then there was Kate's car blowing up. They might have thought it was my car, because she did take me out in it the night before. And if someone is trying to kill me and not Kate, then … oh, I don't know. I really don't. But yesterday a car tried to run me over in the Avenue. Rose warned me only just in time.'

He was bored, going through the motions. 'Did you get the number of the car?'

'No, but Rose said it was a Saab. It looked black to me, but it wasn't really black, I think. It might have been dark green. The number plate was muddied.'

'Dozens of those about, missus.'

And the next question, she thought, would be, Do you know of anyone who wants to do you in?

Ellie felt a shiver run up and down her spine. Both Diana and Aunt Drusilla would benefit from her death.

No, the idea was ludicrous. Diana wouldn't know how to engage a murderer to kill her mother. Anyway, selfish as Diana was, it was not the sort of thing which would ever occur to her.

Aunt Drusilla was a different proposition; she might easily have got to know all sorts of unscrupulous people through that dreadful estate agent. But would Aunt Drusilla really go as far as putting out a contract on her?

No, of course not.

Ellie realized she was overtired. She knew it probably wasn't anything to do with either Aunt Drusilla or Diana, but that was all she could think of. She held back tears with an effort.

'There, there, now! Things get out of proportion at this time of night, don't they? It'll all look better in the morning,' said the policeman, stuffing his notebook back in his pocket.

Armand strode back in, saying that he'd wedged the broken window frame back into place with a couple of chairs, but he really thought it would be best if he slept on the sofa that night … or what remained of it.

Ellie looked at him and saw what had first attracted Kate to him. He was concerned for her. Probably he was at his best when taking care of someone weaker than himself. Kate – being a stronger character – would bring out the worst in him. So let's make the most of it, thought Ellie.

'That's good of you, Armand,' she said, blowing her nose. 'I must admit I don't know what I'd do otherwise. I'll fetch you some bedding down.'

'Don't bother,' said Armand, throwing himself down on the settee, with his greatcoat over himself. 'I'll be quite all right here, and the police promise they'll send someone round first thing tomorrow to make the place safe.'

Ellie thanked the policeman, who left saying that if she were disturbed again, they would come straight back. She left a light on in the hall, retrieved the frying-pan and took it up with her to the back bedroom. Half past three in the morning.

She hoped she'd sleep, but feared she wouldn't. She had too much to think about.

The two policemen were returning to their patrol car when they interrupted the fat man trying to break into his own Saab.

'Hang about,' said one of them. 'Is that chap trying to break into that car? The number plate's suspiciously muddy, too. Do you think it could be the same car which the old dear thought was trying to run her down?'

His mate said, 'And wasn't there a call to the station about a fake gas man seen in a green Saab?'

'So who's that trying to get into it now? A friend of the burglar's?'

The fat man's luck was right out. When challenged, he tried to run away. But with the cast on his leg, he hadn't a chance.

'Excuse me, but is that your car, sir?'

'Yes. That is, a friend's been borrowing it …'

'How did you propose to drive it, with your leg in plaster like that?'

'Hang about,' said his mate. 'Do I smell something on his breath, or do I?'

The fat man began to gasp and perspire, despite the chill of the night, thinking of all the beer he'd drunk that evening.

'What I think is,' said the first policeman, 'that we take laddo here back to the station and ask him nicely if he can produce his log book and insurance papers.'

'And then we could ask him if he happens to know chummy with the jemmy, don't you think?'

'It's your lucky night, mate,' said the first policeman, as he urged the fat man into their own car. 'You get a lift to the station out of the rain, and maybe even a nice hot cup of tea as well; but before that, let's have you blow into this dinky little tube, shall we?'

The fat man despaired. And him without a mobile phone to call for help. He groaned. She had said that at all costs the goods in the derelict house must not be left unattended, and he'd done exactly that. Thousands of pounds worth …

She'd kill him.

Ellie did sleep, patchily. She drifted in and out of night-mares, and woke feeling worse than she had done for many a day. Rose was still snoring next door, so Ellie went down to make sure that Armand would get off to school on time. He was subdued, but very willing to accept her offer to make him a cup of coffee and some poached eggs on toast for breakfast.

With both hands around a mug, he sat hunched up at the kitchen table. After a while Ellie realized he was watching her. Not with suspicion, but speculatively.

She smiled at him. She thought he'd been having a rough time recently, even if it were mostly his own fault.

He said, quietly for him, 'You are in touch with her, aren't you? Is she all right? You needn't tell me where she is. Just tell me that she's all right.'

'She phones me every now and then, but I don't know where from. She is all right. She misses you and would like to come back, but daren't. She thinks someone is trying to kill her.'

His eyes went dark, but he held on to his temper. 'Not me, I swear it!'

Ellie shook her head. 'No, of course not, but the police haven't got anyone else for Ferdy's murder …'

'It wasn't her.' Though he didn't sound quite so sure of that.

'No, rest assured, it wasn't. Believe me, I know.'

His face twisted and he looked away. She averted her own eyes. This man would hate to be seen crying.

She said, 'The police will find the right person soon, I'm sure.'

'And then she'll come back?' He sounded like a little boy wanting to be reassured that everything was going to be back to normal soon.

Ellie sighed. 'Who knows?'

He hunched his shoulders and dropped his head, but said nothing more.

After he'd gone, Ellie checked that Rose was still snoring and took her own coffee into the living-room. She stood by the propped-up French windows, looking up at the church. The wind had dropped. The snow still lay in hollows, but was fast turning to slush. A dreary outlook.

She was dog tired but her brain wouldn't stop turning over the facts and fancies that had occupied her since Frank had died … since she had stood on that spot and seen Kate running down the path from the church, crying.

She tried to think herself back to that time. She'd been half doped.

The weather had been bright, but threatening rain. She'd been worrying about clearing the leaves from the lawn.

No, that was the day that Mrs Dawes had come scurrying down from the church after she'd found Ferdy's body. Which reminded her that she must ring Mrs Dawes and explain why she'd missed choir practice last night.

She wrenched her mind back to the evening of the murder. She couldn't remember anything before she spotted Kate.

She sat down in the big chair and put her head back. Closed her eyes. Tried to concentrate on that one important evening …

18

Rose shook her awake. Rose was fully dressed and looking very lively. Of course, she was the heroine of the hour, wasn't she? Ellie didn't grudge her that but did perhaps wonder if Rose had been experimenting with Ellie's own lipstick. It suited Rose, but still …

'Haven't we had a nice little sleep, then!' said Rose, all smiles. 'I didn't like to wake you, but the builders have arrived to repair the window and I know you wouldn't want to be seen in your nightie.'

Ellie struggled to her feet. She felt terrible, but not as bad as she felt when she spotted the time. 'Nearly twelve!'

'Yes, dear. Now you go upstairs and make yourself tidy and I'll look after the men. Oh, and what do you think you'd like to have for lunch?'

Ellie held her head with both hands. Rose was enjoying herself. Rose had suddenly acquired a bossy nature. Rose was going to move in on her, if Ellie were not very careful. Ellie wanted nothing more than to be quiet in her own house and THINK. So how could she get rid of dear, sweet, helpful Rose?

Well, what did Rose like more than what she'd got here?

Gossip. A little importance in her life.

Ellie said, 'Dear Rose, what would I have done without you? Do show the men in and I'll deal with them. I know you'll be wanting to ring Joyce and tell her you're all right. Isn't it one of your days at the charity shop? Yes, I know you felt you ought to resign just because I'm taking some time off, but you don't really want to let them down, do you? Oh, and I wonder if the *Gazette* has got on to the burglary yet?'

The post had come, including a duplicate copy of the enquiry agents' report. It seemed that Aunt Drusilla had been gradually amassing a number of properties in the area over the years, starting way back when she sold her own house to move in with Frank's father. She now owned six of the flats in the riverside block, plus two large houses divided into flats, just off the Avenue. A lady of property, indeed, damn her eyes!

Half an hour later Rose was gone. Ellie was washed, brushed and dressed, and ready to tackle the answerphone while the carpenters banged and crashed away in the living-room.

Tod's little-boy voice, all excited. '… Is that you, Mrs Quicke? I've brought my mum's mobile up to my bedroom, because I've got to warn you there's a man sitting outside in his car, watching your house. He's been there for yonks. Is he a spy, do you think? Should I phone the police? I've got to go … Mum's coming—'

Ellie smiled at this, and then grew thoughtful. So the fake gas man had been watching her house for some time, had he?

Mrs Dawes. Why hadn't Ellie turned up to choir practice? Ellie made a note to herself to call on Mrs Dawes and tell her. A first-hand account of the burglary would go a long way to soothing ruffled feelings.

Kate's voice. 'Hi, Ellie. How are you doing? I'm dead bored. I'm going to ring you tomorrow at one o'clock so that we can talk. We always seem to miss one another this way ...'

Bill Weatherspoon's voice. 'Ellie, I believe you were trying to get through to me. Unfortunately I had appointments up in town. Ring me, will you?'

Yes, thought Ellie. I will.

There were no more messages, so she rang Bill's office and was put through straight away.

'Bill, this is an emergency. Could you possibly come round here, as soon as possible?'

'My dear Ellie, whatever is the matter?'

She tried to keep her voice steady. 'I think someone's trying to kill me.'

'What? Ellie, did you say ...?'

'Yes, I know it sounds crazy, but it would relieve my mind enormously if you could spare the time to—'

'Of course. You couldn't come here, could you? I've got appointments stacked up all afternoon.'

'I can't leave the house. The police have sent some carpenters round to repair the French windows where this man broke in last night.'

'I'll be round straight away.' The phone crashed down.

Ellie checked that the carpenters were all right ... they wanted to take the old window frames out and put in new ones. It was going to take all day.

Bill rang the bell, and she let him in.

'Ellie, you look remarkably calm for a woman under threat of death.'

'Not calm. Worn out. Come into the study, and let me tell you the tale.'

He listened with care, steepling his fingers, frowning and shifting in his seat now and then. When she had finished, he said, 'What do the police think?'

'They think Kate killed Ferdy and that I'm shielding her. Only, she didn't kill Ferdy. I know that for certain. They don't want to think about anyone else doing it, and the only suggestions I can make, they don't want to hear. I do not know who killed Ferdy and frightened his mother away, unless it's something to do with Ferdy's car dealings. The police say they've thoroughly investigated those, but ...'

She shrugged. 'I can see their point of view. I was standing at the window at the time Ferdy was attacked. At least, I suppose I was. I've racked my brains, trying to remember seeing something significant, but I can't.'

'Do the police know about all these other incidents?'

'Yes, but it didn't occur to me until late last night that I was being targeted. I mean, it's not the sort of thing that would normally occur to one, is it? I'm ashamed to say that just at first I thought either Diana or Aunt Drusilla might have been behind these attacks. Oh, of course I soon came to my senses and realized I wasn't thinking straight, but I have had the most dreadful quarrels with both of them about money, and it did seem to me that I needed some professional help with dealing with them.'

'My professional advice is to go straight to the police and tell them everything.'

'I tried doing that last night, and the policeman looked at me as if I'd got senile decay. "Dear old lady losing her marbles, fancying every man in the street wants to rape her". You know? I began to think I must be imagining things myself. That's why I needed to talk to you. I wanted to tell someone impartial what I know and suspect, to make sure I'm not making a mountain out of molehill.'

'That broken window frame is no molehill.'

'No, and I do need help dealing with Aunt Drusilla and also with Diana. They are both so greedy!'

'Right. What do you want done?'

She began to pace the room. 'I want you to negotiate with Aunt Drusilla for me. I don't really want to turn her out of the house in which she's lived for so long, but I do want to keep my options open on selling it … perhaps at some future date when she might be ready to go into a retirement home. Have a look at this …'

She handed over the report from the enquiry agents. Bill's eyebrows rose, and he said, 'I see.'

Ellie said, 'Could you find out how much it would cost to renew the lease on the flat our organist's father leased from her? If it's too much, perhaps Aunt Drusilla could find a smaller, more suitable flat for her, perhaps taking in a lodger to make ends meet?

'Now about Diana …' She sighed. 'It's so difficult. I don't think they can afford to live in the big house they've bought.'

'Then they should downsize.'

'That's not the way Diana thinks. She asked Frank for more money, and he refused. When I got blown up by the car bomb, she tried to rush me into selling here and renting a small place up there. While I was still groggy, she put this house on the market, telling Mr Jolley that she owned half of it, anyway …'

'What! Why didn't you tell me? If I'd known, I would have had something to say to Diana … and to Mr Jolley, too.'

'Don't worry, I said it myself. To him, and to Diana.' She giggled. 'I told Diana I was making my will and leaving everything to the cats' home.'

Bill laughed. 'But you're not really intending to …?'

'No, of course not, but I'd like you to make a will out for me here and now, just in case something else happens to me today … then I can come round later in the week and sign it properly, can't I? The workmen next door can witness it.'

'My dear Ellie! I ought to take you into protective custody until this is sorted out. The police—'

She said wearily, 'They don't take me seriously. Please, Bill …'

'Very well.' He looked at his watch. 'Just let me ring the office and tell them to cancel my afternoon appointments.'

As they were discussing her will, the phone rang.

It was Kate. Ellie said, 'My dear, there's a whole lot of things been happening here that you ought to know about, but I can't speak now. Just answer me one question. Did Ferdy ever mention to you that he'd had an offer for his car business? He didn't. Oh, no, I realize it sounds unlikely. Well, will you phone again this evening between four and five? Oh, and your husband's missing you. Speak to you later, love …'

She put the phone down, and went to back to Bill … then to find them both some lunch … then to sign her will … and make tea for the carpenters.

Finally Bill persuaded her to go across with him to the incident room. She agreed because she'd promised she would make a statement about the fake gas man and the burglary. The inside of the church hall looked drearier than ever. Inspector Clay was out, so she had to deal with a pleasant, but sceptical underling. Which she did. But as she'd feared, they were soon back on the old treadmill. Ellie found herself far better able to deal with their questions when Bill was beside her, but still it was tiresome, and tiring …

'Mrs Quicke, you say you think you are in danger. There is only one person who could be behind a threat to you, and yet you won't help us find her …'

'Mrs Quicke, don't you see that we can't help you, unless you help us …?'

But she couldn't. 'What about the man who tried to kill me last night?'

A knowing smile. 'Burglars do tend to turn nasty when interrupted, you know.'

'What about all the strange things that have been happening to me recently?'

'Yes, yes.' A condescending smile. Translation: did Ellie really think they were going to waste valuable time following up reports of imaginary persecutions? 'Now, getting back to Kate. We'll find her, with or without your help, you know.'

Ellie wasn't so sure of that. Of course, if they knew how Kate had disguised herself, perhaps they might be able to track her down. But they didn't. And she was not going to tell them. In the end Kate might have to come forward. If she couldn't get a job, if her money ran out.

Bill stood. 'May I ask what arrangements you are making to protect my client until this case is cleared up?'

There were thin smiles in response to this. 'Oh, we'll be keeping an eye on her, of course. But the manpower situation being what it is …'

Wearily, Ellie thanked Bill as he walked back home with her.

'Come back home with me, Ellie. I can't leave you here alone.'

'I have to see to the carpenters and glaziers, and lock up. Then I'm taking a taxi to one of those anonymous hotels near the airport for the night. Don't worry, Bill. I'll take good care of myself.'

The estate agent had run out of cigarettes. He couldn't find a parking space in the Avenue on his way home, so he took the first left at the church and drew up outside the derelict house. Having bought his cigarettes, he shut himself into his car to take a drag … ah, the first one of the evening …

… when he caught sight of a familiar Sold sign outside the big house. He knew perfectly well that their agency was not responsible for selling this house. If they had been and could have got planning permission for the site, some developer would have fallen on this property with cries of 'Eureka!'.

The rain had stopped, so he got out to take a good look. The place looked deserted, but somewhere nearby water was dripping from an overflow. From upstairs. Ugh. That meant squatters were in. What's more, there was a brand new padlock on the garage doors …

And the back door was swinging open. The ground floor rooms were empty, but somewhere upstairs a cistern was dripping. An empty beer can rolled over his foot as he climbed the stairs. The first floor was empty, except …

He reached for his mobile phone.

Ellie's house was still full of workmen when she returned. The answerphone light was winking. The workmen said they were nearly finished, but tomorrow they'd come back and give everything a lick of paint. She gave them more tea, more biscuits.

She put a note through Armand's door asking him to call round when he got back from school. Maybe she could persuade Kate to speak to Armand that evening. Maybe.

She played back her messages. Someone wanting to sell her double glazing.

John, from the charity shop, to say that Madam's friend had changed her mind and wasn't going to join them after all. Madam had been crawling on the phone to Rose, trying to get her to return, and Rose had eventually said she would. John thought that was funny, but warned Ellie that Madam might be trying her next.

Diana. Sounding very upset, but trying to control it. Would mother please ring her? She wasn't working today, so please ring, any time.

That was all.

Ellie sighed. Better get it over with. Diana must have been sitting by the phone, waiting for her call.

'Mother, please listen to me. I didn't mean to interfere in your business, but ...'

'Of course you didn't, dear, you were just looking out for me. But before you say anything else, I want you to know that I've had Bill Weatherspoon here today, to draw up my will. I've signed it, it's been witnessed and it's all perfectly in order. You can keep the car, by the way. Oh, and just to set my mind at rest ... was it you or Stewart who took your father's pen and pencil and cufflinks?'

'Oh, mother! Don't you think Dad would have wanted me to have them?'

'Perhaps. But don't you think you should have asked me first?'

'I did. I'm sure I did.' She sounded far too aggressive to be really sure.

Ellie let her off the hook. 'Perhaps you did. Perhaps I just wasn't taking in what you said at the time. Still, I'm perfectly all right now. Now, you'll want to know what I've decided to do with the money. I've been trying to think how your father would have wanted me to act …'

Diana snuffled at the other end of the phone. 'He wanted me to be happy.'

'Mm. He wanted you and Stewart to stand on your own two feet. He gave you enough money so that you could buy a small house and not have to work while baby Frank was at home. He was too wise to buy you a big house outright. He thought you should work your own way through life. You upset him terribly when you bought a much bigger house than you could afford. He felt you had let him down.'

Diana's voice took on a whine. 'It wasn't my fault that I couldn't get a full-time job afterwards, and the house we've got now, it's a dream house, just lovely, just what I've always wanted …'

'… and can't afford.'

'Dad could easily have given us more …'

'… but he decided that would be wrong. I think it would be wrong, too.'

Diana gulped. 'You mean, you're not going to …?'

'No, I'm not.' Ellie sighed. 'Diana, dear. Please get it into your head. You've had all you are going to get towards a house, but I propose to make you a monthly allowance to be used for child care. This should free you to find a better job somewhere … or if you wish, you can get a smaller house so that you don't need to work until Frank goes to school, in which case, the allowance is for you to spend as you wish. This allowance ends the moment I die. In my will you get nothing, but I'm setting up a trust for baby Frank, to mature when he's twenty-five.'

A long pause while Diana did sums in her head. Ellie knew the sorrow of feeling Diana's ingratitude. At last the question came.

'How much is the allowance going to be?'

Ellie told her. Enough to pay for child care. Not enough to pay the mortgage on the new house. Diana received the news in silence. Then put the phone down.

Ellie felt herself sag, as tension relaxed.

Only to stiffen again as someone pounded on the kitchen door.

It was young Tod, bundled up in a brightly coloured jacket, his schoolbag bumping over one shoulder.

She let him in, smiling. 'Lovely to see you, Tod. Thanks for all the messages you've been leaving on the answerphone. Sorry I've not been around much.'

One of the carpenters came to the door. 'We've just about finished, missus. Want to come and look?'

She inspected their work, thanked them and paid. They'd done a good job, and the result was a much stronger, safer back to the house. She saw them off and returned to the kitchen to find Tod investigating the almost empty biscuit tin. His hair was all on end as usual.

Ellie thought how much she loved him as she put the kettle on again. Now what could she find for him to eat? Perhaps some pot noodles?

He dumped his bag on the floor, and shucked off his jacket. 'Did you know our mum's got a new job? Won't be back till six, prob'ly.'

'You want to do your homework here?' She need not

leave for the night till he was safely back with his mum. She couldn't leave him to go back home alone.

'Mm. Can I watch the telly after?'

'Do you like pot noodles?'

'Wow! Monster!'

'You're shivering! I'll turn the heating up. It's much colder tonight, isn't it?'

'But not snowing yet. We had this plan, see, to make a ginormous snowman by the church. But now the snow's nearly all melted. It could at least have stayed till Christmas. Mum says we never get a white Christmas, nowadays. Why do you think that is?'

'I'm not sure.'

He grabbed the pot noodles, dropped the pot because it was too hot, and swore.

'You shouldn't swear,' she said, wondering where he'd heard the word, and if he knew what it meant. Then told herself that every child used that word nowadays … even if they really didn't know what it meant.

'That's what the funny man at the church said, when he dropped his money,' said Tod, slurping noodles with extravagant noises.

Ellie glanced out of the window, but could see nothing. She had the light on in the kitchen, of course. 'What funny man?'

'The funny man with the tea-cosy hat. Mum's got a hat just like that, that she keeps in the kitchen drawer. She doesn't use it, but she daren't throw it away, 'cause some aunt or other knitted it for her.'

Ellie went to stand by the kitchen door. Something about this story of Tod's was making her uneasy. 'Do you mean that there's a clown out there?'

'Nah. Clowns aren't black, are they? Clowns have white faces and spangly hats.'

'A black man, wearing a big woolly hat?'

'Mm. He was there before, just the once, and now he's come back. But I didn't take any.'

'Take any what?'

Tod stared down at the table. 'Sweets. Mum's always saying, Don't take sweets from strangers, or get in their cars. So I didn't. Some of the others did, but I thought I wouldn't. Not if I was going to have chocolate biscuits here for tea instead.'

He was lying, she could tell. She sat down opposite him, and said, 'Tod, tell me the truth.'

'I am!'

'No, I don't think you are.'

He kept his head down. He said, 'Can I have a chocolate biscuit now?'

'Tell me about the sweets first. You took one ... and ate it?'

He wriggled on the chair, but kept his head down. 'They made me. Some of the big boys. Dared me to. So a course I did. But I didn't eat it, honest. 'Cause they took it off me. And that Darren was off the next day. They said with flu, but ... maybe it was the sweet. I don't know.'

Ellie took a step towards the back door, then hesitated. Her brain was spinning. Was this man the missing piece in the jigsaw puzzle? But if so, how? Ferdy didn't have anything to do with drugs, did he? And this sounded distinctly like drug pushing.

Suppose you looked at it a different way. You could say that the church grounds were Ferdy's territory. That was where he worked on his cars, contacted his customers. And he hated drugs.

Now if you were a drug dealer looking for a new territory to open up, the church grounds were well placed for someone who wanted to contact schoolchildren and people who visited the library. People parked their cars there and walked along the Avenue to the shops. A man lounging around in the church grounds could be in a prime position to have contact unobtrusively with a large number of people … and children.

Suppose a drug dealer had seen the possibilities of the site, and had moved in on it. Perhaps had even offered Ferdy a good price to let him in his territory? What would Ferdy have done about it?

She felt a shiver run up and down her spine.

She said, 'Tod, this is important. Can you remember which day it was this man first came to the church to give his sweets away?'

Tod squeezed his eyes closed and thought. 'Maybe it was a Wednesday … or was it a Thursday? No, prob'ly it was a Wednesday, because I go swimming on a Thursday and so I wouldn't have stopped to see what he'd got. Yes, prob'ly Wednesday. Or maybe it was a Tuesday. Not a swimming night, anyway.'

'And he's a stranger. You hadn't seen him around before that, and he's not been there since – until today?'

'No, I'd have noticed. He's a Rasta, you see. We don't get Rastas around here much, do we?'

'A Rastafarian?' Rastafarians didn't cut their hair, but bundled it all up under large woollen hats; tea-cosy hats.

'Mm. Can I have a chocolate biscuit now?'

'In a minute. Tod, will you do something for me? Come into the living-room and see if you can spot this man you've been talking about. I agree with your mum that he really ought not to be handing out sweets to children he doesn't know.'

'Sure. But can I have a chocolate biscuit first?'

'In a minute, Tod.'

She left the light on in the kitchen, but didn't turn on the main light in the living-room. The side lamp was of course already on. The workmen hadn't bothered to draw the curtains before they left. There were lights on around the church, and in the alley. It wasn't raining. The moon was just visible beyond the steeple.

Tod pressed his face to the glass. She did, too. Gradually their night sight improved. Was there a man standing beside the bench on which Mrs Hanna had been sitting, all those long days and nights ago? Ellie could hardly make him out. Black against black.

'That's him,' said Tod. 'And it's Darren with him, see? Darren had one of the sweets last time. His mum said he was off with the flu, but he said it was scrummy, though he couldn't say what way it was scrummy. The man said he was giving out freebies the first time, but we'd have to pay for seconds. Darren gets lots of pocket money, though. He can afford it.'

'Sweeties!' said Ellie, thinking rapidly. Hadn't Rose told her something about the son or grandson of someone at the charity shop being ill after accepting some sweets? She said, 'Tod, I think that man in black is a drug dealer. First he gives away the sweets, but after that he charges. And he's targeting schoolchildren! He's got to be stopped!'

Had she seen him before? She didn't think she had, but …

'Yeah,' said Tod. 'I thought that's what it might be. Our teacher warned us, ages back. But it's like, well, exciting …'

'But you didn't take any?'

'No.' His head hung low.

'Tod! You did!'

He whined. 'No. But I might have.'

Ellie drew back. She wasn't sure whether Tod had taken any or not. Certainly there was another boy out there at the moment, talking to the black man. At risk. She remembered Liz Adams at the vicarage saying how she couldn't bear to think of drugs being brought into the parish … with the school and the library so close …

A group of five boys came out of the library and crossed the road on to the Green. They hesitated, glancing now at the Rasta and now at one another. Potential clients for the Rasta? Undoubtedly.

And Ferdy had hated drugs.

Suppose he had tried to stop the drug dealer …?

She couldn't spare the time to work it out now. At all costs those boys must be prevented from making further contact with the Rasta. The damage that even one of those tablets could do …

Ellie said, 'Listen, Tod. This is serious. I need a closer look at that man. And I'm going to try to divert those boys before they reach the dealer, and bring them here. Then we must ring the police.'

She knew it was risky, but she must try. Those poor boys … not realizing the danger … she snatched up a coat on her way to the kitchen, and tumbled down the steps into the back garden.

She ran down the garden path, through the gate, into the alley and across it to the churchyard gate. Opened the gate.

This was the opposite to the way Kate had run that night, just before …

Kate hadn't seen anything of the Rasta, or she would have said …

The boys had started to walk along the path towards the Rasta.

Ellie couldn't intercept them in time. She shouted at them. 'Police! Run!'

They knew they were doing something risky. Boys doing something risky are always wary, ready to be warned off.

They scattered and ran …

… leaving her face to face with the Rasta.

Big man. Tall. Immensely strong.

He said, 'You!'

She had never seen him before in her life. She said, 'Sorry! My mistake!'

She backed away, realizing she had strayed into dangerous territory.

He caught her arm and whirled her against the church wall.

'But I didn't see anything …'

How could she have? A black man, wearing black clothes, on a dark night. He would have been invisible to her.

'But I saw you at the window!'

She turned her head and saw the figure of a small boy picked out against the light in her sitting-room. Tod, watching anxiously. She could see him clearly, but he probably couldn't see her very well, in the shadow of the church … in the power of the killer.

She tried to appear calm. 'You killed Ferdy because he couldn't stomach your selling drugs on his territory.'

His teeth gleamed in the dark. She felt rather than saw him raise his arm to hit her.

19

Too late, she understood why Ferdy had died. Why here, why at that time of day.

She wanted to scream at the waste of it. She was only just coming to terms with Frank's death. Now she, too, had run out of time.

She backed up against the door of the church. It did not yield and let her in as it had yielded for Ferdy. Had there been a struggle?

The man grabbed her throat.

So be it, she thought …

… and heard a shrill voice calling her name. 'Mrs Quicke!'

… and felt the pressure tighten around her neck. She was being ground against the church wall … knew she was near death …

'You let her go, you!'

The hands around her neck fell away as the man released her to deal with the newcomer. Ellie gasped and, hands to her neck, stumbled and fell to the ground. Thinking … 'Tod! Must save Tod!'

The killer had flailed at Tod, who was dancing backwards but screaming at the top of his voice. Ellie groped around for a weapon. What could a frail widow and a small boy do against that growling maniac, over six foot tall and heavy with it!

Her coat fell away, the rain was getting stronger, and her ears were playing her up.

'Come on, man!' Another shrill boy's voice.

'Go on, Darren, kick him in the goolies!'

The man was swearing, using that word again. And again.

Ellie tried to focus her eyes. There was a ring round the killer now. A ring of boys, baiting him, running away and jumping at him when his back was turned. He threw one off as another swiped at him with his heavy school bag.

'Police!' Sirens screaming, two cars drew up by the level crossing just as policemen began to spill out of the incident room at the church hall … and plainclothes men appeared in the entrance to the derelict house.

The killer turned to run down the path towards the alley and safety. Tod threw himself in a tackle, clung to the man's leg and wouldn't let go. The man swore, flailed at him, but couldn't release himself from the limpet grip.

Policemen running.

The man screaming obscenities.

The boys jumping him.

Ellie slid down on to the path and let go her hold on the world.

It had been Tod who had called the police, using his mum's mobile phone which he'd taken to school with him to show off to the other boys. Luckily. When he saw Ellie confronting the killer he'd used his head for once, and rung the police for help.

Then bravely gone to her assistance.

Seeing him trying to tackle the killer, some of the other boys had come back to help him. Buying strange sweets was one thing, but leaving Mrs Quicke to be mugged by the dealer was something else. Luckily those particular boys had not had time to buy any of the tempting sweets themselves before Ellie had interfered, so they could present a virtuous front to the police. Ellie didn't ask what Tod had done with the sweets he'd bought. And if she spotted an unfamiliar foil-wrapped packet in her waste-bin in the kitchen the next day, she certainly didn't say anything about it to the police.

The police charged the Rasta with the attempted murder of Ellie. They took him off to the police station, raving about getting even with those who interfered with him earning a living, uttering threats to kill Ellie for betraying him to the police, and screaming that this was all Ferdy's fault for not sharing his territory. If Ferdy hadn't been so stupid, none of this would have happened ...

'But I really didn't see him on the night of the murder,' Ellie protested. She was visiting the incident room to make one last statement about the attack on her, and this time had been received with courtesy. Well, she thought, they owed her that at least.

Inspector Clay was all smiles this time, even summoning up tea and biscuits for her.

She said, 'I really didn't mislead you, you know. He could see me at the window, but I couldn't see him. I had a side light on inside, and he was all in black. How could I have seen him?'

'No, we understand how it was that you didn't see him. However, if we'd been able to talk to your missing neighbour Kate then we might have got somewhere, because it was more than possible that she had seen him.'

Ellie looked meek. Kate was due to return home that evening, after having several long telephone conversations with her husband. But for how long? Would she ever feel safe with Armand? How long before Armand misbehaved again?

Inspector Clay continued, 'We got a taped confession out of the killer before his brief got to him … he's complaining today that he wasn't read his rights and didn't understand what was going on, but it's all on tape, and his pockets were stuffed with Class A drugs as well as 'sweeties' for the kids, so if that's the best defence he can come up with …' A shrug. 'He's got considerable form for dealing with Class A drugs and GBH in the past, so I should think he's looking at a long sentence. Besides, he was a mite careless, so we can prove who he was working for … his mobile phone was programmed with his boss's number. Even before we got him to the station, she was ringing him to find out how he'd done … and naturally we took the call instead of him.'

'A woman was behind the drug dealing?' Ellie was shocked, though she told herself that she ought to be aware that women were at the top of all professions nowadays.

'We've known about her for some time. She's been done for dealing before when she worked out of the council estate. Unfortunately for her, she got ideas about moving up market, which will mean quite different surroundings for her from now on.'

'So were the fat man and the fake gas man working for her as well?'

'Yes. The Rasta was her bedfellow as well as her right hand man. The other two were petty criminals she picked up locally because she wanted to get rid of you before her fellow came out of the woodwork to start up the operation openly. They thought you'd seen him, you see, so they concentrated on getting rid of you with some hired talent …'

'… which turned out to be not so talented, after all. And I felt so sorry for the fat man, getting his leg broken like that.'

'He isn't talking, but the false gas man is and blaming everything on everyone but himself. To help matters on, both their mobile phones connected them with her.'

'Was I right about why the Rasta killed Ferdy?'

'He says it was an accident, that they argued and Ferdy took a swing at him, so he took a swing back. Ferdy fell back through the door into the church, and they went down in a heap with Ferdy underneath. Only he'd caught the back of his head on the edge of a stone step … we found some of his hairs there. We also found some wool fibres from the Rasta's cap and sweater on Ferdy's clothes. We thought they'd come from your neighbour Kate's clothes, of course. They probably got there when the Rasta dragged Ferdy away from the door, so that the central heating engineers wouldn't stumble over him when they got back. Then he lit off in Ferdy's van, took it out into the country and set it on fire.'

'Not realizing, I suppose, that Ferdy had two other cars parked around the church. One has since disappeared. Was that the Rasta, too?'

'No, it was the gas man. He fancies a new car every few days. It's been found, incidentally. It belongs to Mrs Hanna now, I suppose.'

'And was it the gas man who frightened off Mrs Hanna, poor thing?'

'No, that was the fat man – according to his mate, anyway. They thought Ferdy might have told her he'd been approached to share his territory, and they weren't taking any chances. So she scarpered ...'

'... after leaving a note for her neighbour to look after her dog. So have you managed to find her and reassure her yet?'

'We've put the word around and knowing the Polish community, she'll get the message and be back in circulation in no time at all. By the way, you know that big house that's up for sale opposite the church? Someone was curious enough to investigate today. He thought it was squatters ... well, in a way it was, because that was where the gang had been keeping watch on you. We found Ferdy's Bentley and a stolen white van in the garage, and a good stash of Class A drugs upstairs. Also fingerprints all over the place linking the whole gang – not just the fat man and the gas man, but also Mrs Big and the Rasta – with the haul.'

'Had they bought the house, then?'

'No. The gas man had lifted the Sold sign from somewhere else. He's told us all about that, and about how difficult it was to scare you off. He rigged the car to blow up, of course. He thought it was yours, not your neighbour's. Has she returned home yet, by the way?'

Ellie shook her head. If Kate wanted to talk to the police later, she could do so.

Ellie had a parting shot to deliver. 'Don't you think someone ought to recommend Ferdy for a medal? After all, he lost his life trying to save the neighbourhood from a drugs gang!'

The house was beautifully quiet. A little dusty. The houseplants needed attention, the silver needed buffing up. The azalea which Archie had given her drooped. Ellie never had been as good with houseplants as with those in the garden. She tried to remember what Mrs Dawes had told her to do with the azalea. Something about hot water and a basin? She shrugged. She'd do what she always did with azaleas, which was to stand it in the sink and let it soak.

She did that.

It was dusk again. She went to stand in the living-room, looking out over the darkening garden and up at the church spire. The moon was rising. So was the wind.

She missed Frank. She thought she always would. He had picked her up as a green girl, folded her in his loving care and looked after her until the day he died. Perhaps he had been a little over-protective. He had not wanted her to grow up, to change in any way … to be his equal.

She drew back from that thought, and then fingered it in her mind. No, he had not wanted their marriage to be a partnership of equals, and she had accepted her place in his scheme of things, without trying to alter it in any way.

Now that the warmth of his protection was withdrawn, she had found the world to be a colder, sometimes unfriendly place. But also more exciting.

She turned her back on the night, drew the curtains and switched on all the lights.

She patted the back of Frank's chair and went out into the hall, where the answerphone for once was still.

She went into the study and switched on Frank's computer.

She was not going to be beaten by a mere machine. Somewhere in there were details of the PCC meeting, and she was determined to find them.

Switch on. Incomprehensible gibberish. Flag. Propeller whirling. Mouse on Word. File. Open.

Take your pick.

What was it that Gilbert Adams had suggested? Frank might have put the notes under the committee that he was in? Try Property.

Bingo.

PCC notes.

Open. Bingo again. The date was right. Three pages of notes.

She scanned through them. Fine. Now to print them out.

Uh-uh. How did you print them out?

First find the manual for the printer. Mm. Put the mouse on the typewriter symbol. Whoops, something had started whirring. Alarming, this.

Whirr. Whirr.

A new insert appeared. Paper unfolding itself in an icon of the printer. Pretty.

Whirr. Whirr. Countdown to delivery.

Wow. A piece of paper unfurled itself and settled into place on top of the printer. She picked it up. It looked perfect.

Amazing.

Amazing that she'd beaten the computer at its own game.

A second page was delivered into her hand, and then a third.

Splendid. What a relief. She would put them into an envelope and take them over to the vicarage, and Gilbert could see to photocopying and distributing them.

Ah, there was one more thing she had to do. What was it? She took the folded sheet of paper out of her handbag. On it Gilbert had written down all the things that she intended to do in her new life. She crossed them out one by one.

Then looked up a number in the phone book, and keyed it in.

'Is that the driving school? I would like to book some lessons, please.'

2/02 13 7/01
12/03 14 1/03